I0588108

CABO 2 COZUMEL

A DEE SANDERS ADVENTURE

LP SNYDER

Cabo 2 Cozumel is a work of fiction. Any references to historical events, real people, or real places are used fictitiously. Other names, characters, places, and events are products of the author's imagination, and any resemblance to actual events or places or persons, living or dead, is entirely coincidental.

2021 Sky Blue Stories Paperback Edition

Copyright © 2021 by LP Snyder

All rights reserved. No part of this e-book may be reproduced in any form or by any electronic or mechanical means, including information storage and retrieval systems, without written permission from the author, except for the use of brief quotations in a book review.

www.skybluestories.com

Cover art by Vince Conti

ISBN: 978-1-7355084-2-9

CAST OF CHARACTERS

Dee (Sierra) Sanders
Gina Dubulgee
Jamal (Juliet) and Angelic Jones
Mike (Mike) and Keno Williams
Liah Maria Hernandez Sanchez
Cristina Sanchez
Roberto (Romeo) Sanchez
Ernesto (Ernie) (Echo) Hernandez
Alicia Hernandez
Juan Gonzalez
Miguelito Cortes
Alpha One
Beta One
Charlie One
Delta One
Papa One
The Alpha Nephews
Conchita Alvarez
Ike Mann

Elizabeth Adassa
Diego Schwartz
The Ex-Military Team
The Cartel Group
Juanita Jimenez

We lie in the sand
the tide breaking at our feet,
and watch the sun sink into the water
out there on the edge of the world.
How quickly it is gone,
leaving us behind
in its dimming light,
to face our darkness
alone.

—Dee Sanders

PROLOGUE

Sea of Cortez
1536 (the year)

Hernando Cortes stood on the bow of the *Castillo* and looked south. *Just maybe this would work.* The wealth of Montezuma, the gold of the Aztec's, was his for the taking. Loading it in the supply wagons on the expedition to northern New Spain (modern day northern Mexico) had been inspired. Plus, he'd discovered the sea he now sailed on, hoping to reach the Pacific before the Spanish fleet reached him.

Perhaps it hadn't been the wisest decision to attack the Aztec's. In fact Velasquez, governor of Cuba, had ordered him not to do so, but Cortes had attacked anyway, and he had succeeded. He claimed the Aztec empire, and then further south, and now further north, for the kingdom and glory of greater Spain. Yet his enemies persisted. In fact, they were coming for him, and he knew there was little time.

Then Cortes saw them, steaming north, Spanish warships sent to intercept, capture, and return him to Spain to suffer manifest indignities. *Maybe not!* He quickly marked the direction and latitude of the ship for his friend Juan Bautista Castillo, namesake of the ship and well-known painter. Cortes then detonated explosives he had planted on the hull. The ship slowed abruptly and began to wallow.

Cortes didn't know the depth of the sea. He had tried a lead line and free divers. He had run out of line and none of the divers he had sent down had found the bottom. Several in the attempt had not made it back to the top. Nonetheless, Cortes felt certain that in a sea this small the ship could be found again.

He climbed aboard a skiff and rowed for the shore. He took a last glance as the crew screamed and ran about the decks while the Spanish cannons lit the waters around them.

Those long guns were a new thing. Cortes hadn't counted on them. He saw open ground ahead as he rowed for the shore. A hundred feet from the bank, a garrison of Spanish soldiers sprang from the brush and surrounded him. It looked like he would be returning to Spain after all.

CABO 2 COZUMEL

SEA OF CORTEZ

Present Day

Jamal Jones stood in his scuba gear on the deck of the pontoon boat. He was ready while the others dawdled. The sky, the ocean, Angelic, his wife's one piece, were all a brilliant, radiant blue. Not a cloud in the sky or troubles to be found. His life was in harmony.

He slipped the big glass mask over his face, and while the others told him he looked like a space alien, he reminded himself that he was a dry space alien as the mask fit his face well and allowed him a large, unobstructed view. He nudged Angelic, and she gave him a thumbs up. He glanced around and saw Dee and Gina still talking and Mike and Keno still gearing up. Jamal nodded to them, and he and Angelic rolled over the side of the boat into the bright blue of the Sea of Cortez.

Jamal settled into the water and located Angelic. She was still adjusting her gear. He saw the other two couples on the dive platform readying to enter the water. He glanced down toward the sea floor where he saw a dark mass on what looked like a shelf that thrust out into the water. It looked to be about eighty feet, just about the limits of visibility, but the sky was so bright and the water so clear, it might be a hundred feet. There was only one way to tell.

He flashed Angelic the "okay" sign, and she nodded and returned it. He pointed down with his finger and they descended. *Maybe he could find something interesting for them to look at.* He marveled to himself. *As a kid he had nearly drowned in a shallow creek. He had never cared for the water after that. Then he met Angelic, and she loved the water. He'd had to suffer through it. Then they meet Dee and got stuck on the island and Jamal had subsequently learned to dive, surf, and swim. He now thought of himself as a sort of Aquaman. Life was crazy sometimes.*

As they drifted down, Jamal noted there was a long point on one end of the mass that ran down and accumulated into a larger shape, like a portion of a bowl. Then he realized, could that be a ship, a wreck, certainly, but still, it was encrusted and silty with sea life. This could be interesting, and maybe dangerous.

Jamal had a degree in art history from the University of Georgia. He had been recruited to play football and had been a two-time all SEC wide receiver. After a brief stint with the NFL he had gone to work in corporate fitness. It had been too good an opportunity to pass up. He'd originally planned to teach art history. That was the thing, art and history, the two went together.

He was immediately fascinated and turned to Angelic to point at the wreck. She held her hands up, not comprehending. He grinned inside the big mask and watched her roll her eyes at him. He pointed back down, and they resumed their descent.

The closer they got, the surer Jamal became. He saw the

lines beneath the sea growth. He'd studied design and taken drawing classes. Ships were often the subject of a still life, and he recognized the form. It was smaller, old, probably wooden, not a warship, maybe a merchant carrier, or cargo, or a private vessel, a galleon perhaps. And it was only a part of a ship, but it was definitely a ship.

Jamal reached for what he thought to be the mast and slowly swam toward the fragment of hull. Angelic followed along, watching him. Jamal's eyes darted back and forth as he tried to ascertain the dimensions and overall shape of the vessel. It was encrusted heavily in places, but far less so in others. There wasn't much coral in the Sea of Cortez. It seemed odd that the growth or silt or sediment wasn't consistent. As he swam around what he thought must be a portion of the deck, he made out several shapes that looked like the base of the mast, making him think it was, in fact, a galleon.

He motioned to Angelic and swam over the side toward what would have once been the hull of the ship. Only it wasn't there. The bottom gaped open and Jamal saw into a partial interior. There was debris scattered along the ledge. Jamal held a finger up to Angelic, telling her to stay, and then swam a few feet away from the ship out into the sea. He looked down, and the water disappeared into a black void beneath him. He swam back to Angelic.

The shipwreck was indeed sitting on a shelf that extended from the seawall. It was perched, as if placed there, awaiting discovery. A few feet either way, and it would have disappeared into the inky depths.

It was amazing. What had they found? Jamal hesitated to probe about as he had no idea what the maritime law might be, territorial Mexican waters? He wasn't sure. *Surely this had been seen before.*

He looked up to see Dee, Gina, Mike, and Keno had

descended just above him and hovered next to Angelic. Dee held out his arms and Jamal nodded his affirmation.

Jamal led them on a swim about the ship, pointing at things as he went. Then they made for the surface and the pontoon boat.

They scrambled on deck and broke down their gear as they gathered under the canopy.

"That was a shipwreck, probably a galleon!" exclaimed Jamal.

"What kind of wreck?" asked Keno.

"It's probably an old Spanish galleon, a merchant ship, or a pirate, perhaps. It was too small to be a warship."

"How could you tell?" asked Gina.

"Jam was an art history major," replied Angelic. "He loves art and history."

"I recognized the shape from some of my drawing classes and some of my history classes. I don't know much about this area of the world or these waters. Spanish, I guess," he said, with a glance at Dee.

"Far as I know, it was mostly Spanish explorers. This is, or was, the Sea of Cortez, more commonly known now as the Gulf of California. So, I'm guessing, Cortes ... that sound right to you, Jamal?"

Jamal nodded. "It's just hard to tell the time period. It wasn't that badly encrusted. It could have gone down in the last hundred years. The waters can be so turbulent here. It could be a private yacht or something, although it looked older from a design point of view."

The women were pulling off their wet diving tops and their bikinis or swimsuits were a mess. It was a good thing everybody knew everybody, and no one was terribly shy. That seemed to be a habit Angelic and Keno had picked up from Gina.

Gina was making her way toward the open deck on the

front of the pontoon. "I'd like to get some sun and dry off," she said. "Ladies, want to join me?"

Keno and Angelic started toward the front, peeling away the rest of their swimsuits.

Jamal turned to Dee. "Let's go back down. Mike, are you in?"

Mike had been looking away. He pointed to the south. There was a large yacht that had appeared on the horizon. It was sitting anchored.

"Maybe I'll stay up here and keep an eye out. I'm not as trusting as I once was. Can I use the scope?"

Dee reached into his backpack and tossed the scope to Mike.

Mike caught it and said, "Don't stay away too long, just in case."

"Not everybody's a pirate," laughed Jamal as Dee grinned with him.

Mike just shook his head.

The ladies sprawled out on the deck in the sun. Mike sat under the canopy, studying the luxury yacht. Jamal and Dee suited up and went back over the side.

WHEN THEY GOT BACK TO THE WRECK, JAMAL MOTIONED DEE behind him. He wanted to approach the items along the shelf cautiously. Jamal wasn't sure why he was being so careful. It just seemed like the right thing to do. Not that there would be booby traps necessarily, but if this thing was that old, it would or could be very unstable. Plus, if the currents picked up, it could move, and if he or Dee got caught up in it they'd head straight for the bottom, which looked to be a long way down.

Jamal pulled his dive knife, as did Dee, and they gently probed along the shelf the ship sat upon. It was mostly gravel, rock, and plant life. Fish swam idly past them. As Jamal and Dee swam closer to the remaining hull, it appeared that they were in what was once an area of the ship's hold. They hadn't brought lights, and it was darker in the shadow of the hull. They probed for several minutes and found little. Then Jamal stuck his knife into a dark object and felt something solid. He moved the knife slightly and continued to feel the resistance. Finally, he reached the top of the object and then tried to draw the knife around the shape of the item. He motioned to Dee, who swam beside him, and pointed. Dee brought his knife in from the other side of the object and the two of them slowly worked their way around it. The object wasn't that large, and it was cone-shaped. The men continued to probe until they got fully around it. They were both wearing gloves, but neither was anxious to grab the item. Dee finally reached forward to try to get a grip. When he tugged, the item didn't budge. Dee looked to Jamal. They both grabbed the item and slowly were able to pull it away from the hull area.

Jamal brushed at it with his gloves and some residue floated away. He continued to pat the item down, and Dee did the same. They realized shortly that whatever the item was, it had a handle that ran from one side across the top and to the other side. As they got away from the hull, Jamal pointed to the handle, then to himself and Dee, and then to the pontoon boat.

They each grabbed a section of the handle and swam upward. Progress was slow. The item was heavy. Neither Jamal nor Dee could imagine what it was. After several minutes, they reached the float deck of the pontoon boat. As they struggled to lift the item onto the deck, Dee called out to Mike.

"Mike," shouted Dee, "come and help us!"

Footsteps hurried toward them, then Mike leaned over

from the deck and pulled. He was a muscular guy, but even he set the item back down as Jamal and Dee's grasp gave way and Mike carried the full weight.

Jamal and Dee clambered aboard and stripped their diving gear. The sun was moving lower in the sky and a breeze had picked up. The girls, who were back in their suits, stood and giggled and pointed at the item.

"What did you find, Jam?" called Angelic.

"Don't know, heavy, whatever it was."

"We'd better start back," noted Mike. He went to the helm to fire the engines.

"What happened to the yacht?" asked Dee.

"They went on north," replied Mike.

Dee pointed behind Mike and said, "Looks like they're coming back."

Jamal and the women gathered around the object and begun wiping at it and speculating.

"Jamal," hollered Dee, "we got company."

The yacht was close and there was a dark-skinned man in a white shirt with a large tattoo or birthmark running up one arm and then out onto his neck and up part of his face.

Jamal threw his towel over the object.

As the yacht passed, the man did not smile or wave, but he watched them intently. The yacht motored on.

"Wonder what that was all about?" questioned Angelic.

"He was creepy," threw in Keno.

2

LA PAZ

The yacht quickly disappeared to the south of them and they slowly made their way back to La Paz. They had come up from Cabo to see the sights in La Paz, and after a day in the city had decided to spend another day on the Sea of Cortez for some snorkeling and scuba. The waters around Cabo were potentially more treacherous than further up in the Sea of Cortez, but they had been warned the currents and wind were still an issue.

For sure, the water was cooler, and there were much stronger currents than what they had just left in Costa Rica and the Caribbean.

Jamal toweled the object down and looked up in surprise.

"It's a bell, maybe the ship's bell," he exclaimed.

Dee looked in and said, "It seems kind of small. I'd have thought that a ship's bell would have been larger."

"You guys said it was heavy," added Gina. "Could that be part of it?"

Jamal kept wiping, scrubbing the surface. "It's got some tarnishing and some swirls on the surface, but it's coming pretty clean." Then he stopped.

He pointed. "Look, it's a name. *Castillo.* Do you suppose that was the name of the ship?"

"Makes sense that it could be," commented Angelic.

"I still think it's too small and too heavy," added Dee. "A ship's bell from any period other than recent times would be brass or bronze, which would tarnish easily and deteriorate, and it wouldn't be that heavy for its size."

Jamal looked at him. "But you agree it appears to have come from an older ship, possibly a galleon?"

Dee nodded in return.

"That's an interesting gold color," observed Gina. "Not as shiny as the stuff we found on the island, but that was heavy."

Dee looked up at her, nodded and said, "A gold bell doesn't make any sense."

Jamal continued to wipe down the bell. "It would be a lot older, might depend on the quality of the gold or how it was cast. Maybe the name *Castillo* will tell us something. I don't really want to part with it until I get a little backstory. No telling what we've found."

"We'll have to box it to transport it, if we take it out of Mexico, which may not be a good idea," said Dee.

"Surely, we can keep it long enough to get some kind of answer before we turn it over, but to whom? Could that be determined by what it is?" replied Jamal.

Mike called out from the helm, "Probably country of origin versus territorial waters, and who has the best lawyers."

THEY PULLED INTO THE DOCK AS THE SUN WAS SETTING. Jamal and Dee had placed the bell in one of the sturdier dive bags. They would still have to carry it by the handle to move it. Keno was going to pull the Range Rover close to the dock so that it wouldn't be so far to carry, and they could try to keep the item undercover or unobserved. During their return, Jamal had tried to Google the name *Castillo* on his phone, but he couldn't get any service or only very slow service that timed out.

BEFORE THEY WENT TO DINNER THAT NIGHT THEY HAD discussed leaving the bell in the Range Rover but decided to bring it in as Jamal wanted to try again to determine its history. They chose a restaurant around the corner from their inn and walked the short distance to eat.

Returning to their rooms, they heard the blaring of a car alarm and stepped into the parking lot where they saw their Range Rover with the doors forced open, the tires slashed, and the windshield broken. Fortunately, they hadn't left anything inside it.

Dee and Mike bolted for the rooms, which were second-story inside the courtyard. The doorways were visible from the ground. They did not appear to be open or damaged. When they got to the rooms, nothing was disturbed.

Mike reported the break-in at the desk and they called the authorities. Angelic called the rental company, who made arrangements to pick up the vehicle and replace it with another in the morning.

As they stood on the balcony afterward, Jamal said, "What do you suppose that was about?"

"The desk captain said it happens occasionally, random break-in on a suspected tourist vehicle," replied Mike. "La Paz is a larger city and has some crime issues."

Jamal looked at both Dee and Mike, then said, "What do you guys think? I mean, nobody knows we have that thing, except maybe the guy on the boat and he couldn't see what we were looking at. It might have been a seashell for all he knew."

"It doesn't seem likely," replied Dee.

"It's just odd," added Mike.

The women were admiring the view from the balcony, then turned and slipped an arm around each of the men's shoulders.

"We'd better get to bed if we plan to drive back early tomorrow," observed Keno.

Dee exhaled and Gina looked up at him and smiled.

Angelic slid her arm around Jamal's shoulder and said, "Time for bed, great explorer or discoverer of old sunken stuff."

THE NEXT MORNING, THE CAR RENTAL COMPANY HAD PICKED up the damaged Range Rover and left them a brand new one.

"Do you think anyone might follow us?" asked Mike.

"There's only one road back to Cabo, so anyone else headed that way would likely follow us," replied Dee. "There is a harsh beauty to the countryside down through here, but it's desolate. No one's going to stay, just pass through the area. Plus, Cabo is the only airport. We're pretty clearly tourists. Anyone tracking us doesn't have to look very far."

AS THEY CONTINUED ON FOR CABO, A DISCUSSION AROSE ON what they wanted to do next. Discussions about another cruise, under the premise of having the time to do so, the adventure of it based upon the last cruise, the fear based upon the last cruise—they'd been stranded on an uninhabited island in the Pacific for a month, and the desire to get back on another ship, the old falling off a horse syndrome, was in play.

"I think we should do it," said Dee.

"But why tempt our fate?" asked Keno. "We were so lucky to get off that island."

"You have to face your fears," added Angelic.

"I thought we did a pretty good job of that last time," replied Mike.

"Jam, what do you think?" asked Dee.

Jamal looked at Dee in a mock-threatening glance and said, "Only my wife gets to call me Jam," he replied with a grin.

Dee nodded. "Sorry."

Jamal looked out the window and then back. "Dee's right. This is a desolate place. Who knows what someone might do for a chance to get out of here, whatever the circumstances. But, to answer your question, yeah, I think a cruise is a good idea. I need time to research the bell and we won't really be too far from Mexico, right?"

Gina jumped in, waving at herself, Angelic and Keno, "We saw a cruise that would work."

They had seen information in Cabo that told of a Cabo-to-Cozumel slice cruise. By plane, it would hardly have been an hour. But by sea, the cruise had to travel the Pacific length of Mexico, then Central America, turn and reenter the Caribbean through the Panama Canal, and turn north back to Cozumel. It was a journey of several days. But the best part, according to Keno, was that they would never be very far offshore. In fact, the coastline would likely be visible for much of the trip. That was something they could all feel comfortable about. The group had really enjoyed their time in Costa Rica, and getting back to the Caribbean had lots of appeal. Plus, the cruise would give Jamal time to determine a feasible disposition of the item. The bell was going to be difficult and heavy to carry around.

Upon returning to Cabo, the women made arrangements for the Cozumel cruise while the men found a building supply store which did not have what they were looking for.

Dee had decided that building a crate for the diving equipment, with the bell tucked safely in the middle, might allow them to ship the equipment, especially since during the cruise they would not likely need their gear, and the crate could be stored in the ship's hold. They wouldn't have to keep it in their rooms that way.

Jamal agreed and took numerous pictures with his phone, although the only real telling item was the name cast in the metal.

The men eventually found what they were looking for at a shipping facility and asked to have it delivered to their hotel.

Later that afternoon, the women advised the cruise would port in Acapulco, San Salvador, and Panama City, Panama before reaching Cozumel. The ship would cruise offshore between those locations. Jamal would have several days to research.

3

CABO 2 ACAPULCO

They boarded the next morning. Dee's theory about the box paid off as the cruise ship sent porters to gather their luggage, who then deposited the crate into one of the passenger luggage holds.

Strolling the ship's deck after they checked in, Jamal was excited about the bell's prospects. "Even if I don't have good coverage, the ship should have decent internet. I can research *Castillo* on my tablet."

Dee, Mike, and the women all laughed at him.

"Jamal, you got to give it up," said Mike. "It's a big heavy chunk of metal."

Dee nodded his agreement. "Try to figure out what you can between here and Acapulco. We should probably hand it over before we leave Mexican territorial waters. We know they'll have a claim on it, regardless of where it might have originated."

"See what you can find, baby. 'X' doesn't always mark the spot," said Angelic as she took Jamal's hand and smiled at him.

Jamal shook his head in return. "I'm going to go research. I'll meet y'all at dinner."

SEVERAL HOURS LATER, THEY SAT TOGETHER AT ONE OF THE large tables. They were all casual. The women had gotten some sun and Dee and Mike had sat in the bar and talked.

Jamal had been waiting for them. He didn't look happy.

"What did you find?" asked Dee.

Jamal twisted his face in a slight scowl, then said, "*Castillo* is Spanish for house, which doesn't tell us anything, it's also the name of a very famous soccer player for one of the European football teams, and it's a relatively unknown painter from the 16th century. There was no mention of a ship or an explorer or anything like that. I also tried more current news stories for shipwrecks or boating accidents."

"Tough luck man," said Mike.

"It's probably nothing," added Keno.

"You tried, baby," said Angelic.

Gina just smiled at him.

Dee looked thoughtful for a moment. "You know, you mentioned explorers. Sometimes ships were named for patrons. Cortes would be the likely explorer in old Mexico, if the ship was in fact from that era. You might look into Cortes to see what his ships were named or how he financed his expeditions. Many, maybe most of them, were by a king or queen, but who knows. It might be something else to look at. We have some time before we get to Acapulco."

Jamal nodded.

They ate dinner and forgot about the bell for a while.

THE NEXT MORNING JAMAL CAME RUNNING UP TO DEE WHO was standing on the rail idly watching the sea.

"You'll never guess," Jamal exclaimed.

Dee turned to him, grinned and said, "Probably not, so why don't you tell me?"

They both turned toward the sea.

Jamal said, "You mentioned patrons last night. Cortes apparently financed a lot of his own expeditions, but he did use patrons. Velasquez, the governor of Cuba, who charted Cortes to make the journey, also helped finance Cortes' on his initial voyage to Mexico in 1519.

"The only thing I can find on the painter, Castillo, is that he did a portrait of Cortes in the early 1500s, which means they likely knew each other."

"Could you determine how successful Castillo was as a painter? Or how prominent he was at that period of time?" asked Dee.

Jamal shook his head.

"If he was successful enough, even just at that moment in time, he might have helped finance Cortes and been a patron. Although naming a ship would usually require a significant contribution. And, I still think the bell is too small," continued Dee.

Jamal stood quietly for a moment.

"Could the bell be ornamental or commemorative?" he asked.

"Why is it so heavy?" responded Dee.

"Because, it is gold," replied Jamal. "You said Cortes, Aztec, gold of Montezuma, actually Motecuhzoma II, who was ruler at the time of Cortes. Motecuhzoma thought Cortes was one of the Aztec gods come to life and back to reclaim his kingdom. The Aztecs met Cortes with many gifts, most of them gold. Suppose he kept some of it? Maybe cast the bell in honor of Castillo and put his name on it. Maybe the ship was headed to Spain to deliver the gift."

"Well, that's an interesting idea, but the ship was on the

Pacific side and there was no canal. They would have hauled the bell across country and sailed from the east."

Jamal stood still for a moment before he spoke. "I'll keep digging, there's more to this here."

Dee nodded and replied, "It would appear you are onto something."

ANOTHER DAY PASSED AND, AS ACAPULCO APPROACHED, THEY gathered as a group to talk about going ashore.

"I don't think there's anything I want to see. I'm happy on the ship," noted Keno.

Gina nodded her head in agreement. "They have a nice pool and I can see from here."

Angelic followed up, "I don't think it's the tourist haven it once was. In fact, I think there's a good bit of crime. It's not worth it for a few hours. We've seen a lot of tourist towns."

Jamal nodded. "I'm still researching."

Dee looked at Mike. "What about you?" he asked.

Mike shook his head slightly. "I'm game for a couple of hours. Let's go see what we can see."

LATER THAT AFTERNOON, DEE AND MIKE TOOK THE LAUNCH from the ship to the dock. They wanted to see the cliff divers at La Quebrada. They took a cab and chatted along the way with the driver, whose name was Hector, in bad English and worse Spanish, about what to look for and where to stand. Also, anything they should not do.

"Who comes to see the divers?" Dee asked their driver.

The driver grinned in the mirror. "Tourists," he replied. "Divers have been going off those cliffs for hundreds of years. Who knew they'd one day get paid for it."

"So, we won't see any locals?" asked Dee.

The driver shrugged. "There will be a few, always, looking for tourists to hustle. Pay attention, amigos."

He pulled up to the site and dropped them at the curb. Mike tipped him generously.

"I'll be here when you come back," the driver stated. "Give me a wave and I'll pick you up."

Dee and Mike sat in the restaurant in the shade, overlooking the cliffs. It was a two-hour show. They watched one spectacular dive after another. At one point, his mug running empty, Mike turned to the bar and held the mug in the air.

"Dee," he said.

Dee was still watching the divers.

"Dee," he said again.

Dee turned slowly around.

"Don't look quickly, but isn't that guy at the bar the one from the yacht? That tattoo, or looks more like a birthmark, is hard to miss," said Mike.

Dee shifted slowly and looked toward the kitchen. As he brought his eyes back toward the cliffs, he passed across the man who was now looking at him and Mike. Dee continued to face the cliff and the divers but said softly, so that only Mike could hear, "Yes, and he appears to be watching us."

"Any chance it's coincidence?" replied Mike.

"Could be, it seems kind of unlikely, but if he was traveling down the coast, he could have stopped here, just like we did."

"The show will be over soon. Let's get back to the ship," answered Mike.

A few minutes later Dee said, "I'm going to run to the men's room before we go back."

He started for the bar and noticed another man, beside the tattooed one, push off and start in their direction.

"Mike," Dee whispered.

"Yeah, I see him," Mike replied. "If you're not back in a minute or I'm not here, we'll know what happened."

Dee started on for the bathroom and the man passed by Mike, headed in the same direction. *We are getting really paranoid*, thought Mike, but he nonetheless watched the man disappear into the men's room behind Dee.

Upon entering, Dee saw that the doors to the stalls in the men's room opened outward. He quickly stepped inside and took a seat. Pulling out his phone, he waited for the door to open and then began an imaginary conversation about how the trip was going. He heard the man turn the water on and then step in front of Dee's door. Dee spoke quickly.

"Yeah, we were diving and ran across an old chunk of metal." Dee saw and felt the man move closer to the door. Moving quickly, Dee stood and slammed the outward opening door into the man, who doubled over, clutching his knee.

"So sorry," noted Dee to the man and quickly exited.

Dee walked calmly over to Mike and leaned close. "Let's go."

Mike nodded. "The dives are ending for the afternoon."

Dee and Mike made their way to the taxi stand. While doing so, both men casually admired their surroundings and kept an eye out for either of the two men. Neither saw either.

They waved toward Hector, and he chugged over in the old taxi and picked them up.

Once riding in the car, Mike sighed.

"Maybe it was just a fluke."

"I hope so," replied Dee.

Back on the ship, they met the others for dinner. Dee and Mike had decided not to mention their sighting of the man and his accomplice to the others. They would just pay more attention on the ship or at any other stops.

•   •   •

GINA SAW HIM FIRST. THE GROUP WAS SEATED AT AN outdoor bar and the man was leaning against the rail, close enough that he knew they would see him.

"What's he doing here?" she asked.

"Maybe he's just traveling like us," replied Angelic.

"He had a yacht. Why would he be on this ship?" Gina replied.

"Maybe he was just a visitor on the yacht, and he's a tourist like us," added Keno.

They watched him for a few moments. The man had a drink in hand, which he seemed in no particular hurry to finish. When he finally did, he left the glass on the rail, turned in their direction, waved at them, and then strolled past and into the night.

THEY ALL MEET IN JAMAL AND ANGELIC'S ROOM.

"What are we going to do?" asked Keno.

"Be calm," replied Dee. "He may have just seen us looking at him and was being friendly."

"Do you really believe that?" asked Mike.

Dee grinned, and replied, "I don't know what to believe."

Jamal said, "If we have a gold bell, and he suspects it, that could be all the motivation he needs to pursue us."

"Why do you think it's gold, Jam?" asked Angelic.

He looked at the group first and then said, "I've been researching. The weight points toward it being something unusual. Bronze and brass don't weigh that much and would have been far more corroded. Cortes is reputed to have received or stolen a great deal of Aztec gold. As Dee pointed out, it's too small to be an actual ship's bell. It looks more like a commemorative. I can't say positively, it's just a feeling I have."

"Is it safe with the diving gear?" asked Keno.

"Probably safer there than in our rooms, and safer for us," replied Dee.

"What's the value of something like that, if it is gold?" asked Mike.

"Street value would be several million dollars, based on weight. I have no idea what historical value might be," replied Jamal.

"How do we keep it safe if this guy is really after it?" asked Gina.

"Until we can authenticate it, we don't really know what we have," replied Jamal.

"Or if this guy is really after it," answered Dee. "Let's stay close together for the next few days. Move around in pairs or greater. The bell's in the hold. There's nothing we can really do. Let Jamal try to determine more about it and watch out for one another."

Agreeing for at least the short-term, the group broke up and went to bed. It helped that they were all in adjacent cabins and felt more comfortable nearer to one another.

4

ACAPULCO 2 SAN SALVADOR

They sailed all the next day and saw no sign of the man or his accomplice. By late afternoon, everyone was a bit more relaxed. Jamal had been researching all day, and when they met for dinner, he had some interesting news.

"It turns out our cruise is fortuitous," he said.

"It's what?" teased Angelic.

Jamal looked at her and rolled his eyes. "It's a convenient coincidence," he replied.

"Cortes first landed in Mexico at Cozumel. We'll see where. He was on his first voyage after being commissioned by the governor of Cuba to sail west and determine what was out there. Cortes landed and encountered a rival tribe to the Aztecs. In their midst was a captured Aztec princess, rumored to have been Montezuma's daughter, and a Spanish sailor who had survived a shipwreck from a previous expedition a few years earlier. What worked out for Cortes was that both the captives spoke the native language. Cortes could speak to the Spanish sailor, who translated to the local tongue for the Aztec princess, and she could translate into the Aztec language. Cortes had a direct pipeline to communicate. This impressed Montezuma considerably. Montezuma already thought Cortes to be the living embodiment of an Aztec god named 'Quetzalcoatl' who had come to reclaim his kingdom. I'm not clear why Montezuma thought that, but it made it easy for Cortes to approach him, particularly with the help of the interpreters and the return of the Aztec princess. It led Montezuma to shower Cortes with gifts of gold, which may have led to the Spaniards' decision to attack and destroy the Aztecs."

"What's all that mean to us?" asked Keno.

Jamal grinned. "Nothing specific, but it points to the Spanish greed for the Aztec gold and the lengths they may have gone to remove it from the country. I think it's a piece in determining how this bell came to be, if I can work my way through it."

"Changing the subject, we'll be in San Salvador tomorrow. Do we want to go ashore?" asked Angelic.

"I think we dock outside the beach area, La Libertad, which is about an hour from the city. There is an overlook called Puerta del Diablo, or the Devil's Door, between the beaches and the city. It might make a pleasant hike and we could see inland toward the city and back toward the coast to the ocean," said Gina. "Or we could go into the city for the national palace or some cathedrals."

There were murmurs among the group. "Some exercise might be good," noted Jamal. "We've stayed pretty close to the cabins."

"I'm for it," added Mike.

THE NEXT MORNING, THE GROUP GOT UP EARLY AND TOOK the excursion for the hike to the Devil's Door. As they climbed toward the top of the mountain Keno noted, "This is as steep as portions of the trail back on the island."

. . .

THE ENTIRE EXPEDITION WAS BREATHING HEAVILY BY THE TIME they finally reached the top. But the views were breathtaking. The sky was that limitless blue they had grown accustomed to while being on the water, and the lush green of the valley ran off in both directions. The air was clear around them and then turned hazy as it met the horizon. They could, in fact, see down to the city and back to the ocean. They were standing on the summit, almost as if they could look back in time or forward to the future.

THE GUIDE FILLED THEM IN ON THE HISTORY OF THE AREA. "This was the site of a Mayan sacrificial altar. Early Catholic priests were mortified at the practice, trying for years to abolish it, and then finally naming the area 'The Devil's Door,'" he shared. "Over time, the name stuck."

Angelic turned to Jamal and said, "Didn't Aztecs perform human sacrifice as well?"

"Yes," he whispered, "I'll tell you about it later."

Shuffling around the peak and taking in the views from each direction, it seemed like the group could see and feel the past civilization. It was as if the sacrificial practice had left an indelible presence on the site.

The guide then led them to a small cave just below the summit. He packed the entire group from the ship and, what appeared to be a few additional tourists, inside. He made his way to the front of the cave and addressed the group.

"This was the ceremonial room for the sacrifice," he said. Around the crowd, several people stepped anxiously about, looking at their feet or the walls.

"Not to worry," continued the guide, "The practice was

discontinued many hundreds of years ago." A few smiled anxiously. As the crowd shuffled about, Mike nudged Dee.

"That guy in the corner, in the sunglasses and hat, is he the one from the bar that followed you into the men's room?"

Dee turned slowly and saw the man and another standing next to him. Dee looked around at the crowd. Everyone had on shorts except the guy in the cap. He had on baggy pants. Perhaps there was a bandage on the knee beneath.

"Looks kind of like him," Dee replied.

"I really noticed the sunglasses first, here in the dark," replied Mike. "Then I got to looking at him." He turned toward the other fellow. "It looks like there might be several of these guys."

"Did you see them on the boat or on the launch while we were traveling to shore?" asked Dee.

Mike shook his head. The guide led them from the cave.

The excursion stopped shortly afterward and ate lunch in a picnic area. A little later in the afternoon they made their way back to the ship. Some of the presence from the hilltop site must have lingered because no one said much, and they all looked forward to getting back to the ship and their rooms. The two men did not appear to be a part of the shipboard passengers.

When the group got aboard and back to their staterooms, the doors were all ajar.

Stepping cautiously inside, Dee, Jamal, and Mike all witnessed the same thing. The rooms had been ripped apart. There was nothing left in the drawers or in the closets. Things were scattered about the deck and left in a huge jumble. Dee summoned a security officer, advised him of what they had found, and had the officer review the suites.

"We rarely get this situation," the security man said. "Did you have anything valuable or anything anyone might have known about in the cabins?"

While Dee and Jamal had been talking to the security officer, the others had gone through their cabins and put things back in order. Each of them reported in as they finished cleaning up.

"Keno and I aren't missing anything that we notice. A few things are broken or damaged, but nothing seems to be gone," reported Mike.

"Same for Dee and me," stated Gina.

Then Angelic came out and added, "Most of our stuff appears to be on hand, except Jamal's electronic tablet that he was performing the research on is gone. That appears to be the only thing missing."

"What type of tablet or notepad? What were you working on?" the security officer asked.

"It was an electronic tablet, and I was researching some local history. You know, I was just trying to add some color to the cruise. It makes no sense."

"Do you have the 'Find' app?" asked the security man.

"Yeah," replied Jamal, who reached for his phone. He pulled up the app but the header on his program showed only *no known location*.

"Could be no power, or signal, or maybe destroyed," said the security man. "Did you have anything on there of value?"

"It would just be personal data which would have to be accessed by someone with passwords, not that hard to bypass, if you know how. But, no documents or original material that would be of any value to anyone but me," replied Jamal.

The security officer nodded and gathered the group around to make some notes.

"The cruise line is insured so we'll make good on anything broken or stolen. I need each of you to list those items and we'll get the process underway."

The group really had little except for the loss of Jamal's e-tablet.

After the officer left, they stood and talked for a moment.

"What are you going to do?" asked Keno.

"Can you find all that information again?" questioned Mike.

Dee and Gina just smiled at him.

"I can replace it with another tablet from the electronics stores on board," he added. "And get back to work researching. It's good that I hadn't documented anything except a few thoughts in pencil on my notepad, which they didn't take." *This is starting to get serious,* Jamal thought.

5

SAN SALVADOR 2 PANAMA CITY

They set sail the next morning knowing they would be at sea for a day while they cruised off the coasts of Honduras, Nicaragua, Costa Rica and finally Panama. They would eventually queue up there in a line of ships to anticipate passage through the canal and their return to the Caribbean.

The women lounged by the pool, Dee and Mike worked out in the gym, and Jamal went about reestablishing his research.

He found a nicer, newer, larger screen tablet in the shipboard store and thought to himself, *Perhaps that wasn't such a bad thing, as long as they aren't dangerous. We didn't really lose anything, and I don't think they learned anything. But, they are persistent. If they get the tablet open, the best they can do is call up websites I've visited. There's really nothing unusual there, for this part of the world. And now I've got a much better piece of equipment.* He smiled to himself and went to work.

Jamal had made some notes on a writing pad. He didn't really have much, but he felt like there had to be a connection. *There was a friendship or an alliance between Cortes and Castillo, the painter, and the gold bell was part of it. Where should I start? How had the bell ended up in the Sea of Cortez? I don't know Spanish explorers, and I don't know the Sea of Cortez, but I know art. Let me start with the painter. But first, let me take another look at the Aztec material. There was a lot of art there as well.*

Jamal spent the morning reviewing the internet sites regarding the Aztec culture, the interaction with the Spanish, Cortes in particular, and the saga of Montezuma. It was a rich culture, highly developed, very structured and defined in the people's roles, their actions, and their interactions with one another and with their religion. That's when he saw something that made him shiver. It had to be a complete coincidence, but there it was. The Aztec god Quetzalcoatl, the feathered serpent, was illustrated with a mark, maybe feathers, which crossed his face, ran down the side of his neck, and onto his arm. The placement was very much like the markings on the man from the yacht. *That's just bizarre*, thought Jamal as he moved on to the next item.

Dee and Mike came into the room then and called out to him, "Jamal, let's get the girls and go eat."

Jamal had just switched to a site on Juan Bautista Castillo, the 16th century painter. He wanted to take a quick look, but resigned himself to do so after lunch. He got up and joined the other two men. They left the cabin to meet the women for lunch.

"I just heard that we are going to dock in Panama City or Panama, as the locals call it, for most of two days," said Gina. "It takes a full day to get through the locks and we can disembark or stay aboard."

"I think we should stay aboard? We're safer on board," added Keno.

"Do you know if most passengers are staying or

disembarking?" Dee asked Gina. She didn't know and shook her head.

Angelic walked up. She had gone to the room looking for Jamal just after he had left with the other men. Hearing the last of the conversation, she added, "Most people are disembarking since we have a couple of days. What can we do?"

"We won't be able to get back to the ship, will we?" asked Mike.

"Not while it's in the locks," replied Jamal.

"I know a woman," said Dee, and Gina turned sharply to look at him. "I went to school with her. She and her husband," emphasizing the latter word, "and her family owns a bed-and-breakfast here in the city. Let me see if I can get in touch with them for a place to stay."

"That would be fun," said Angelic.

"We can see the city," added Mike.

"We should leave the bell here, it's safest," said Jamal. "We can try to see if anyone is following us."

"It's been quiet today. Maybe it would be good to get out," murmured Keno. "Since they didn't find what they wanted, maybe they'll go away."

"Not likely," replied Jamal. "We can put some distance between us and the bell. They either haven't thought of the hold or they've already taken it. I'd like to go check on our gear but I'm afraid to give away its location."

Dee had walked up and heard the end of Jamal's conversation. "I agree about checking, but everything is crated up and it wouldn't be easy to get to anything. I've rather left it undisturbed. They, the man on the yacht, don't apparently know what we have, only that we had something. They don't know the size and appear to be looking for something smaller."

Jamal nodded in agreement. "Until we can be sure what

the bell represents, I'd like to keep it as safe as possible. I can't help but worry. If they figured it out, they could have taken the bell and be long gone."

"They couldn't have gotten off the ship yet. When we disembark, we can watch the hold and see if anything comes out," replied Dee. "Probably the best we can do. I'd rather they take the bell than we get in harm's way." Jamal nodded.

Lunch arrived, and they settled in to eat. While doing so, Dee explained his friend.

"I went to school at the University of Tennessee Knoxville and one member of the women's gymnastics team was this girl, Liah Maria Sanchez, she was half Panamanian, her mother, and half American, her father, American military. She came up on scholarship and later participated on the Panamanian Olympic team. She was very good. Anyway, her degree was a double major in marketing and history. She worked for a time after graduation and then went home to help her family with the B&B. She met and married her husband and they have a little girl. And, perhaps most importantly, they have room for us. It might be a little tight. They weren't expecting six more people but said they could make it work."

The P.A. came on and announced that off the port side of the ship was the Costa Rican coastline. Looking that way, all they could see was water, so it looked little different from the Nicaraguan coastline had looked a few minutes earlier.

"It's too far offshore for me," noted Mike, and Keno giggled.

"I'll lend you my scope," called Dee, and Mike gave him a thumbs up.

. . .

THEY STILL HAD A HALF DAY OR MORE BEFORE THE SHIP approached Panama and the canal. Jamal invited them all back to the room.

"When I went to the ship store earlier I inquired if there was a library," he said. "They told me there was a small one with several photo books, which was exactly what I was looking for. Maybe I can get you all to help me?"

The ladies had all the sun they wanted. The men had worked out, they all felt safer close together, there was nothing on the ship they really wanted to do, and the curiosity was getting to all of them.

Jamal handed out photo or picture books on the Aztecs, the Sea of Cortez, and Mexico. He pulled out the e-tablet to return to his work on Castillo.

Angelic and Mike had books on the Aztecs. Dee had a book on the Sea of Cortez and Keno and Gino had books on Mexico.

There was silence for a time as each of them thumbed through their book and tried to look for anything that might be relevant.

Dee was the first to speak. "There have been a couple of galleons found on the fringes of the Sea of Cortez. Mexican authorities have taken responsibly for and authority over them. That may answer who will assume control of the bell when we turn it in to authorities. There's nothing about treasure or Cortes, so far. There seems to be issues with the currents being really strong at times and the movement of the wrecks by the waters. That might explain why we only found part of the ship."

Jamal nodded. "Yeah, it was just a fragment of the hull. Don't know how long it was sitting on that shelf. It could be gone by now."

Gina popped up next. "It says here that Cortes founded Vera Cruz, translated as 'the true cross' and set up a training facility, barracks and a city around them. There might be something to see."

Jamal nodded. "Yeah, I guess Cortes was all over modern-day Mexico. Maybe we could find something helpful there."

Then Angelic said, "The Aztecs were really well organized and structured. It says here they excelled in art, architecture, and athletics but that they were very much a caste society and were savage in their enforcement of it. They had slavery and mass sacrifice."

"Most of the world still has slavery," noted Jamal.

"On a positive note, it credited them for inventing chocolate," replied Angelic, "but, their torture included skinning victims alive, dismemberment, decapitation, and wrenching out the hearts of their victims, while they were still alive."

"Sounds like a means of control or an exhibition of power," added Mike. "Not a religion."

"Also sounds like modern day drug cartels," added Dee, "highly structured, very efficient, savage, and they believe in blood sacrifice. They're not somebody to mess with."

The group sat silently, taking in Dee's description.

"Surely that's not who we're dealing with," noted Keno.

"No, probably just treasure hunters," replied Jamal.

For the rest of the afternoon, the group sat mostly silent and reviewed the books. When they reached the end of one, they swapped and went through the other books. They grew tired and stopped in the late afternoon.

"Does anyone know what Panama looks like?" asked Gina.

When no one answered, Dee spoke up. "Liah says it's flat around the canal, that it was a swamp area originally, and in the distance are rolling hills. There are five locks and it takes seven hours for a ship to pass through them. She says we should enjoy the old city and the historical sites, also the visitor area around the canal."

Slowly everyone closed their books and Jamal shut off the e-tablet.

"Let's go eat," he said, "My eyes are tired."

6

PANAMA CITY - CASCO VIEJO (OLD CITY)

The group disembarked in Panama the next morning. Liah was waiting for them. She was tall and slender with long legs. Her thick dark hair reached nearly to her waist and contrasted with her paler skin and eyes. She ran up and hugged Dee, and then to his relief, each of the others.

Turning, she pointed and said, "This is my daughter, Cristina," with pride and love apparent on her face and in her eyes. The little girl stepped forward and waved at the group.

"Welcome to Panama," she giggled and twirled from side to side.

Gina looked at Dee, and said, "She's beautiful."

He nodded in reply and returned her smile. "Yes, she is."

"Would you like to see the visitor area or go to the old city and see some of the historical locations?" Liah asked. "My family is readying your rooms, so we need to stay busy for a few hours."

"I think I'd like to go into the city," said Keno. "Get away from the water for a little while."

Angelic and Gina nodded their agreement.

Liah looked at Dee, Mike, and Jamal. They also nodded.

"Let's go learn something new," replied Jamal.

"Good," answered Liah, "We can start with 'Casco Viejo' or the old city, and tour a bit, and then grab some lunch from one of the rooftop cafes, and after that if you still have some energy, we can travel out to 'Panama Viejo' which was the original site of the city. The ruins are quite fascinating. The original city was laid to waste by a 17th century pirate named Henry Morgan."

Keno turned to Angelic and Gina and said, "As if we haven't had enough of pirates." They all three giggled while Liah continued.

"Casco Viejo, the current city, was established in 1673, just two years later. It's quite a history."

Dee, Jamal and Mike had been absorbed in her story, and they all nodded enthusiastically.

LIAH LED THEM DOWN COBBLESTONE STREETS WHERE BRIGHT pastel-colored, multi-storied homes with wrought-iron balconies mixed with cathedrals, museums, and retail shops. It felt like a mixture of Paris, Havana, and New Orleans all rolled into one.

"You must love living here," remarked Angelic.

Liah nodded. "Yes, I couldn't wait to get back. Until then I didn't know how much I loved it, and missed it."

"It doesn't look much like Knoxville, does it?" said Dee.

"No, it doesn't, but Knoxville was charming in its own way, as was the university. I got tickled at their idea of 'old' buildings. But I enjoyed my time there. Then I went to work in Atlanta and it was nice also, but I wanted to come home. My mother kept telling me about Roberto, and that I needed to meet him."

"That's your husband?" asked Gina.

Liah nodded. "Yes, I am so glad I came home to meet him. I was on the national team for a short time."

"You mean the Olympics?" asked Keno.

Liah nodded. "Yes, I was a gymnast."

"Dee told us," replied Angelic. "If you don't mind my asking, how did the competition go?"

Liah smiled. "It was fun, it was worth all the time and training I put into it. "

"Did you do well?" asked Keno.

"I won a bronze in beam and a silver in rhythmic," she replied.

"It must have been hard to quit?" asked Angelic.

Liah shrugged. "I met Roberto, and Cristina followed shortly after. I was working with my family. It was time for something different. I'm very happy. I've gotten to do everything I wanted."

Dee, Jamal, and Mike had been walking along behind listening to the conversation and viewing the sites. Dee kept turning every few minutes. Mike did the same.

"Are you guys just a little paranoid?" asked Jamal.

"You should be, too. It was your tablet they stole," replied Mike.

Liah stopped the group. By this time, they had walked several blocks around the old city after making the drive over from the canal. "If you're hungry, I'll take you up to my favorite rooftop café? It's located down the street in an older historic building with lots of art and architectural detail. It's beautiful. On top, the view of the city is amazing."

Everyone nodded. Cristina squealed.

"She loves to go to the rooftop," said Liah.

TWO HOURS LATER THEY WERE SITTING IN THE UMBRELLA'S shade of their rooftop table. Brunch had been delicious, and they were finishing their drinks and looking out over the city. Cristina played quietly beside them.

Liah filled them in on the B&B and what to expect, also about her parents and Roberto.

They felt relaxed for the first time in days.

Mike was facing the entrance to the café, and Dee noticed him stiffen. Dee's eyes followed Mike's gaze. Two men came through the entrance and headed for a table across the rooftop. It had a line of sight for the group.

After they had passed, Mike said, "Didn't one of them look like the guy in the cave at Devil's Door?"

"Maybe a little. I didn't get a good look either time," replied Dee.

The men sat down, and in a few minutes Dee noticed them looking toward the group.

"They appear to be curious about us," noted Dee to Mike.

Mike nodded.

Dee stood. "Need to stretch my back," he said to the group. Dee got up and walked to the edge of the roof. He glanced down the streets and, while not seeing anyone familiar, noticed several men lounging in doorways or in the shade. *Nothing wrong there. Shade makes sense. We are really jumpy.*

Dee returned to his seat and leaned in to Mike. "Could be a couple of others down on the street. We have been here for a while. Maybe they thought we got lost."

Mike nodded.

"If you guys still have a little energy or need some exercise, we can take a couple of minutes and run by 'Panama Viejo' before heading for the B&B," stated Liah.

Everyone looked at one another and nodded.

"A little exercise would be good," replied Jamal.

"The food was delicious," noted Angelic.

Liah smiled and rose, and the others followed. The two men at the table didn't move.

A HALF HOUR LATER THE GROUP FOUND THEMSELVES strolling the grounds or ruins of 'Panama Viejo.' There were several people around the site wandering about, taking pictures and fanning themselves.

"'Panama Viejo' was founded in 1519 by a Spanish conquistador and is the oldest European settlement on the Pacific coast of the Americas," said Liah.

"What does that mean?" asked Keno.

Liah smiled. "He laid the city out in a rectangular grid, like European cities. It's amazing these ruins have remained. Nothing was ever done to rebuild them after the survivors relocated to Casco Viejo."

Liah stopped in front of a four-story tower. Its square graduated shape and went from larger to smaller as it rose into the sky.

"This is the 'Old Panama Cathedral' built in 1519 as part of the original settlement. It's a UNESCO World Heritage Site."

She resumed her walk, and the group followed along. Dee trailed behind, frequently glancing around the grounds and to the rear. Twice he thought he saw one man he had seen in the street below the café. For the time being, he kept the thought to himself.

Liah finished the tour and, as they were all getting a little warm and tired, she suggested they head to the B&B.

"I got a text while we were at lunch that said the rooms are ready, if you are."

Everyone agreed it was a good time to check in and maybe grab a swim.

. . .

Liah made the short drive back into the city. She was in an older Ford Excursion, so the group had plenty of room. Liah sat in front, with Keno in the passenger seat. Cristina was in a car seat in the middle row, flanked by Gina and Angelic. The men sat in the back row of seats. Their luggage was stacked comfortably behind the men. While the women were chatting about the sights they passed, Dee leaned across to Mike and Jamal.

"When I stood on the rail at the café, I saw several men in the street below. I saw two of them in the ruins. Could be coincidence, but it feels like there's something still going on? I think we're being followed."

"Are you sure?" asked Jamal. Dee shrugged. "They've broken into our vehicle and into our rooms, stole your tablet. I don't think they are going to give up."

"What do you want to do?" asked Mike.

"I don't think involving the police is going to help. All we have right now is suspicion. Liah's dad was military. We should probably tell him. Maybe he knows someone."

"Do you really think we should alert him? I don't want to scare anyone or cause trouble. He'll think we're crazy," added Jamal.

Mike shrugged.

Then Dee said, "Let's meet him and see if we can get a feel for how he might react."

"Almost there," called out Liah as she swung the car into a short driveway.

7

PANAMA CITY - PALACE PANAMA (B&B)

Liah rolled the vehicle into a side lot and stopped. She turned to the group and spoke. "This was the estate of a foreign diplomat in the middle of the last century. There were some issues with the Panamanian government and the property was abandoned. My mother's family took it over. They were trade brokers and coordinated activities around the canal. They made their money there. When my mother's father passed, her mother, my grandmother, feared she would lose the place to the government, or to a rival, or to her own bad management. My parents were newly married, but my father stepped in to help. He was still active military and was gone a lot but he could see that his mother-in-law was well cared for and the property maintained. After my grandmother died and he retired, my parents converted the house to a bed-and-breakfast. I hope you will enjoy staying here, it's quite elaborate inside."

With that, she got out of the car, and the group followed her. Liah went around to the side door and unhooked Cristina. When she sat the little girl down on the ground,

Cristina ran toward a man whom had appeared from inside the house.

"Papi," she called.

A short, dark-skinned, muscular man swept her up in one arm.

"Cristina," he bellowed and swung her around. She giggled radically.

He stepped toward the group and said, "I am Ernest Hernandez, welcome to my home, the Palace Panama."

Liah giggled. "That's not really the name," she sighed, "but my mom wanted to call it that as the B&B, and Dad went along."

Ernest grinned and continued to swing his granddaughter in one arm.

The men stepped forward to greet him. Jamal stuck out a hand. "Ernest or Ernesto?" he asked jovially. The man shrugged and said, "Call me Ernie."

Dee stepped forward and shook Ernie's hand. "Retired military?"

Ernie grinned. "I was a SEAL."

Mike shook his hand. "Thank you for your service."

"It was my job," Ernie replied, and grinned again. Then he turned and started toward the house. He waved an arm, "Come with me."

As Ernie led the group toward the home, they saw a multistory stucco and stone house with an arched doorway and double wooden front doors.

"This was the embassy for one of the former South American regimes. It turned over in the 1950s and my wife's family acquired it. You'll be staying upstairs in the main quarters. There are three bedrooms but alas, only one bathroom. It is an older house," he said with a smile.

He opened the massive double doors with one hand, as

Cristina was still on his arm, and made his way toward a curving staircase that ran along and up one wall.

"Roberto will get your luggage while Liah and I show you around," Ernie added.

ERNIE HAD DEPOSITED EACH OF THEM IN A LARGE SUITE MADE up of a bedroom and a small sitting room. There was one large bathroom centrally located. There was marble and hardwood throughout, under high ceilings and ceiling fans. Windows located high on the walls were cracked to catch the breeze and circulate air. It felt very comfortable and also like stepping back in time.

As they turned to the center landing, all their luggage sat stacked against the wainscoted wall.

"Roberto has been here, I see," said Ernie, and smiled. "You'll meet him at dinner." Nodding to Liah, he said, "Let us go and let them unpack and get comfortable. Dinner will begin in a couple of hours. There is a small pool directly behind the house if you'd like to take a swim."

Ernie, Liah, and Cristina headed down the stairs.

After they had gone, the women swung around, looking at the rooms and taking in all their surroundings.

"It's beautiful," noted Angelic.

"I wouldn't mind to stay a few days. It's a delightful change from the ship," added Keno.

"It feels wealthy," added Gina, who turned and looked at Dee.

"I bet it's a PITA to keep up, and expensive," responded Mike.

"Agreed," noted Jamal, "but it is stunning craftsmanship," he continued as he moved closer to the wall and the door frames, examining the framing and carpentry. He was awed by the intricacy of the wooden inlay.

"It's very nice, and very nice of them to let us stay," added Dee. "Does anyone want to take a quick swim before we clean up for dinner?"

Keno looked at Mike. "I think I'd rather get cleaned up, maybe soak a little, since we only have the one bathroom. I'm dying to try out that clawed foot tub."

Mike nodded. "Y'all go ahead, and we'll get a start on the bathroom and be out of the way when you get back."

DEE, GINA, JAMAL, AND ANGELIC SAT AROUND THE RIM OF A narrow but long lap pool that dominated the area immediately behind the house. It had hedges and plant beds that separated it from the rest of the yard. It was tiled in various shades of blue and had two small ledges surrounding the length of the pool that stepped down into the water. To the side of the pool deck, there was a small woven-reed and bamboo cabana stocked with towels and pool toys.

"The pool and the grounds are as beautiful as the house," noted Angelic. The others nodded as Gina slid into the water. The other three sat on the pool edge for a few more moments and then Gina, further down the pool, called and waved. "Dee, get out here, Mr. College Swimmer. Let's see what you got."

Angelic giggled and elbowed Jamal as Dee slipped into the water and paddled toward Gina.

"Jam, have you noticed how much more attached she seems to get to him?" asked Angelic.

"Really?" he replied.

"Really," she answered. "Are you being facetious or stupid?"

"Neither, I hope. But, what I have noticed is that if she had any less clothes on, she'd be naked."

Angelic punched him in the shoulder and pushed him into the pool.

"You'd better start swimming before I drown you," Angelic called as she jumped in and swam after him.

TWO HOURS LATER, THEY WERE ALL GATHERED AROUND A large, elaborate wooden table in the formal dining room. Along with the group were Liah, Cristina, and Ernie. Liah's mother, Alicia, and Liah's husband Roberto served the group.

As the servers brought food Ernie commanded, "Please, go ahead and begin."

"If you don't object, we'd like to wait for Alicia and Roberto," replied Dee.

Ernie smiled at them and replied, "Yes, thank you. That would be marvelous. Alicia, Roberto, please come in and sit down." They both hurried in and sat down the last of the food and took their seats.

Ernie held up his glass and toasted, "To new friends and gracious people, let us eat."

They all toasted and began to feast.

Angelic spoke to Alicia, "You have a beautiful home and the food is delicious."

Alicia replied, "Thank you. We are so happy to have you. Liah was so excited when Dee called. They were good friends at school. She invited him down one year, but he wasn't able to make it."

"It's so beautiful here. I'm sure he would have enjoyed it," answered Angelic.

Next to them sat Gina, opposite Roberto, who was thin but muscular, even wiry, with medium toned skin and close-cropped hair. His eyes were so dark they were almost black.

But now, his face was lit up with a smile. "Are you enjoying the cruise?" he asked.

Gina returned his smile and nodded. "Yes, but we've had some issues."

Roberto arched his brows, as if to inquire.

"Our suites were broken into on board the ship and our rooms were trashed about. They stole Jamal's e-tablet," she replied.

"Something they were looking for or just a random break-in?" Roberto asked.

"I'm really not sure," Gina replied.

Dee, sitting beside Gina, broke in. "We were scuba diving in the Sea of Cortez and accidentally ran across an old artifact. Apparently there were other people actually looking for it or seriously interested in it. They broke into our vehicle at La Paz. Then we noticed them trailing us on the ship and our suites were broken into."

"And they only stole your friend's e-tablet?" asked Roberto.

Dee nodded in reply.

"There are lots of stories and old legends about gold in the Sea of Cortez, lots of crazy people running around chasing after it. But," he paused, "they can be dangerous, too."

Mike was seated next to Ernie, who sat at the head of the table.

"Where does your cruise take you next?" asked Ernie.

"We sail for Cozumel late tomorrow afternoon," replied Mike.

"I'm really enjoying the house," added Keno, "I'd love to stay here longer with you."

"Perhaps after your cruise, you could return," replied Ernie. "We would love to extend our hospitality."

Liah, at the far end of the table, next to Roberto, heard Mike say Cozumel was their next destination.

She turned to Gina and said, "Cozumel is such a beautiful place. The beaches are wonderful and there are excellent restaurants and some nightlife. There are also ruins in the area if you like that kind of thing."

Before Gina could respond, Jamal, who had overheard Liah, leaned in their direction. "Yes, we, or at least I, am fascinated by the Aztec's. I've been researching them and Cortes."

Liah smiled. "Central American history was one of my majors in school. Cozumel, Cancun and the surrounding area are full of ruins. Cozumel is where Cortes first landed. There is a museum there with multiple exhibitions and information on that period in time. It's a wonderful place."

Jamal smiled. "We'd love for you, and as many of your family as might want, to come with us."

Liah sat back, as did Gina.

"I don't know. I doubt they could spare me, and Cristina," Liah replied.

"Bring her, it will be fun," answered Jamal, growing excited at the prospect.

Gina looked across at the little girl playing in her food and smiled as well.

"I'll talk to Roberto and Mom and Dad but I don't know."

"You could stay for as long or as little as you like, but I'd really love to have you show us, or me, the area and the museum. I'm doing some research on an artifact we found, and I bet you would enjoy the challenge."

Liah smiled and nodded her agreement.

8

THE PANAMA CANAL (COLON)

That night, after dinner, the group met in the sitting room of Jamal and Angelic's bedroom. Jamal explained he had invited Liah and Cristina to go with them.

Angelic responded, "Do you think they can?"

"Won't they need them here?" asked Gina.

"I can't imagine Roberto or Ernie would be too happy," stated Mike.

"I hope they can, it'll be fun," replied Keno.

"I have no idea," said Dee.

The next morning, with Liah as their tour guide, the group explored more of the city and then stopped at the Canal visitor area late in the day before leaving to board the ship. Liah had left Cristina with Alicia and seemed excited as she happily chatted away for most of the morning. Just before lunch, as they pulled into the parking lot of a local restaurant, Liah turned to them all.

"I spoke to Roberto and my parents' last night and if you still want me to go, Cristina and I will accompany you to

Cozumel and show you around for a couple of days. Roberto will join us if he can."

"That's great," exclaimed Jamal. "It will be so helpful."

The others murmured appreciatively.

"How will your parents manage?" asked Angelic.

"Roberto is staying to help them, and it's only a small group we have coming after you. Once he gets them settled in, he will join us," she replied.

"It'll be fun," added Dee. "I hope he can join us."

They lunched and did a bit of shopping until time to go to the Canal visitor area.

Once there, they toured the facility quickly, stopping only to marvel at the pictures of the early landscape and slow progress of the building of the Canal.

Liah pointed out several things as they toured.

"Officially, over five thousand people died while building the canal. Unofficially, the totals are estimated to be between twenty and forty thousand. The French tried to build the Canal in the 1880s and lost most of their workers. Later, the United States bought the French out. The United States originally wanted to build a Canal through Nicaragua but took over here in 1904 and finished the Canal in 1914. It was still a miserable task, but has been a boon to Panama, at a great sacrifice to many."

"It made the world a smaller place," added Dee.

"Hopefully safer, too," replied Liah. She continued.

"Roberto and Cristina will meet us at the parking lot to pick up the vehicle and drive us to Colon. It should take just over an hour and we can board there. He contacted the cruise lines and Cristina and I can travel along for the last leg of the trip," explained Liah as they departed the dock.

Roberto, standing next to the Excursion, waved as the group approached. Cristina jumped from his arms and ran to Liah, who embraced her as she got close to her mother.

"Roberto's taxi," he said with a grin and ushered them all into the vehicle.

"Ernie dropped Cristina and me off, so I could drive you. It should take us a little over an hour. It's mostly rolling countryside, but you can feel the presence of the water, of the ocean, and we're mostly parallel to the canal. You can't get away from it." He laughed and then smiled.

It was an uneventful trip, although Dee and Mike both thought they saw a couple of the same vehicles trudging along behind them at a steady speed. They just couldn't get over the idea of being followed.

Arriving at the port in Colon, Roberto helped the two men unload the luggage and whispered to them.

"Did you notice anything on the trip over?"

Dee and Mike looked at one another, and then Dee spoke, "Maybe we're just paranoid, but we felt like a couple of those vehicles stayed the same distance behind us the entire trip, while others sped up, slowed down, or pulled away."

"Very good," noted Roberto. "I felt the same. I got a tag number that I'll check out, but it's probably nothing. Nevertheless, continue to keep a sharp eye, let me know if you need anything. I'll try to be there in a few days."

They all nodded, and Dee and Mike shook hands with Roberto.

Jamal and the women were crowded around Liah and Cristina while porters helped them with their luggage. Jamal quickly shook Roberto's hand and thanked him.

Roberto smiled at them all, kissed Liah quickly, and then picked up Cristina and swung her around.

"I'll see you in a couple of days, little one."

She squealed and hugged his neck.

• • •

They got settled in their cabins after re-boarding the ship. Liah and Cristina were just down the passageway from the others. Dee checked with the staff and was assured that their boxes of gear in the hold were secure. The Canal passage had been uneventful.

Before dinner they all met and showed their newest visitors the sites of the ship. Even though they wouldn't be on board long, the ship was scheduled to cruise through the night and all the following day. They might need something to do. There were no more stops until they reached Cozumel.

After dinner they strolled the decks and watched the night sky, now full of stars. Just before dark Gina had noted the softer blue of the Caribbean water and Keno added that the wave action and sway of the ship seemed less. For whatever reason, once the cruise resumed, they all felt better being back in the Caribbean, as if in crossing the canal they had left their problems behind. After walking the decks a bit, they took a table in one of the outdoor bars.

Jamal cleared his throat and spoke to Liah, although the entire group leaned forward and listened.

"The artifact I mentioned to you, it's a gold bell, about half the size of a ship's regular bell. We found it in an old galleon in the Sea of Cortez. I was hoping, with your background, that you might help us learn more about it, and what to do with it."

Liah's eyes got big and her face flushed. "You found a gold bell and brought it with you?"

Jamal nodded. "We didn't know what to do with it and we were heading back to Mexico so we could turn it in, but I wanted to research it for a few days."

"The National Institute of Anthropology and History and their archeologists will not be happy with you," she replied.

"We can take them back to where we found it. The galleon sat on a ledge and I was afraid it would wash away. I have no idea how deep it was below," answered Jamal.

Liah paused for a moment, as if considering her next actions.

"The museum in Cozumel isn't that large, but they have an excellent collection of material and pride themselves on Cortes' history, background, and information. Perhaps we can find something helpful?" said Liah, while swirling her drink and keeping an eye on Cristina who was playing by the table.

"You'll need to do something before you leave Mexico again," she stated.

There was a soft breeze and the rest of the group were all lying back in their chairs and soaking it up, relaxing and listening.

"Absolutely," replied Jamal. "We were assuming it was probably Aztec gold originally. Do you think there'd be any manifests or ship logs, or government records at the museum?"

"Those aren't the things that are normally on display. But, the Spanish kept pretty excellent records and many of them are still available. The museum might have something or know where to look. But, speaking to the origin of the records, like any government organization, there was corruption, and ignorance, and bad accounting. It's hard to say. Although, an item like that bell should stand out somewhere. A solid gold bell that size would be quite a prize for someone."

She looked around the group. They all nodded to her.

"I guess that's why somebody kept chasing us," noted Keno.

"Apparently it wasn't the authorities," Liah replied, "Or they would have arrested you."

"It felt more like treasure hunters from the actions they've taken," added Dee.

"There's a lot of that around Mexico, but also Central and South America. These waters are full of sunken Spanish, and other nationality, ships—English, French, and Portuguese. There are many people that dream of treasures, but they are more dreams than treasure," replied Liah.

"I'd just like to figure it out, so I know what happened, and then we can give the bell to whomever it belongs," added Jamal.

"Mexico will most certainly claim it. But should it be Cortes, Spain might make some attempt to challenge ownership," answered Liah. "It could be from anywhere."

9

COLON 2 COZUMEL

The next morning, they all met for breakfast. The women and Cristina were going to get some sun and shop a little at the ship's boutiques. Dee and Mike were going to get some exercise, and Jamal was going back to his e-tablet and his research.

"I can look at research with you after lunch if you like," said Liah.

"That would be great," replied Jamal. "I'm mostly just searching Aztec and Cortes history, also the painter Castillo, to see if I can find any references to a bell or gold casting, or anything that strikes a bell," added Jamal, finishing with a grin.

"Oh!" hissed Angelic. "Jam that was bad."

He grinned back at her.

"Liah, what can we see and do in Cozumel?" asked Angelic.

"We'll harbor in San Miguel, and there are several attractions there around the docks and in the immediate surrounding area. The museum is there. There are ruins inland, as well."

"Aztec?" asked Angelic.

"No, they're Mayan. It was a similar type of civilization that occupied Cozumel and the Yucatan on the mainland. Their empire ran further south, while the Aztec empire was more central Mexico or what is known as the 'Valley of Mexico.' The Mayans were who Cortes first encountered when he landed in Cozumel," replied Liah.

"I think we saw Mayan ruins in El Salvador, the 'Devil's Door' it was called," said Angelic.

Liah nodded. "Their empire extended across Central America and into northern South America."

She resumed her story of Cortes. "The Mayans told Cortes of the Aztecs and the gold. It eventually led to the Spanish conquest and the destruction of the Aztec empire. To be fair, the Aztecs could be savage and bloodthirsty in their own right. It is suspected that the Aztecs conquered and absorbed the previous great society of central Mexico, called the Toltec's. Many Aztec customs and parts of their religion are directly borrowed from the Toltec's. Civilizations recycle all the time, it's messy," she concluded. "I'm sorry that's probably 'TMI' for your questions, but yes, there are ruins, they are interesting. But once you get outside the San Miguel area Cozumel is largely undeveloped and primitive, mostly sand, sun, and water. It, along with much of the surrounding area, is called the 'Mayan Riviera.'"

"We have one of those in South Georgia where I'm from," added Jamal. Then he grinned and added, "Sand, sun and water, but we called it the 'Redneck Riviera.'"

Liah smiled. "I know it well, spent several Spring Breaks frolicking in the sand. It wasn't quite home," she laughed, " but it was fun. After all, it was the northern Caribbean."

Everyone had leaned in listening and, hearing Liah's comment, chuckled.

"Never thought of it that way," said Keno. "Mike and I

went down several times. No beach is really close to St. Louis."

"I've done PCB, Panama City Beach, Florida, several times," added Gina. "The water is beautiful."

Everyone paused for a moment. Then Dee and Mike rose from the table and waved to the others. "See you at lunch," called out Dee.

The women got up to head for the pool, Liah holding Cristina by the hand.

JAMAL SAT ALONE AT THE TABLE. HE WAVED TO A SERVER AND asked for an iced tea and if he could sit there for a while longer. The server nodded and smiled graciously.

"Stay as long as you like, senor," he replied.

Jamal nodded and called, "Thanks." He reached to the deck for his backpack and pulled out the e-tablet. Opening the screen, he switched it on, and then in his notebook flipped to a clean page.

Jamal spent the rest of the morning reviewing what he knew or thought he knew about Cortes' landing in Cozumel, the encounter with the Mayans, and the circumstances surrounding the Mayan captives that provided Cortes with interpreters. Jamal wasn't really finding or learning anything new, however.

Nearing lunch, Liah found him still at the breakfast table.

Jamal explained what he had found so far. Liah listened, and when he finished, she spoke.

"Let me add a few details to what you have, which is accurate, as we understand it, but a little incomplete. Cortes landed on Cozumel and met the Mayans. In their ranks, the Mayans had a Spanish sailor named Aguilar who had been captured from an expedition nearly ten years before. The ships had capsized and a band of survivors had been taken in by the Mayans. Aguilar learned to speak the language and when Cortes arrived Aguilar could translate from Spanish to Mayan. Cortes took the tact of being a peaceful and helpful but threatening force if needed. The Mayans quickly determined that they'd prefer if Cortes moved on, so they told him about the Aztec gold."

"Having an interpreter must have been really helpful to Cortes," noted Jamal.

Liah nodded. "Yes, but there's more. The Mayans also had in captivity an Aztec woman, and this is where it gets speculative. She was thought to be one of Montezuma's daughters. Aztecs were polygamist and Montezuma would have had many wives and children. Nonetheless, the Mayans saw an opportunity to make peace or gain a little favor with the Aztecs by sending this woman along with Cortes and Aguilar. That way Aguilar could translate from Spanish to Mayan and the woman could translate from Mayan to Aztec and Cortes had a direct line of communication with Montezuma. This would be not only advantageous in communicating, but it gave Cortes the appearance of having greater powers, as perceived by the Aztec. This is thought to be one basis for the Aztecs believing that Cortes was the embodiment of one of their gods, Quetzalcoatl, and receiving the grand treatment that he did upon arrival. This is presumed to have led to the Aztec's mistaken trust in Cortes."

"It sounds like he was a lucky man, at least for a time," noted Jamal.

Liah nodded. "There's one more thing. This is unsubstantiated, but a common theory that has circulated about. Cortes and the Aztec woman were supposedly intimate. When in that state, the woman saw that Cortes had a birthmark that started on his arm, ran across his shoulder and up his neck. It didn't come out upon his face, but nearly so. This was the same marking as on Quetzalcoatl, and on her father, Montezuma. The woman was both terrified and enamored of this and told her father shortly after her return."

"I thought Quetzalcoatl was the 'feathered god?'" replied Jamal.

"He was. But, in the Aztec art it's difficult to tell what is feather and what could be body markings, whether tattoo or birthmark," answered Liah. "Her telling of this to her father may have also influenced Montezuma's treatment of Cortes."

"All of which is a way to say that Cortes may have had a large cache of gold given to him as well as more that he may have taken," Jamal responded.

"He was actually in a potentially incredible position of authority with the Aztecs, but it appears he got greedy," replied Liah.

"That's a lot to absorb," noted Jamal.

"Politics is never simple," quipped Liah and smiled.

"But, changing gears for a minute, with all that gold, however he came by it, Cortes would have needed to transport it. Since much of it may have been gifts, it probably took various forms and not just gold bars," said Jamal.

"Correct," replied Liah. "The Aztecs were quite gifted artisans and the gold would have come in many shapes and sizes."

"Cortes could have recast it into shapes more appropriate for gifts from him, like a bell," noted Jamal.

"Commemorating a ship," finished Liah, with a smile.

"What do you think we can find in the museum tomorrow?" asked Jamal.

"There are several exhibits and some museum archives, I'm sure," replied Liah. "We'll introduce ourselves and ask to look around. We'll tell them that our curiosity has us on the trail of Aztec gold. Most museum curators love to hear themselves talk, it's really just a question of whether they have anything to say that we want to hear."

THE REST OF THE GROUP, WITH ANGELIC AND GINA HOLDING Cristina by each hand, approached the two of them and wanted to know what was for lunch.

"Jam, don't wear her out on the first day. We have lots of things to see and do," scolded Angelic.

"I wasn't. Liah was just filling me in on my incomplete research," he replied.

Liah smiled up at Angelic. "He got most of it right, I just added a few details."

"Do we know the answer yet?" asked Keno.

Jamal grinned. "We got small pieces, but we're getting there. Tomorrow is going to be a big day."

"What are we going to do first?" asked Gina.

"I'd like to go to the museum early and find out what we can," inserted Jamal.

Liah smiled. "We can do that and, any of you that want to go with us, I think you'd find it interesting, but there's also several shops, restaurants, and attractions in the dock area if we take too long in the museum."

"I want to see the ruins," added Angelic.

"I hear there's a tequila factory," said Mike.

Dee and Jamal nodded.

"We can start at the museum and go from there. I think I can find something to make everyone happy," giggled Liah, while picking up Cristina and setting her in her lap.

10

COZUMEL (THE MUSEUM)

The ship had docked during the night, and the following morning onshore excursions began. As this was the official termination of the Cabo 2 Cozumel slice cruise, the ship would harbor for two days, to allow excursions on the first day and deboarding of the current passengers on day two, before disembarking for Vera Cruz and then Key West where yet another slice cruise would originate.

The group was up early, eating, chatting, and planning for the day. First stop was the Museo de Cozumel (local museum), to be followed by lunch and then the women would head slightly northwest of the city for the Zona Arqueologica San Gervasio (San Gervasio Archeological Garden, site of pre-Columbia Mayan ruins) while the men headed slightly southwest of the city to Hacienda Antigua (a local tequila distillery tour and tasting). On an island eleven miles wide and forty miles long, nothing was very far apart and having seen no further evidence of being followed since entering the Caribbean, the group felt like a small separation in touring wouldn't hurt.

.   .   .

COMING ASHORE, THEY STROLLED A SHORT DISTANCE TO THE museum. Liah led Cristina by the hand and the others followed along, craning their necks at various sights and other tourists passing by them.

Upon entering the museum, they spent an hour being introduced to the area and its history by their tourguide. As the initial tour wound to a close, Liah stepped forward and, after congratulating the guide for a job well done, asked if she could speak to the curator.

"Might I inquire of the curator if there is additional Cortes information available or where we," she paused, pointing to her group, "might pursue further information?"

The young man, whose name tag read *Juan Gonzalez*, replied, "I'm afraid the curator is unavailable. He's off the island." But then, seeing Liah's crestfallen face, continued, "Perhaps I might help you. I am about to go on break, so I have a moment. The museum has further information on Cortes and I can show a couple of you," he paused, looking at Cristina, "what is available if you are quite careful."

Liah smiled and nodded.

"Aren't you Liah Hernandez, the gymnast?" he asked.

She looked at him for a moment, as if attempting to recognize him.

"We've never met. I competed in parallel bars, rings, and floor. But I didn't make the national team," he replied.

"For Mexico?" she asked, and he nodded.

"You were a double medal winner that year. You were amazing to watch."

Liah blushed. "Thank you," she stammered.

"I'll show you what we have," he continued. He held out an arm to usher the group down the hall.

· · ·

JUAN SHOWED THEM AN ENTIRE ROOM OF CORTES information. It was all neatly filed and boxed with multiple indexes as to the contents.

"You may look through these, most of which are copies, as the originals are under thermal protection," Juan explained. "But please be careful. The curator is mad about organization."

Liah, Jamal, Dee, and Mike stood and looked over Juan's shoulder as he showed them how the files were arranged. Angelic, Keno, and Gina agreed to look after Cristina and sat in the adjacent room around a break table and chatted about the afternoon's excursion.

Juan stepped away and left them to their work.

"I think we should start with correspondence and manifests," said Jamal. "That way we can see if the bell is mentioned in any letters or if it appears as an onboard item or elsewhere in any of the manifests."

Liah and Jamal started on manifests, ship's records, whatever they could find, while Dee and Mike started on correspondence. While the entire room was full of information related to Cortes, much of it was from later in time and dealt with his early life or his later life after the return to Spain. They were churning through the applicable material quickly.

"It ought to be simpler," huffed Jamal while sitting down one box and picking up another.

"Many of the larger museums and the National Institute digitize material, but then there's nothing to display to the tourists," replied Liah with a grin. "Plus, you still have to go through it when you're looking for something."

"There just doesn't seem to be much information from that early period," added Mike.

He moved closer to Liah and Jamal and they stopped for a moment to rub their necks and stretch their shoulders.

Jamal looked over at Dee, who hadn't spoken and seemed not to be paying attention to the others.

"Dee, come over, take a break," called Jamal.

Dee held up a finger, his eyes not leaving the document he was scanning. Then he walked over to them with the piece of paper in his hand.

"It's a letter from Cortes to Velasquez, the governor of Cuba, the man who sent Cortes on the expedition and funded about half of the first voyage. Apparently Cortes left in a hurry from Cuba as Velasquez was coming to relieve him of command," Dee explained.

"Cortes was a favorite early in his tenure in Cuba, but, as this voyage approached, Velasquez felt like Cortes would not be loyal to him and was going to remove Cortes from command," added Liah.

"So it seems, there's much flowery apologizing for the departure and stressing the need to get underway, the tides, and the importance of the event, all very self-serving," Dee paused, "but then Cortes says that there are local reports— the letter appears to be written while he was in Cozumel—of enormous amounts of gold and precious stones inland under the control of the Aztecs."

"That would have been true, and the Maya were eager to send Cortes on his way and rid themselves of him," added Liah.

"This is where Cortes picked up the two interpreters, right?" asked Jamal.

Liah nodded. "They were instrumental in Cortes' ability to deceive the Aztecs."

"Here's the best part," continued Dee. "Cortes says that he intends to make presents of the gold and jewels for all deserving dignitaries and patrons. And I quote, 'I should like to change its form' end quote."

"Cortes, at that point, didn't expect the Aztecs to be the

artisans and craftsmen that they were. Their work with gold and jewels was beautiful. It was quite intricate, delicate, and ornate," added Liah.

Dee continued, "Cortes then says that he will set sail and follow the coast around to the north where he will land at a beach called 'Chalchihuecan.'"

"Modern day Vera Cruz, or the 'true cross' which he founded and where he began his big move to escape Velasquez and set himself up as governor of 'New Spain,'" added Liah.

"We got to go to Vera Cruz," exclaimed Jamal. "That's probably where it happened."

"Possibly, but Cortes was in Mexico for several years. He conquered the Aztecs and then moved south to expand. Then toward the end of his time he moved north and claimed more land and discovered the Sea of Cortez, before he was taken captive and returned to Spain."

"But it all fits together so far," exclaimed Jamal.

"Yes, but we need to narrow the time frame. The bell is likely a single instance. Cortes might have had items cast at many different times and places. There were ships routinely sent back to Spain to provide the king with his one fifth royalty tribute," said Liah.

"You mean the king got a fifth of the treasure, just for being king?" asked Mike.

Liah nodded. "That was how it was supposed to work, and it did function in that fashion, it's just that all the findings or discoveries were rarely reported. But a fifth of something was better than nothing," replied Liah.

"The cruise ship moves on to Vera Cruz and then Key West. We can book it to there," said Dee.

"Alright," said Jamal, who turned and looked at Liah. "Could you come with us?"

She smiled nervously. "I don't know. I'll have to check. I

admit, I am curious now, but will have to see what my family needs."

"Do we need a copy of that letter?" asked Mike.

Dee looked at Liah to confirm. "I don't think so. It doesn't really establish the bell. It just shows that it's possible, even likely, but the letter doesn't seem direct enough."

Liah nodded her agreement. "It doesn't establish provenance, although it helps with intent."

Mike looked at Liah.

"We need something that actually describes or identifies the bell to authenticate it. The bell has the name *Castillo* stamped on it. We have to find the link to that name," she replied. "Let's go back to work, see if there is anything else."

THEY MOVED THROUGH THE REMAINDER OF THE FILES WITH little success. Standing and stretching, they heard Angelic as she stuck her head through the door.

"We're hungry. Are you done yet? Did you find it?" she asked.

Jamal looked at her and grinned. "It's a big puzzle, but we found an important piece."

They heard footsteps and saw the tour guide, Juan, approaching them.

"Did you have any luck?" he asked.

Liah stepped in front of the group and smiled at Juan. "A little," she replied, "we mostly satisfied our curiosity. Thank you so much for allowing us to review the files. We tried to leave everything just as we found it."

They shook hands, and Juan held her fingers for an extra second.

"If I can help further, please let me know."

Liah flashed him a very broad smile. "Come on, Cristina, we need to let this nice man get back to work."

11

COZUMEL (THE TOUR)

Liah led them from the museum to one of the beachfront restaurants near the docks. They gazed out at some of the bluest water they had seen so far. The sky was high and cloudless. A light breeze moved across them as they were seated.

"I noticed you shared little with the tour guide," noted Jamal to Liah.

She smiled at him and addressed the group. "When you're researching, you never know who else is as well. He seemed very helpful and wasn't intrusive. So I was probably overly cautious. It's just a habit for me. I hope I didn't offend him."

"I don't think he was offended. In fact, I think he was quite taken with you," observed Angelic.

Liah shrugged her shoulders, "Men, what can you say."

Dee, Jamal, and Mike in unison 'humphed' at her. Then everyone laughed.

"So how are we going to do this?" asked Angelic.

"The women can catch tours from the plaza by the docks to the ruins, and the men can catch one to the distillery," replied Liah.

"What will we see?" asked Keno.

"We, the women," replied Liah, "are going to the San Gervasio Mayan ruins. They were dedicated to 'Ix Chel,' who was the goddess of fertility and childbirth, among other things. Mayan women would make pilgrimages to this site at least once in their life to make offerings and or give thanks."

"That seems appropriate," giggled Gina.

"Absolutely," noted Liah. "Family was very important to the Maya."

"But what about us?" said Jamal.

"You are going to the 'Hacienda Antigua' which is a replica of the hacienda in Guadalajara," replied Liah.

"No," sighed Mike.

Liah smiled. "It's okay. They walk you through the process of distilling tequila with pictures and exhibits and you taste test all along the way. I imagine you'll enjoy it. That's one reason to take a cab or a tour, in case you enjoy it too much."

Keno jumped in and addressed Mike. "You'd better not enjoy it that much. We'll be out in the hot sun toiling along and you'll be sitting in the shade soaking up high-quality tequila."

"Somebody's got to do it. You make choices in life," replied Dee.

"You have to be in the right mindset to visit the site of a fertility goddess, not fooling around drinking," laughed Jamal.

"It'll be fun for all of us," added Liah.

.   .   .

SHORTLY AFTERWARDS, THEY HAD FINISHED LUNCH AND FOUND themselves standing in the plaza. They had decided to take taxis so that they could come and go as needed and get back to the ship when they felt like it, rather than being trapped in a tour vehicle.

The men boarded for the Hacienda and the women for the ruins. They waved and started out. The taxis followed one another out of the city, but soon separated as the women turned left and began the trek further north. The men continued on the main road. In a little less than fifteen minutes they arrived and were ushered inside the Hacienda. Another twenty minutes later, they knew more about tequila than they thought possible.

They sat in the shade on a veranda and enjoyed the last of the complimentary twenty-two-ounce margarita they had been given upon entering the facility.

Jamal finished up, and even though they had tried small shots of several varieties of the drink along the tour, he said, "How about another? This is the first time I've relaxed since we left Cabo."

Mike nodded and held up his glass.

Dee looked at his watch and said, "Yeah, I guess, the women are going to be awhile yet, anyway. We can sit here and enjoy ourselves for a bit longer before we start back to the docks. We can stay out of the sun here as well as there. We could taxi over to see if we could find them?"

Jamal and Mike looked at him and shook their heads.

"Let's leave them and their fertility goddess alone," said Mike.

Jamal ordered them all another round. Then, sitting down between Dee and Mike, he said, "Do you think we're ever going to find anything out about this bell? I mean Liah seems pretty intent about turning it over to the government.

Plus, it's heavy. I don't know about toting it around much longer once we get off the ship."

"I agree," replied Dee. "I'm not sure how we move it, or where we're going. We need a decision."

"I just wish I had some answers," stated Jamal. "We turn it over to the government and it'll disappear forever."

"You don't think they'd put it on display?" asked Mike.

"Not if they can't establish ownership. They wouldn't want someone else claiming it. It'll end up in a box in a warehouse," replied Jamal.

Dee and Mike both looked at Jamal inquisitively.

"Well, it will," replied Jamal, crossing his arms.

The drinks arrived, and the men settled back to enjoy them along with the slight breeze that had picked up.

SLIGHTLY TO THE NORTH AND MUCH HOTTER, WITH SWEAT running down their faces, despite the light breeze, the women trudged through the ruins, with Liah leading the way. The women took turns holding Cristina's hand and leading her or carrying her when she got tired.

They started on the main path into the ruins and crossed under the ceremonial arch as if they were on a pilgrimage of their own. They passed from site to site, listening to the guide and looking at signage. Liah was also knowledgeable about the ruins.

"While these remaining ruins aren't very large, compared to many, they were the second most important site in the Mayan society," she said. "The women came here as young girls before they were women to ask for fertility and they returned after childbirth to give thanks. It was a heavily visited site."

They were nearing the end of the tour and were standing

in front of a ruin called 'Nohoch Nah' or 'Big House' which was the most complete structure they had seen so far on the tour. The guide described it as a temple which had an altar at its center where offerings were made by the Mayan women. Directly behind the structure was a thick canopy of forest. The women were at the back of the group and stopped to inspect the structure. They heard the guide say the group would move on to the 'Central Plaza' before dispersing.

Liah and Angelic were marveling at the small structure.

"All those thousands of women who passed through here," whispered Angelic.

Liah nodded. "It must have been something to see."

Angelic turned and looked as the crowd moved away toward the plaza. She looked back to Liah. "Do you suppose we could stick our head inside? I'd really like to see the altar."

Liah froze for a moment. "For many years you could walk among the structures, but tourism has gotten so heavy that it's restricted now." Liah turned and looked at the receding crowd. "I suppose it would be okay for a minute." She waved to Keno and Gina, who were busy with Cristina. "Come on, just for a minute." They trooped up the steps together.

They stood for a few seconds, glancing about the little room and then staring at the small altar.

Keno had Cristina by the hand and turned and picked her up and placed her on the altar.

"Look, Mommy," Cristina giggled, "I'm a Mayan princess."

Liah scowled, but then smiled quickly and said, "Get down from there. We'd better go."

They turned and exited the structure and, reaching the bottom of the small stairs, stopped to look back one more time. Keno again had Cristina by the hand at the front of the group. She turned and waited for the others to finish.

As the others turned from the temple, they realized Keno and Cristina were surrounded by a group of men with guns at their sides. The crowd had receded in the distance. Standing in the center of the group, right beside Cristina, was the man with the birthmark, from the boat, from the Sea of Cortez.

"He's back," whispered Keno.

The man spoke, "My name is Miguelito Cortes and you all will be coming with me."

DEE, JAMAL, AND MIKE HAD FINISHED THEIR SECOND margarita and caught the taxi back to the dock. They waited patiently. Jamal finally called Angelic and got no answer. In fact, the call went straight to voicemail.

"Okay," said Jamal ending the call," Angie never shuts her phone off, she likes to talk too much."

Mike tried Keno, and Dee called Gina. There were no answers, and the calls went straight to voicemail.

"We better get out there," said Dee.

They turned and started looking for taxis when Mike jumped forward and walked over to one parked across the way.

It was the driver from earlier that morning who had taken the women to the ruins.

Mike held up his hands. "The women from this morning?"

The driver looked at him.

Jamal pulled out his phone and popped up a group picture they had taken on the ship.

"You took them to the ruins earlier this afternoon," said Jamal.

The driver nodded. "I stayed until the end of the tour but I didn't see them again. They must have ridden back with someone else. I was looking for them, they tipped well."

"Can you take us back out there?" asked Dee.

The driver nodded. They started to get in the car.

"Dee, Jamal, Mike," they heard a voice and turned. It was Roberto. They waved for him to jump in the cab with them, and then the driver pulled quickly away.

12

COZUMEL (THE SEARCH)

"I just flew in and made for the ship. Liah had texted me you were touring this afternoon. I was lucky to see you. I had Dee's number and was going to call," explained Roberto as they rode to the ruins. Arriving as the site was closing for the day, the men jumped hurriedly from the cab. Dee handed the driver a large tip and asked if the man could stay and wait for them. He eagerly agreed.

Jamal ran to the entrance gate and asked if the grounds were closed, if everyone had been cleared. The woman in the booth seemed a little surprised.

"Our wives and girlfriend," Jamal said, waving his hand at the group of men, "came out for the afternoon tour and have not returned. We can't reach them on the phone. Have there been any issues, heat stroke or anything?"

The woman in the booth shook her head. Another woman, a little older and uniformed, came toward them from across the plaza.

"Is there a problem, senor?" she asked, although she faced the entire group of men.

Jamal repeated himself, "Our wives came out on the afternoon tour and haven't returned, nor have they answered their phones."

The woman looked at Jamal and then at the group. She took a radio from her belt and said something quickly and softly.

"The two tour guides will be here in just a minute," she reassured the men.

They stood in the sun for a moment and two younger women approached from the grounds behind the uniformed supervisor.

The woman turned and said, "These men are looking for their wives from the afternoon tour."

Jamal stepped forward and showed the guides the picture he had previously shown the taxi driver.

One shook her head, but the other pondered for a moment. "They were with me. I remember the little girl. She was so cute. They took turns with her, like a group of aunts. They were with me most of the way through the tour, although I don't remember seeing them at the end in the 'central plaza,'" the guide responded.

"What was the last previous stop?" asked Roberto as the other men turned to look at him. He nodded briefly and stepped forward to the guide.

She pointed beyond them and to the right. "It's called the 'Big House.' It was a ceremonial temple where the Mayan women made sacrifices."

Roberto turned and looked at the other men, his face tight. He turned back to the guide and said, "Can you show us?"

The guide looked to the supervisor, who nodded.

"Come this way," said the guide and started for the ruin.

The grounds were empty around the structure and it stood silent, reflecting the sun in a soft, late afternoon breeze. The guide stuck her head inside. "There's no one in there."

Roberto stood for a moment, the men surrounding him.

"That's not like them," said Mike. "Keno's not a rule breaker. Could they be somewhere else on the grounds?"

The guide shook her head. "The other guide and I just finished our walk through before we lock up. There's no one on the grounds."

"May I walk around the back side of the structure?" asked Roberto.

The guide nodded.

The other men watched as Roberto walked slowly around the building. He disappeared. Dee and Jamal were both scanning the grounds in opposite directions.

"Guys," Roberto called, "come around here."

Jamal, Dee, Mike, and the guide all trooped around the building.

Roberto was squatted on his heels, looking at the dirt and sand of the pathway around the building.

He pointed with one hand. There were a large number of tracks, including a small one, and the men knew he meant Cristina, along with several larger ones, and they weren't sure what he meant. The tracks led back to the jungle. He stood and walked along beside them.

"I'll look," he said.

They watched him stride back to the edge of the jungle, looking at the sand and dirt of the footpath and into the foliage beyond.

He stopped again and pointed. "You see how it's trampled a bit here around the perimeter?"

Dee, Jamal, and Mike all moved a little closer toward him. Only the guide hung back.

"I'm going to go just a couple of feet," he said and started into the foliage.

The men moved closer and then stopped at the edge of the jungle. They could partially see and hear him. He was bending over.

He came back toward them, his hands full. He had a pile of phones which he sat on the ground. He reached for a small one.

"This is Cristina's play phone, which means Liah may still have her phone. I don't see it in this group and didn't find it. Maybe she fooled them if they counted the number of phones. Can you guys identify these others?"

Jamal reached out and pointed. "That's Angelic's," he said.

Mike pointed to Keno's.

Dee picked up the last phone. They were all turned off. He turned it on and a picture of Gina and him came up on the screen. He nodded to Roberto. "Gina," he said.

Roberto turned to the guide, who was still several feet away. He pointed to the jungle.

"Is there anything out there, buildings, airstrip, or boat dock?" he asked.

The guide shook her head, her eyes sad and her face long. "Just jungle until you get to the beach.

Jamal was looking at her, watching her as she answered. "What's the matter?" he asked her.

She shook her head. "I fear someone has taken them."

"Do you know something?" asked Dee.

She shook her head violently. "No, senor, only what I see, and I'm thinking of the little girl. Rich tourists sometimes get taken."

Roberto grimaced. "How far is it to the ocean?" he asked the guide.

She looked at him for a second.

"Probably two-and-a-half miles north and a little west to

Isla de la Pasion, three miles north and a little east to the Cozumel Pearl farm, four miles due east to the beach, and maybe four and a half miles northeast to Castillo Real," she replied.

"What is Castillo Real?" asked Roberto.

"It's an isolated Mayan ruin, probably a lookout point for the open sea, amazing views, not near anything," she replied. "You have to ATV or bike or walk into it."

"Four miles?" he asked.

She nodded. "But it's mostly jungle and marsh. There are crocodiles in the marsh, just so you know. I wouldn't walk it from here."

"It would take quite a while to walk it even without rough terrain," added Dee.

Roberto nodded to him.

"Do the ruins have an ATV?" Roberto asked the guide.

She held up two fingers. "Two," she answered.

"Can we use them, can you show us?" he asked.

The guide paused for a moment. "Yes, under the circumstances, I'll take you to them. But shouldn't you call the police?"

Roberto nodded to her. "Definitely, as soon as we have something to report."

He stood. "Dee, you want to go with me? Jamal, you and Mike go back and secure the taxi. We'll need to bring the ATVs back here, so this is the best place to stay. We'll call you as soon as we see anything."

Dee could see that Jamal and Mike didn't like being left behind.

"Could we double up on the ATVs?" asked Dee.

Roberto glanced up at him, and then at the other two men. "Let's see what size they are," he said and nodded to the guide to lead the way.

Back at one of the utility sheds on the site, the guide pointed at the two ATVs. They were older and small. They clearly were meant only to motor around the site.

Roberto looked up at Dee and the other two men and said, "We'll be lucky if they get two of us there."

Jamal and Mike nodded.

"What can we do?" asked Jamal.

"Secure the taxi so we have a way back to the docks, and try to be patient. It's a lot to ask, I know. We'll call you as soon as we see something."

Jamal and Mike nodded and walked toward the entrance and the parking lot beyond. Roberto rolled the larger of the two ATVs out and nodded Dee toward the other.

"Have you ridden one of these?" asked Roberto.

"A few times, I have friends that hunt with them or climb mountains," Dee replied.

Roberto grinned. "No mountains here, but we are hunting, you can be sure of that. Follow me, but not too close. I'll try to keep an eye out for you."

And with that, he roared away.

Dee waved to the guide. "Thank you, we'll put them back when we return." She nodded, her face still strained. Dee floored it and scrambled to follow Roberto as he led them behind the ruin where he found the phones and disappeared into the jungle.

They broke through the canopy a few minutes later and were on more of a rocky pre- beach landscape where they rolled up and down and tried to avoid marshy areas and drop offs.

Roberto flew along. Dee guesstimated he was headed northeast toward Castillo Real, for whatever reason. Then Dee noticed they weren't really on a path, but they were following what looked like someone else's trail of bent and broken grass, scattered rock, and disturbed terrain. If someone had taken the women, they too must have had ATVs or some kind of transportation. The terrain wasn't walkable unless you were really desperate.

Roberto cruised along and finally slowed. He motioned Dee up beside him.

He pointed at the track they had been following.

"Whoever this was didn't try to conceal their trail," he stated.

"Did they think we wouldn't look or that it would grow dark or..."

"Could have been, or they may have just been arrogant," answered Roberto.

He gunned the ATV and took off again.

A few minutes later, after wondering how Roberto seemed so capable, Dee saw the ocean in the distance. They were still moving northeast. It wouldn't be long.

A moment later, Dee saw the ruin. It sat on a little knoll, and it looked a bit like a mini lighthouse. Standing on it would have provided a magnificent view out to sea.

Roberto slowed and stopped several yards from the rock. He parked the ATV and moved cautiously toward the ruin. Dee followed.

There was a sandy patch close to the overlook. Roberto made straight for it.

He stopped several feet away and pointed to the ground. "See all those footprints?" he asked, then he pointed a little further inland. There were two parallel tracks, and the ground looked as though it had been windswept.

"Rotor wash and helicopter landing gear, a big one, four women, a little girl, four or more big men, it would have to be good sized, probably a Huey. I might be able to find it." He pointed to the ground. "They stood here, waited for it to cycle down, and then were picked up."

Roberto walked back toward their ATVs. He saw

another piece of a sandy area that lead around the ruin and down to the beach. He approached it slowly, then stopped and waved to Dee.

"Tire tracks," he said, then turned and pointed. "Our bikes are over there. Could be anyone, but they look fresh, not windblown or caked into the sand. Let's follow them."

He moved further down the bank and toward the beach, monitoring the tracks. When Roberto got to the beach side, he stopped and looked back up at the ruin. There were still tracks. He followed them toward the base of the ruin. As he reached the rock footer, there were several scrubby bushes and brush against the base. The tracks ran into the brush. He motioned to Dee and then cautiously pulled the bushes back and away from the rock base. The space was empty, although the sand was littered with tire tracks.

Roberto stood there for a moment, studying the patterns.

Dee called out, "Roberto, there're tracks down here, all the way to the water."

Roberto turned from the bushes and the base and walked out to Dee, holding something in his hand. He knelt by the tracks.

"Someone picked up the ATVs after the others left on the chopper," he replied. "This was very well organized," he paused, "and expensive."

Roberto stood up and scanned the sea to the horizon. There was only empty ocean.

"They could have flown to a ship, but that's a big bird. They probably circled the island and returned to the mainland. Up here on the north and east side there's not much traffic. Less chance anyone saw them in the air or on the water."

He turned back toward Dee and held up a phone. "It's Liah's," he said. "I found it by the rocks and it has an unsent text message. It says 'mainland.'"

Dee looked at him for a moment, then said, "What do we do?"

"We go get them," replied Roberto, who fired up his ATV and roared away.

13

COZUMEL (LATER THAT NIGHT)

In only a minute, Roberto stopped. As Dee pulled up, he saw Roberto pull out his phone, but then he looked at Dee and grinned.

"Would you call Jamal and Mike?" he asked. "I don't have their numbers."

Dee nodded. "What exactly do I tell them?" he asked.

Roberto looked to the west, at the sun sinking low in the sky. He turned back to Dee.

"We should be there shortly, hopefully before dark, and we'll head back into town and decide what to do. They were taken by helicopter to the mainland. There's no known reason, yet."

Dee made the call, and they zoomed away toward San Gervasio.

THE FOUR MEN SAT AT AN ISOLATED TABLE ON THE DECK OF the seaside restaurant where they had eaten lunch, which now felt like so long ago. It was dark, and the soft illumination from the string of lights above them highlighted their faces.

During the taxi ride into town, Roberto had briefly explained to Mike and Jamal what he and Dee had seen.

Dee spoke to Roberto, but also for the benefit of the others, "Back on the beach, you said something about being able to track the Huey. You seem really knowledgeable and capable. Which is great but how..."

Roberto nodded and allowed a brief grin. "My friends, and I hope I can call you that," he looked around the group and everyone nodded, "Before I married Liah, I was Panamanian special forces. That's where I met Ernie, on a joint training mission, parachuting into the jungle of a country that shall remain unnamed. It was at night on a HALO jump, that's high altitude low opening, you go out of the plane early and you fly around to get where you are going and then you open late or at the lowest possible altitude. It can be risky, especially at night, anyway Ernie took a hard landing on some broken ground, busted up his knee. He was the field commander on the mission. He's been doing insertions for many years, he's highly decorated. Anyway, I assisted him during the balance of the mission. He's a tough old goat, but the knee eventually led to his retirement.

"After we got back from that mission, he asked me if I was married and I said no. Then he said, I have a daughter I'd like you to meet. I couldn't believe it and he made me kind of nervous. You never know what to expect. Then he pulled out a picture of Liah and my knees went weak. I recognized her. Olympic heroes are very well known in my country. The rest is history. I went to reserve duty so I could help at the B&B and be with Liah, and then Cristina. I was a street orphan. It was go to the military or go to prison. Ernie and Alicia, Liah and Cristina, they are the only family I've ever had.

"But, getting back to the question, I have connections, as you might imagine, that should be able to track down a Huey or any helicopter flight plans and locations. It depends on who it is. My friends," he leaned closer to them and lowered his voice even though they sat away from the other patrons of the restaurant, "this is an 'active' part of the world. There is a lot of military surplus around, but Huey's stand out, there is cartel activity, and there are a lot of other ambitious elements in my country and in this country as well.

"I do not know why someone would take the women. It might be a straight up ransom, which would actually be best. Those types of people can be dealt with, and no one will look in our direction. But, I worry it may be related to what you found in Cabo.

"Taking them was a bold extraction. To kidnap them from a public place, in broad daylight, take them cross-country, fly them out, and remove the ATVs, it was well organized and expensive. I fear who we may deal with."

"You have an idea?" asked Jamal, leaning forward.

"Not a specific name, no," replied Roberto. "Just the magnitude and scope of the operation so far. If it's blackmail, we should have a ransom note by morning. If it's traffickers, we're going to have to move fast. There are four beautiful women and a little girl." He shook his head slowly. "I don't want to think about that."

"What do we do?" asked Mike.

Roberto actually grinned for the first time. "We call Ernie. He will not be happy, but he will know what to do."

. . .

Roberto made the call. At first, Ernie couldn't believe him and made Roberto repeat the story. But then, when Ernie believed him, Ernie took action.

They spoke for a moment, and then Roberto sat the phone in the middle of the table, in speaker mode, where they could all hear. Ernie spoke slowly, calmly, softly, and in generic terms. Anyone overhearing the call, which didn't seem likely, could not tell that anything unusual was going on.

"We'll get some friends, Roberto, you get two and I'll get two. We can start our vacation there where you are. I'll get all the gear together and meet you later today. I want you to contact your friends at the airport and see about helicopter flight information," instructed Ernie.

"Will do. See you soon. We'll stay in the dock area. I'll text you a location," replied Roberto.

"Affirmative," replied Ernie, and the call went dead.

"The best thing you can do is get some sleep," said Roberto to the other men.

"We want to help," replied Mike.

"I know you do. I'm not sure what will be best, but right now it would be good to get some rest. You don't know when you may get to sleep again," answered Roberto.

"Surely we can help you with something now," added Jamal.

"I have to do some planning. Ernie will have ideas as well. I can't say for sure what will happen or if you will go with us," said Roberto.

"We will be going with you," answered Dee.

"You are not soldiers. I do not want to see you die," replied Roberto.

"We don't want to see that either, but they are our wives

and girlfriend, and we will not abandon them to anyone. We survived on a deserted island for six weeks, dealt with evil men, pirates, killers, and we lived. Do not underestimate us," said Dee.

Roberto smiled. "I would expect nothing less from you, my friends, and I welcome your support. But we must plan how to be efficient and effective. Ernie will have much to say and he will lead the way. You must do as he says. He will expect that you want to be part of the rescue. Let us see how he plans it. In the meantime, let me reach out to some friends for support, equipment, and information. I still have that tag number from the drive to Colon that I didn't have time to run down. Perhaps that will tell us something. Meantime, get some rest. Ernie will be here by dawn and then we will move quickly, I promise."

The group broke up with Dee, Jamal, and Mike heading back to the ship. Roberto stated he would stay somewhere in the immediate dock area and meet up with Ernie when he and their other friends arrived.

"Don't leave us behind," said Dee to Roberto as the men stood to leave.

"We wouldn't leave without sharing our status with you. Most likely Ernie will have a task for you. Do not worry. Ernie will move the heavens and the earth for his daughter and granddaughter, and their friends. He is not a man to be taken lightly."

The group nodded to Roberto, who already had his phone out and was dialing away.

As they walked back to the ship, Dee spoke.

"We'll need to make arrangements with the cruise lines for our luggage and equipment and extending the tour to Vera Cruz and Key West. I got a friend in Key West that might help us."

"You got friends everywhere," noted Jamal, and Mike grinned at them both.

"We need help," replied Dee.

"Yeah, I'm grateful," replied Jamal. "What are you thinking?"

"We'll book passage to Key West and I'll plan for Ike—his name is Ike Mann—to pick up our gear when the ship ports. That way we don't have to worry about taking possession or keeping up with our stuff or the bell. Be sure tonight to get all the passports."

"Ike Mann the tennis player?" asked Jamal.

"Retired," replied Dee. "We were in school together. He was one of my roommates. He works around the tour now. I hope I can catch him at home. He's got a little 600 square foot house in Key West where he keeps his stuff when he's not traveling."

"Let's get some rest," said Mike. "Breakfast at five and we'll work through it and wait to hear from Roberto."

They bumped fists and went into their respective suites for a short night and a little sleep.

14

COZUMEL (THE RESCUE)

Ernie and four friends and two boxes arrived at seven the next morning. They said they flew in from Panama.

Roberto had called Dee and told him to bring Jamal and Mike and come down to the dock. The three men had met for breakfast and planned with the concierge for the group's continued passage to Key West. They hoped that the rescue might go quickly and safely, and perhaps they could catch the ship in Vera Cruz. Dee had reached Ike, and he was available to look for them or their gear in Key West if the rescue took longer. They were set to go, if Ernie had a place for them.

The entire group met at the end of a long fishing pier. No one else was around.

Ernie waved at the four men and then turned to the others. "From now through the conclusion of the operation, we will use code names. It's safer for everybody. If we get split up, no one knows anything specific." Pointing back to the four men, he concluded, "These are Alpha, Bravo, Charlie, Delta, and I'm Echo. We're the 'A' team."

Dee noted that two of the men were older, closer to

Ernie's age, and the other two were younger, closer to Roberto in age. *Perhaps they'd work with the man who recruited them. What would that mean for himself, Jamal, and Mike? We are probably the reason for the code names. These guys know each other.*

Ernie pointed at Jamal. "You're 'Juliet.'"

Jamal looked at Dee, "You Romeo?"

Ernie, now Echo, shook his head, "'Sierra.'" Then he pointed to Roberto, "He's 'Romeo.'" Then he pointed to Mike, "You're 'Mike.'"

Mike nodded. "I might remember that one," he grinned.

"Romeo," Echo said and waved his finger at Sierra, Juliet, and Mike. "And you guys are the 'B' team. Each group will have a specific assignment, carry it out to the letter, do not fail."

They all nodded in agreement.

Two hours later, they found themselves at the back of a small hangar at the Cancun International Airport. They'd taken the ferry from Cozumel to Playa del Carmen and then taxied to the airport. There was a twin engine Beechcraft sitting just beyond them. There was a man working on the plane. Dee, Jamal, and Mike—now Sierra, Juliet, and Mike—looked at him uncertainly.

Ernie waved at him and spoke, "He's 'Papa' the pilot. He's one of us."

They sat in a small circle in folding chairs, the boxes just behind them. One of the four men spoke. It was Alpha or Bravo.

"We brought some toys for our vacation. It should be fun," he said.

Ernie grinned at the man. "Don't scare them." Then, turning to Sierra, Juliet, and Mike, he said, "I heard the story about your stay on the island and how it ended. That was very impressive. This will probably be even more dangerous. We need you to do just what you are told."

Sierra, Juliet, and Mike nodded to him.

Romeo said, "There was no ransom note this morning, no reports on the news of kidnapping, or murdered women. This looks like traffickers or something else more specific."

The entire group shook their heads in reply.

"Romeo, what did you find about the Huey?" asked Echo.

"There are several in the area. Two of them did not fly. There was a third that flew between Mexico City and Costa Maya, which doesn't seem probable for us, and then the last two. The first one flew from Cancun to Campeche, and the second one flew from Cancun to Oaxaca."

"Anything similar about the flights?" asked Echo.

Romeo replied, "The flight paths would both have crossed the lower Yucatan near the three-state border of Quintana Roo, Campeche, and Yucatan before separating for their respective locations."

"How do we know they flew beyond Cancun? If we believe they came to the mainland?" asked Alpha.

"We don't," answered Echo. "We're just looking for patterns."

Romeo continued, "I put out feelers for human trafficking in the three-state area. My sources say there is some because of the tourists, but the cartels don't want to discourage or frighten them, so there is more drug trade, prostitution, and only the occasional kidnapping."

Charlie responded, "So what does that mean to us?"

Romeo held up a hand. "There is another piece of information, in several parts. Let me explain."

Romeo paused for a moment, as if collecting his

thoughts. "Echo, there was another item that I failed to tell you about before I left Panama. When we drove to Colon, several vehicles followed us. I caught a license number on one of them in order to check it. We got busy with the new arrivals at the B&B and I failed to immediately look it up."

Romeo looked to Echo, his face anxious. Echo nodded to him. "Please continue."

Romeo caught his breath and started again. "The vehicle was registered to a company I'd never heard of before. When I checked the company it was owned by another company and that was owned by a third company. With some digging I found the owner of the third company, the primary owner, was Miguelito Cortes."

Echo brought a finger to his lips and exhaled slowly.

Alpha, Bravo, Charlie, and Delta were all looking at one another.

Juliet asked, "What does that mean?"

Romeo looked to Echo again, who nodded almost imperceptibly, and then Romeo said, "Miguelito Cortes is an extraordinarily wealthy businessman and head of the largest cartel in Mexico. He's a powerful and ruthless man, not someone to be trifled with. He has interests in banking, transportation, communication, construction, and drugs. He has his fingers deep into the government."

"Why would he be involved?" asked Delta.

"Something he must want badly," noted Echo. He turned toward Juliet, Sierra, and Mike.

"Tell us about what you found in the Sea of Cortez."

The three men looked at one another and then Juliet said, "We were diving outside La Paz, just to the north. We found a fragment of an old galleon on a shelf about 80 feet below the surface. While we were exploring it, we found a ship's bell, or a replica of a ship's bell. It was heavy, but we brought it up and took it with us."

"How would Miguelito Cortes know this, and why would he care?" asked Charlie.

Sierra continued, "There was a big white yacht that passed us right after we brought the bell up. We don't think they saw what we had, but we can't be sure. Juliet thinks the bell is cast from Aztec gold."

There were head shakes and sighs from Alpha, Bravo, Charlie, Delta, Echo, and Romeo.

Romeo said, "Miguelito, which is Spanish for 'little' Miguel, is the son of 'big' Miguel, or his father, who founded the cartel and established many of the business interests. To Miguelito's credit, he has expanded the legitimate portions of his empire, although there is rumor how he accomplished that. He has many apparently legitimate business interests aside from being the leader of the largest cartel. Miguelito thinks he is a direct descendent of Cortes and there are also rumors that he thinks he is a direct descendent of the Aztec, Montezuma. He has a birthmark on his face that runs down across his shoulder and onto his arm."

"That's him," exclaimed Juliet. "He was on the bow of the ship when it passed us."

"We saw him again in Acapulco and on our cruise," added Mike.

"Then he is definitely after you," stated Echo. "This is bad. He want's what you have."

"Why haven't we heard from him?" asked Sierra.

"Do the women know the location of the bell?" asked Echo.

Sierra, Juliet, and Mike all nodded.

"Then he doesn't need to hear from you. We have to find them quickly," replied Echo.

Romeo spoke again. "He operates primarily out of the central Mexico valley, in and around Mexico City. But he has homes all over the country and abroad. He could have gone anywhere."

"Perhaps," replied Echo, "but I doubt he did. He's safest in Mexico, has the biggest base of operations, and if you're here," he pointed at Sierra, Juliet, and Mike, "he won't want to go too far away from the bell or whatever he thinks you have."

"Would he go to his local habitat, his group in Cancun, one of their facilities?" asked Charlie.

"It would be easy for him there," added Delta.

"Wouldn't it depend on what he's looking for?" said Alpha.

"Might he keep it separate from the cartel," added Bravo.

Echo, who was listening intently, raised a finger to his lips. "If he's looking for Aztec gold, or anything from the Sea of Cortez, it's likely unrelated to the cartel. I think Bravo is on to something."

"I thought this was originally a Mayan area," said Juliet.

"It was," replied Romeo. "But Echo's correct. Miguelito won't go far. Besides, he took them from a Mayan site. The Maya believed in human sacrifice and the Aztec, and the Inca. The era of those civilizations was a hard time in history to stay alive. The three cultures are similar in many ways."

"Does it mean anything that he took them from the Mayan site?" asked Sierra. "If he's that powerful, he could have taken them anytime or taken any of us, anyplace that suited him."

Echo again raised a finger. "I think you might be on to something. What was the nature of the site he took them from?"

"It was a fertility goddess, Ix Chel, I think," replied Juliet.

Echo smiled. "Romeo, you said they flew out of Cozumel from 'Castillo Real,' a lookout point for the Maya?"

Romeo nodded. "Yes, that's correct."

"We have a pattern," said Echo. "He's following or observing or some crazy thing or other, related to pre-Columbian history, tradition, or practice. You'd think it would be Aztec, if it's true what you say he believes, but they are similar and the Mayan sites would be convenient."

"You said Mayans believed in human sacrifice too?" asked Mike.

All the men turned to him.

"They took four women and a little girl from the site of a fertility goddess," replied Echo, "and left through a historical lookout point, but to where, to a sacrifice?"

"Extract the information and sacrifice the victims, especially if he thinks he's looking for Aztec gold," answered Romeo, sitting back in his chair.

Alpha, Bravo, Charlie, and Delta were murmuring among themselves.

"Where would they go for such a thing?" asked Sierra.

"Chichen Itza would be the closest and most obvious choice," answered Romeo. "But that's a huge tourist attraction and heavily populated."

"What else is in the area?" asked Juliet.

"Nothing," answered Romeo.

"Wait," said Echo. "The two helicopters crossed the Yucatan, correct?"

Romeo nodded.

"What's out there?" Echo asked.

"Nothing," Romeo answered again. "I mean, it's a rock plain made of sand, gravel, limestone. There's almost no one out there, it's extremely desolate, dry, and empty."

"Are there ruins?" asked Mike.

Romeo shook his head. But then Alpha spoke up. "I have family in this area. They say the limestone is riddled with caves and that there are many Mayan sites underground.

They aren't open to the public because they aren't near the beaches or spectacularly grand like Chichen Itza. But they are there."

"Romeo, what is the point of divergence of the two helicopters?" asked Echo.

"It's near the three-state border, where Quintana Roo, Yucatan, and Campeche meet. It's nearly due south of Chichen Itza," replied Romeo.

"What's important about that?" asked Mike.

"Until that point, the helicopters are on the same path. If they stopped at or near the convergence, we have two chances of locating the women. After that, we have to run down each path individually. It's just a thought, mid-desert, low traffic, feels right," replied Echo. "Even though it is a Mayan site, while the Aztec would feel superior in their status, they would make use of a facility or a site, if needed."

"We need topographical maps," he continued. "We can search for likely locations of caves near the divergent point. Alpha, does anyone in your family know the area?"

"I'll check. I have a couple of nephews that trail ride, motocross. They may know of something," Alpha replied.

"I'll get the maps," said Romeo.

"We'll break out the toys," said Charlie, nodding to himself and Delta.

15

COZUMEL (THE RESCUE-PART 2)

Two hours later, they were reassembled at the hangar. Romeo had several topographical maps spread out across the now-empty boxes. Charlie and Delta had assembled a cache of weapons that leaned against or sat beside the boxes. Alpha and Bravo had gone to meet with Alpha's nephews to talk about the Yucatan interior. Echo had sat and made notes in a spiral-bound book while Sierra, Juliet, and Mike had paced the hangar and chatted among themselves.

"Who has something?" asked Echo.

Both Romeo and Alpha spoke up. Romeo deferred.

Alpha stood. "I think your maps will help in a moment," he replied to Romeo. Then, turning to the others, "Bravo and I went and talked with two of my nephews. They motocross, race and practice, around much of the Yucatan peninsula, which encompasses all three of the local states. They spend a lot of time practicing in the tristate border region because it is so remote, and the terrain varies widely, lots of caves, so lots of ridges and bluffs and valleys. They're not high elevation, just widely varied. There is an area, in the state we are in, Quintana Roo, just south of the tristate borders, where they say there is some fencing, some 'private property' signage, and sometimes armed guards. They stay clear of it. I think we could spot it on your map."

Romeo nodded, turned to the map, and put his finger on a spot. He studied the terrain for a moment. "It could be a cartel stronghold," he replied.

Echo shook his head. "Defensively it would make sense, but heavy traffic in and out of a desolate area would create awareness that the cartel wouldn't want. It makes little sense strategically. The peninsula is surrounded by water. You could come and go easier that way. They have safe houses. Why would anyone want to be burrowed away in the interior?"

Romeo spoke again. "They're hiding something that they want few to know about and in which they have complete control over."

Echo nodded. "Like a place that you might take or make a sacrifice, if you believed in such things."

"What's the point of the sacrifice?" asked Mike.

There was silence for a moment, and then Romeo said, 'It's basically about power. It's about the ability to take a life with no consequences, to glory in death. It's a ritual that supposedly gratifies their pagan gods and brings them good favor. Basically, it intimidates the people, or makes a point about what happens if you defy the leadership."

"But they just want what we found? Getting that information from the women, or from us, shouldn't be that hard. Why is it necessary to kill them?" asked Juliet.

"Short answer, he's crazy," replied Roberto, "Longer version, he's eaten up with this whole idea of being the descendent of both Montezuma and Cortes the explorer and he feels he has some divine right of ownership to the Aztec gold. Again, it's basically an underlying attempt at influencing or intimating people and maintaining his power and peoples fear so that they do not intercede in his activities. It's colorful, frightening, and deadly, people fear it."

The group murmured and shuffled in their seats.

Echo stood and moved to the center of the chairs. "Romeo, take two of the men and research the area near where the helicopters separated. Use the topographical map for what you saw and any other likely sites, and see if you can establish the perimeter of the guarded area without being seen. Look for their surveillance-motion detectors, lights, cameras, booby traps, whatever obstacles they might have laid out. I'll work on the overall plan and the rest of the men can check their gear and prep."

Romeo nodded to Alpha and Charlie, and they broke from the circle and headed for the doors.

Sierra watched them go and thought to himself, *One from each group, the old and the young. They must all work well together. We need to integrate with them as best we can.*

A short time later, Bravo and Delta instructed Sierra, Juliet, and Mike in loading their packs and in the basics of their weapons.

Bravo pointed to Delta. "We're not sure what your assignments will be yet but we can go over a few basic things and get them out of the way," he said.

He grabbed one of the packs and started pulling items from the smaller boxes that had been unloaded. "You'll have a first aid kit, some protein bars, a canteen, a poncho."

"We expecting rain?" asked Mike.

Bravo shook his head and laughed. "No, but if we don't find what we're looking for quickly and night turns into day, you'll be glad you have some shade. It gets really hot on the peninsula, and it's very dry. Try to ration your water."

"Flashlights for the dark?" asked Juliet.

"Yeah, you'll have a flashlight, but we'll go in with night vision. You guys will probably tandem in on a chute with three of us. All you have to do is not panic and we'll get you on the ground."

"I've done a little skydiving," said Sierra.

"That's good," replied Delta, "but this will be a HAHO most likely, that's high altitude, high opening. We'll exit the plane at a high altitude and open the chutes almost immediately but some distance away from the site, and drift or fly in to minimize being heard by anyone on the ground."

"Why will we go in that way?" asked Mike.

"It's just an abundance of caution, it gives us an opportunity on approach to get a good overview, to see anything that might occur in the surrounding area, and time to make adjustments," answered Delta.

Bravo had picked up a rifle. "I understand you guys have some experience with AKs," he said.

They all three nodded.

"This is an M-4. It's like an AR-15 to civilians. Ever use one?" he asked.

They all three nodded again.

Bravo spoke in reply. "What we hope to do is 'insert, extract, and withdraw.' What we don't want is the 'engage' that often comes between 'insert and extract.' But, we'll do what we have to get the job done. Look these over, see if you have questions. Worse case, you can spray and pray, you know that one?"

Sierra grinned at him. "We've had some experience with it."

"Just be careful where you discharge, we don't want any 'friendly fire.'"

Bravo paused for a moment. "You'll have extra mags for the weapon, a combat knife, and we'll need to get you fitted, or suited up, I should say. Romeo guessed at your sizes. We'll go in with a desert camouflage pattern uniform."

"Just like a soldier of fortune," noted Mike.

Bravo and Delta both looked at him, and then Bravo spoke. "Not exactly. Echo will have a support role for you. If we're lucky, you won't have to do much of anything but tag along. He must think pretty highly of you guys to allow this. But, let's see what he says first."

They talked a while longer, and Bravo and Delta answered what questions they could. Everyone but Echo took a break and grabbed some lunch, relaxed, and waited until Romeo, Alpha, and Charlie returned. Echo kept scribbling in his notebook.

LATER THAT AFTERNOON, THE THREE MEN WHO'D BEEN ON assignment rolled back into the hangar, looking hot and sweaty. They were wiping their faces as they sat in the folding chairs and stripped off some of their gear.

"It's brutal out in the interior," stated Romeo. "No one would survive long without water and shade, at least not on the surface. We rented a couple of old trucks, no air conditioning. It was miserable, but we looked authentic."

"What did you see?" asked Echo.

Romeo smiled. "It's desolate out there, nobody around. And even when we came upon the fences, there was no sign of life. The entire area was silent, like there was some type of cloud hanging over it. But, there was a property sign and, in small print, at the bottom, it said 'Azteca Industries.' It has to be our guy. There were no guards and no visible security. It's very low profile, except for the sign. We took a couple of minutes and went in some other accessible caves further down the bluff line. They're larger inside than you might imagine, maybe the size of a basketball court a couple stories high. They drop into the ground. There's not a lot of surface elevation. A posted guard with night vision could see a long way. It's also very still. We will have to be cautious."

Echo stepped into the middle of the group again. "Did you see any sources of power, generators, or transmission lines, any communication equipment?" he asked.

"Negative," replied Romeo. "It appeared very low profile. I wonder if it's not a dead end."

Echo paused for a moment before he said, "What if Miguelito is in fact following some ancient ritual, then modern conveniences are not likely being used or serve only as a backup or emergency. We do not want to underestimate him."

Alpha jumped in and added, "In two nights, there is a new full moon. It's the second this month. It's called a 'Blue Moon.' Would that be significant?"

"Is the new moon related to the sacrifice, or to the sacrificial process?" asked Juliet.

No one spoke for a moment. Then Romeo cleared his throat. "I think it could be. I know that eclipses and other solar events were viewed as important omens. The full moon or 'Blue Moon' could be as well."

Echo spoke again, "Here's what we will do. Let's take a day and set up a surveillance on the site. See if anyone comes or goes or if there is any other type of activity. If we see something we'll take it into account. If not, we'll go in HAHO tomorrow night. There are ten of us and our gear. The plane would be full. I just don't think we have time to waste. But," he paused as if thinking, "we need transportation out. That will be your job," he said, turning and pointing at Sierra, Juliet, and Mike, "Land Rovers or, better yet, off-road Jeeps. They will be more durable than the old rental trucks. You will be just outside the perimeter of the operation. We will maintain radio contact and direct you.

You can carry extra supplies and move about as needed. It should be safer for you and less of an issue for the HAHO and the plane."

Alpha spoke up again, "What if we plant two men in a fixed position and then two or three more on motor bikes moving around the basin. That would draw anyone observing's attention and perhaps allow our watchers a better view of our prey."

"That's an excellent idea," replied Echo. "Can you arrange it with your nephews?"

Alpha nodded. "Who rides?" he said.

Bravo, Charlie, Delta, Juliet, Mike, Romeo, and Sierra's hands all went up.

Echo smiled. "I see we have plenty of volunteers."

Alpha called his nephews and arranged for them to meet the group at the hangar in the morning. They would bring three extra bikes. Echo assigned Romeo, Bravo, and Sierra to ride with the nephews, while Alpha and Charlie would cover fixed position surveillance. Echo, Delta, Juliet, and Mike would continue to plan, manage the communications, continue to research Miguelito, and watch for any news breaks or unusual happenings.

They wrapped up the session and broke into small groups for dinner. Echo and Romeo left together, Alpha, Bravo, and Papa went the opposite direction, Charlie and Delta followed them, leaving Sierra, Juliet, and Mike to go in the direction of Echo and Romeo. There were many restaurants and bars. They did not wish for all of them to be seen together. It was easy, to the casual eye, for them to blend in among the many tourists. However, a trained observer might notice so many hardened men together, and the group did not wish to raise any concerns.

16

THE YUCATAN (BY DAY)

They slept in the hangar, even Sierra, Juliet, and Mike. They didn't want to go back to the ship and be separated from the others in the group, and they knew there would be an early start the next morning.

Alpha's nephews rolled in right after dawn. Sierra spoke to Alpha as his nephews entered the hangar.

"Tell them to take it easy on us. If we look too bad, anyone watching will be suspicious."

Alpha nodded and smiled. "They're good. They'll make you look good too. Just relax and enjoy yourself."

Romeo, Bravo, and Sierra climbed into the back of the truck with one nephew. The other two rode up front. As they pulled away, Romeo spoke to the nephew.

"Do you know where we could rent a couple of off-road vehicles, Jeeps or dune buggies?" he asked.

The nephew nodded. "How many do you need?"

"Two should do it," replied Romeo. "Can we pick them up this evening?"

"We'll deliver if you like," the boy replied.

"I'll get you the coordinates later today," answered Romeo.

The group rode on in silence as they left the city behind.

ALPHA AND CHARLIE FOLLOWED AFTERWARD IN ONE OF THE old trucks. They would drive to a position approximately opposite the fenced and gated area and then hike in to a fixed base to observe. The others on the bikes would ride in the small valley between the two points.

Echo, Delta, Juliet, Mike, and Papa would remain at the hangar to plan, monitor, and assist in whatever fashion.

The truck pulled off the track deep in the Yucatan peninsula, just inside the state of Quintana Roo. It was remote. The road had become little more than a track across the rock and sand. Sierra glanced about anxiously. He thought to himself, *I hope we don't get caught in the dark out here. If I get turned around, I'm going to be so lost.*

They unloaded the bikes, and one nephew explained the track they would follow to circle around the valley floor.

"Have some fun, give it the gas, and get some air. You'll love it. But, it will be hot," he said. Then he grabbed a box and pulled out some leather chaps and jackets and vests. "These are going to be hot, but you will have a breeze. We got plenty of water but you can only pick it up when we come around the circuit. The chaps are better than landing in the rock on bare skin. We'll wear the vests. You guys wear the long sleeves." Then he handed out helmets. "These are all miced so we can communicate. Shout out if you go down hard. Otherwise, get up, get back on, and keep going."

The nephew in front led the way around the track for the first time. The second nephew rode in the middle of the pack with Romeo, Bravo, and Sierra, while the third nephew brought up the rear. The leader rode slowly and stopped at several places, pointing out features of the valley and highlighting obstacles.

"When we come back around on the second loop, we'll pick up speed and spread out a bit. This is not a race or a journey. We are practicing. You should expect starts, stops, and spills. Have some fun, cut doughnuts in the sand, ride wheelies, motocross riders are crazy guys," he said, just before he gunned the throttle and started away on the second lap, pulling a thirty yard wheelie. The others took off after him.

Romeo, Bravo, and Sierra were a little tentative on the next couple of laps, but then Bravo went down in a turn and came up laughing and brushing himself off. He jumped back on, pulled a small wheelie, and raced away. One nephew veered to the right and shot off a small rise, getting an impressive amount of air before landing on the far side and pulling back onto the track. Romeo and Sierra glanced to one another and, with an unspoken word, simultaneously pulled short ten yard wheelies, standing up on the pegs of their bikes and screaming. Everyone circled the track furiously and frantically.

A dozen laps later, the nephew in front waved everyone over to the truck. They were sweat-soaked, dusty, in some cases dirty, and had big smiles on their faces. They pulled over and shut the bikes down. The nephew tossed out bottles of water.

With his helmet off, he spoke softly to the group, "Uncle, Alpha, contacted me on my headset and said there was a guard who appeared and watched us for a few minutes. Then he disappeared, back into a cave, he thinks. It looks like the area around the sign is an entrance of some type. We'll go back to riding and see if he or Charlie can spot anything else. We normally break by early afternoon. It gets too hot to continue. We have some lunches in the truck. We can eat and see if Alpha needs anything else."

They went back to riding and circled the track for another hour. At one point, a nephew went down. He made several practice remounts and when Bravo stopped, they worked for several minutes on dismounting and remounting while moving slowly, as if on a restart from a fall.

The nephew who had gotten the big air on the early jump waved Romeo and Sierra over near the point he had made the jump. He motioned for them to sit at the top of the rise. Then he rode down to the bottom and turned back toward the top. He raced the bike's motor and then came roaring up the rise. He sailed up over the lip and right past Romeo and Sierra. It looked impressive, but from the reverse direction he was only a few feet off the ground. He motioned to Romeo and Sierra. Sierra looked over, and Romeo had a big grin on his face. Romeo gunned his bike and spun around, heading for the bottom of the rise. A few seconds later he came roaring up and passed by Sierra, several feet in the air.

Sierra thought to himself, *I guess it's my turn*, and he spun around to make the ride and the jump.

They pulled over for lunch just after midday. It had gotten continuously hotter. They were soaked and their chaps were dripping.

The nephew spoke again. "Alpha says there is some activity around the sign. The guy they saw earlier and another guard seem to be watching the road for someone. He says they have paid little attention to us. After we eat and pack up, he wants us to head in the direction the guards are watching. Just to see if we pass anyone or see anything. We'll take off in a few minutes. That road starts toward Campeche but veers back around toward Cancun and Cozumel. It probably has a better approach, to where the guards are located, than the road we came in on."

Everyone nodded and started in on the sandwiches that the nephew passed out. Reaching into the cooler, the nephew looked up. "Water or cerveza?" he asked.

THEY LOADED THE TRUCK AFTER LUNCH AND STARTED THE trek toward the road Alpha wanted them to take. Crossing the valley floor, they tied in to the other road and started toward Cancun.

They were still deep in the peninsula when they saw dust on the horizon. Something was coming their way. In a few minutes the driver called back, "It's coming up, a box truck, looks like an old Fed Ex." Shortly after, the truck rattled past them and the four riders in the back watched as it drove away. The vehicle was moving fast and bouncing hard.

"It's in a big hurry," said Romeo.

"On its way to a sacrifice?" asked Bravo. "It was big enough to hold six to ten people, depending on how tightly packed they are."

"It's good we're going back tonight. I don't think we have much time," replied Romeo.

THEY REACHED THE HANGAR AND OFFLOADED FROM THE truck. Romeo waved at the nephew and said, "Later tonight, can you meet us on the Campeche road with the dune buggies?"

The nephew nodded.

"I'll call you with the time. Alpha has your number?" Romeo continued.

The nephew nodded. All three of them threw up their hands in farewell, and the truck pulled away.

Alpha and Charlie pulled up in one of the old rentals and passed the nephews on their way out, as Alpha and Charlie were on their way in.

Bravo, Romeo and Sierra stood together and waited for Alpha and Charlie to join them. They all strode into the hangar together. At the far end, they could see Echo, Delta, Juliet, and Mike busy at work.

"Let's go see what's happening," said Romeo and he led the way, the others falling in behind him.

17

THE YUCATAN (BY NIGHT)

Echo looked up as the men made their way across the hangar. He raised a hand and waved to them. "Be seated. Let's catch up," he said.

Everyone filed in and sat down. Mike went first.

"I contacted the ship to see if we had any messages. There were none," he said. "They also advised they had stored the luggage from our rooms with our equipment in the hold. So, apparently no issues have occurred with that so far."

"Apparently, then, Miguelito does not know what you have, or the size of it. Taking it from the ship's hold would be fairly simple for him," stated Echo.

"What must he be thinking?" asked Jamal.

"If he didn't see what you had, he must have been looking in or for the area where you were diving. He must have had a report or a sighting he was pursuing. And if he thought he saw you with something, he's going to want to know what it is," replied Echo. "He's chased you around the country, the long way. It must be something he considers very important."

Mike then continued, "With Delta's help, I searched the news and media for any notices, requests for reward, statements, anything like that. There was nothing."

Juliet went next. "I spent the day researching Miguelito Cortez. I was looking for his history, his interests, any recent sightings of him, anything that could tell us more about what he might do or how he might act. He appears to have an Aztec fixation. His birthmark can be identified or traced to the Aztec feathered serpent, Quetzalcoatl, who was the god of death and resurrection, appropriate for a sacrifice, perhaps. The birthmark also traces to Cortes the explorer, his supposed namesake. The story has it that the Aztec princess or captive that Cortes took from the Mayans and used to converse with Montezuma, eventually became his mistress and the mother of Cortes' male child and thus established the connection between Montezuma, the supposed descendent of Quetzalcoatl, Cortes the explorer, and in whatever fashion, Miguelito Cortes the drug lord, businessman, and treasure hunter."

Delta went next. "Aside from helping Mike, I planned the route for the night drop and for the exit from the site, while Echo worked on the strategy of the extraction." He nodded to Echo.

Echo stepped forward. "Based on the information Alpha and Charlie shared with me while returning from the observation site, I have a plan." He paused and looked around a room full of rapt faces.

"The full moon rises at sunset and reaches its highest point in the sky at midnight. I did a little research myself and that seems to be the strategic moment of the 'Blue Moon,' the peak of its power, so to speak. My guess is that any ceremony that Miguelito wants to perform will happen then. But, to be safe, we'll leave here at dusk and fly over for the

HAHO. Romeo and Sierra will be in one of the exit vehicles and Juliet and Mike will be in the other."

Romeo jumped to his feet and blurted, "I need to go with you. It's my wife and child."

Echo looked at him for a moment. "You are my second in command. I need you to manage the 'B' team and execute our escape. They are my daughter and granddaughter, they mean as much to me. If something should happen, you are much younger and stronger than I. You can care for them better than I, in my absence."

The two men looked to one another for a moment, and then Romeo nodded slowly and sat down.

"It's not a very detailed plan because we have so little information. We have a site and we think we may have some participants. It would be nice to know more, but there is little time. We will fly in from the HAHO and land near the gated area, unless we see some signs of activity, in which case we will land further up the cliff face so that we can approach the area from an elevated position. We'll have to read the situation on the way down. There should be plenty of light with the full moon. Once on the ground we will rendezvous, use night vision if we need, and move to the entrance.

"We will eliminate opposition as necessary and quietly as possible. Everyone will have combat knives and suppressors, which will only help so much. Once inside the cave or tunnel, we'll have to evaluate and decide in real time. I'll lead, flanked by Alpha and Charlie, as they have seen the guards and should recognize them or not. Bravo and Delta will bring up the rear and provide cover. Papa will fly us over the drop zone, return to base, and prep the plane for departure to Panama. Hopefully, we won't be coming back in hot. Once we locate and extract the captives, we'll exit to the gated area and to the Campeche road where the 'B' team will pick us up in the dune buggies.

"It'll be tight coming out. We'll put the women and the girl in the seats and the extraction team will split two or three to a vehicle and strap on to the supports where we can be hands free and provide cover. We'll stop and switch to the old truck as we come into town so we don't attract attention. It'll be late so there shouldn't be a great deal of traffic or they'll be partying and won't care. It's not much, but it's what we have. We'll go in heavily armed. We have M-4's, RPGs, hand-held grenades, flash bangs, and pistols. We have multiple magazines or rounds for all the weapons. We have level IV body armor. I wouldn't expect Miguelito to have a huge number of people present, just some security, and maybe a couple of other participants."

"Participants?" asked Juliet.

"He'll need other men to help him with the process of the sacrifice. Guards or strong men at the least, to manage the women and present them in the order he desires," replied Echo.

"Do we know what that order might be?" asked Sierra.

Echo paused for a moment and then shrugged. His voice was thick with emotion. "The little girl will probably be first or last. She would be the virgin sacrifice. The others are some kind of token. It's hard to know what twisted logic he might follow."

Alpha asked, "What if we don't find them?"

Echo looked thoughtful for a moment. "That would be unfortunate," he replied. "If we find nothing, we exit in the same fashion. If we see anything, or find anything, or anyone that can tell us something, we'll need to decide if we can pursue the information at that moment"

"Questions?" he asked.

"Any restrictions on engagement?" asked Delta.

"Bring the women and the girl out alive, do what you

have to accomplish that," Echo replied. A grim bunch of nods went around the group.

"We have a couple of hours. Check your gear and get some food and some rest. We'll mount up around dusk. The drop zone is only a few minutes away."

A COUPLE OF HOURS LATER, EVERYONE WAS GEARED UP AND ready to go. Echo, Alpha, Bravo, Charlie, Delta and Papa headed for the plane. Romeo had called Alpha's nephews and told them where to meet on the Campeche road. He, Sierra, Juliet and Mike climbed into one of the old trucks and got underway.

Romeo drove, Sierra sat up front with him. Juliet and Mike were in the back, against the cab. They shouted back and forth through the open rear sliding window.

"How are we going to know what to do or where to be?" asked Juliet.

"Echo will radio us positions and status," replied Romeo. "Sierra and I have been out here. I think we have a pretty good idea where to hold up. I want to be close enough to assist if they need us. Hopefully, it will be clean, quick, and non-lethal."

Sierra looked at him. "Do you really think so?" he asked.

"We can hope," replied Romeo.

SEVERAL THOUSAND FEET ABOVE THEM, THE OTHERS IN THE group made ready to jump. They were cruising at 12,500 feet, at the limit for no supplemental oxygen. They were nearly two-and-a-half miles high. HAHO's were typically 15,000 feet or greater and nearly three miles high or more, so this one was a little short, but Echo didn't want to use supplemental O2 and he wanted to open as soon as possible on the approach.

ROMEO PULLED OFF THE CAMPECHE ROAD IN A LITTLE ravine. He had seen it on the return trip earlier that day. Two nephews sat at the wheel of two beat up but sturdy looking dune buggies.

As Romeo and his group approached, one of them called out, "We brought the biggest ones we had. We thought you might need the space and the power."

Romeo nodded, and they shook hands. "Leave them here when we return?" he asked.

The nephew shook his head. "Yeah, you need us to take the truck for now or leave it here for the swap?"

"You can leave it. I can't give you an approximate time. Can I call if things change?" Romeo asked.

"No problem," replied the nephew as he and the other driver jumped from the dune buggies to climb into a late model pickup that the third nephew drove. They waved as they pulled away.

Romeo and Sierra jumped in one vehicle with Romeo driving, and Juliet and Mike jumped in the other, with Mike driving. They left the keys to the truck on the floorboard for whomever got back first. Anyone that wanted to steal it could hot wire it, anyway. Maybe it would be there when they returned. It was a pretty remote location, Romeo wasn't too concerned. They pulled onto the road and made for the drop zone.

IN THE PLANE, NEARING THE DROP ZONE, THE OTHERS IN THE group made ready. They were going out on high performance chutes that they would drop shortly after jumping. They had on flight suits, and there were low winds other than the expected altitude turbulence. The moon was up and full. There was plenty of light.

Ernie stood at the door and acted as the jumpmaster. He raised a hand at Papa's signal. He looked to his men and nodded before he shouted out as he dropped his arm, "Let's get this party started."

18

THE YUCATAN (ROUND MIDNIGHT)

Romeo and Mike pulled off the road at the foot of a small grade. Romeo spoke through his headset, "At the top of this rise the road levels out and is visible from the gate and signage. I don't know if they could see us from their interior position or not, if we were to get closer. We can be there quickly from here and, if anyone comes or goes, we're less conspicuous."

Mike came back. "What now?" he asked.

There was an audible sigh. "We wait," replied Romeo.

Thousands of feet above them, the last man had gone out the door of the plane. Echo waved at Papa, and then circled his finger, telling Papa to return to base and ready the plane, and then Echo rolled out the door. He stabilized quickly under his chute, checked his altimeter and compass, then cut away and flew for his target.

The moon was bright, and he could see the other flyers below him and the ground below them. *These were good men. They were not new to a fight. We have an adequate plan. Miguelito should not be expecting us. We will succeed.* Those were Echo's thoughts as he made his way to the target. He saw no sign of activity on the ground below, and he could see his men lining up for a close landing. His knee twinged a bit, but now was not the time for it, and he braced himself for what was ahead.

They landed in a tight pattern just above the entrance to the cave or the tunnel. Night vision equipment would not be necessary, at least until they got inside and circumstances dictated otherwise.

They peeled the flight suits off and grouped up. Echo hand signaled Alpha and Charlie to circle around, check the entrance, and remove any obstacles as needed.

They were back in only a few moments. Echo had not heard a sound. Alpha whispered into his headset, "The guards have been silenced. They were the two we had seen earlier. There is no one else around—that is visible, anyway. The entrance appears to be a tunnel leading into a cave. We'll need the night vision, at least for a time."

Everyone broke out their night vision and readied for the cave access. They moved around as a group, with Alpha and Charlie in front. They passed the sign and came to the cave entrance. Alpha held up a hand and motioned to Charlie. The two of them fitted their night vision and moved down the corridor. They disappeared around a bend and all was quiet for a few moments.

They reappeared quickly and quietly from the darkness. Alpha waved them back to the entrance. They stepped outside and Alpha spoke.

"The tunnel opens into a large cave. It's a couple of stories high and has an altar. It's like a pyramid with steps, except that it's flat on top with what looks like a stage and the altar. It's at the far end and is nearly at the level of the tunnel entrance. Ideally there would be a way around the top. If not, we have to go down and go back up to reach the altar."

"The women?" asked Echo.

Alpha nodded, and Charlie said, "They appeared to be in a pen at the bottom of the steps in the deepest portion of the cave. There were several men around the pen in street clothes. I didn't see Cortes or anyone in any sort of Aztec or Mayan garb. I think they must be here. The men around the pen seemed very vigilant, like others were around. No lounging, no laughing, they were serious."

"Do you think we could slip in, silence the captors, and ease the women out quickly?" Echo asked.

Charlie looked at Alpha, who then said, "It's several stories down. It is low light, but I saw some wall lamps so I think there's power. We could be caught flatfooted halfway down if they heard anything."

"So, we need stealth," answered Echo.

"Yes," replied Charlie. "Delta and I can slip down there and eliminate the problem and start the women out. A couple of you can meet them part way, and the others provide cover if needed."

Echo looked up at Alpha.

"I expect they are stealthier than me," replied Alpha.

"Happy to do it," added Delta.

"Let's go back inside," replied Echo.

They stopped as a group where the tunnel turned into the cave. They could see the altar across the distance of the cave and the women in the pen at the bottom.

Echo nodded. "Go, be safe, be successful."

They nodded and slipped away.

Echo turned to Alpha and Bravo. "Each of you, work your way around to the left and right and see if we can reach the altar without going down and back up."

They nodded and slipped off to each side, leaving Echo alone at the entrance.

Echo stood watching Charlie and Delta work their way down the cave along a path that descended toward the bottom. He had lost sight of Alpha and Bravo.

It was like a big, sloping crater, as Charlie and Delta moved slowly toward the bottom. They were about halfway down when the cave filled with light and the night vision equipment left them momentarily blinded. Shots rang out, and Echo dropped to the ground for cover.

By the time he could see again, rounds were echoing and ricocheting around the cave. None had been close to him.

"Spotrep, Charlie," Echo called into his headset, "Spotrep Delta." Echo heard footsteps and turned his weapon toward the sound. Alpha and Bravo came from each direction. Each man shook his head.

They slid in beside Echo and provided him cover.

"Spotrep Charlie, Spotrep Delta," he called again.

He heard a gasp, and then Charlie's voice crackled across the transmission. "I'm down, got stitched in the chest. Must be big NATO rounds, armor piercing."

"Spotrep Delta," Echo called again.

Charlie came back on and said, "I can hear him over there, but I can't see him."

There was more gurgling coming through on Echo's end. He turned to look at Alpha and Bravo.

Alpha said, "My side ran out and overlooked a steep drop to the bottom. It was like a balcony with no exit."

Bravo followed, "Mine was the same, but across the way I saw another entrance that looked like it had a path that led up to the back of the altar. That must be where Cortes and any others are. Who saw our guys?"

Echo shook his head. "They were doing great, and then the lights came on. I didn't see or hear anything."

But then he did, as there were more shots, and they heard Charlie scream. They turned to look and Charlie had jumped from his position on the left when the two guards from the pen had approached Delta, who was moaning in agony. They fired several rounds before Charlie realized what was happening and sprang up to spray them with his weapon. The guards and Charlie went down.

"This is turning to shit," mumbled Echo.

Alpha nodded to him and pointed at the pen. "The women are unguarded. Bravo and I will go get them. You provide us cover. I think your opposition will come from the altar or the area to the lower left."

Echo nodded and the two men moved out. He slid a little further back to get a wider view of the area, and that's when he heard it.

"Sitrep Echo, Sitrep," it was Romeo screaming.

Echo tried to calm himself. "Charlie and Delta are engaged. They may be down." He didn't want to sugarcoat it.

"On the way!" screamed Romeo.

"Negative," replied Echo, "Negative." But there was no reply.

Echo shook his head and hoped Romeo had listened.

He watched and hoped. His two men had made it to Charlie and Delta's position. Alpha checked Charlie and Bravo checked Delta and the guards. Alpha came back on first.

"Charlie had it right. He was stitched across the chest but then took one in the head. He's down. We'll get the women and pick him up on the way back," he said.

Then Bravo came on, "Looks like Delta took one in the neck early. He was probably down before the guards got to him." There was a pause. "Both guards are down."

Echo nodded to himself. Then he looked up beyond the

two men who were advancing toward the pen. Scurrying back up the stairs was a man in colorful feathered-looking garb, probably Aztec, carrying Cristina under one arm and taking the steps two at a time. Echo brought his rifle up. But the man was bobbing, and Cristina was thrashing about.

Alpha came back on. "I see it, Echo. We'll get the women and I'll go after Cristina."

Just as Alpha and Bravo were approaching the women, one of them broke from the back of the group and ran up the steps.

It was Liah, and she was screaming at the top of her lungs, "Cristina!"

Echo saw Alpha start up the steps behind her and he rose from his position. He heard sounds from behind him and raised his weapon. It was Romeo and Sierra.

"How did you get here so quick?" asked Echo.

"We moved closer to the cave as time passed," shouted Romeo.

Echo pointed to the stairs, and Romeo immediately saw Liah and then Cristina moving up the steps. Without a word, he sprang forward and ran down the cave path to the pen. He started up the stairs behind the others.

Shots rang out, and Echo saw Alpha stumble. He raised his rifle to return fire, but realized all the shooting was contained between the altar and the cave floor. He was in a position of relative safety and he could collect the others here. But he would need to move forward once they arrived.

Bravo had started the other women toward Echo and now Sierra. Echo saw them and pointed to Sierra. "Help them, assemble them behind us," he shouted.

Sierra ran to the bottom of the cave floor, grabbed Gina and Keno by the hand, and pulled them from the pen. "Come on," he shouted and pulled them toward the tunnel. "Angelic, stay with us," he called back.

"If you don't speed up, I'm going to run over you," he heard her pant. "Boy, are we glad to see you," she continued.

They heard more shots, and Sierra turned and flagged the women past him. "Run to the top. Echo—Ernie—is up there, stay with him. Do what he says."

Then he looked to the stairs. Another shot rang out and he saw Liah fall from mid stride. He felt an immediate heaviness, and he ran forward toward the pen and the bottom of the steps. As he approached, he saw two things: Romeo had reached Liah and stooped to hold her. He squeezed his arms tightly around her. At the same time Sierra saw the man in the costume stumble over a stair, or maybe his costume, or maybe a squirming Cristina, because the man pulled his hand away sharply and Cristina fell from his arms. She hit the steps running.

"Daddy!" she shouted.

Romeo released Liah and stood where he was, bringing his weapon to his shoulder. More shots rang out, and he fell to the side as the man in the feathered costume jerked backwards and screamed. At that same moment, Sierra saw Alpha unload with his weapon into the altar area.

"Romeo is down!" he heard Alpha scream into his headset. And then more softly, "Romeo is down."

Sierra ran up the steps and met Cristina as she was coming toward her parents. He grabbed the little girl who began squirming and shouting, "I want my mommy and my daddy!"

Sierra struggled to hold her. Then he pointed up the path. "Your grandfather, Ernie, is at the top. Run to him and I'll get your mommy and daddy. Hurry, go!" he said and pushed her away. She looked back for a second, then ran up the path.

Suddenly there was shooting from the right side of the rim. Sierra thought, *Echo or Bravo must have changed positions.*

The women and Bravo had reached Echo, and he placed the women in the tunnel behind him. He radioed Mike and said, "Come and get them. Then start for the hangar. Forget the truck. Don't look back. Don't worry about us. We'll be along."

Then he turned to Bravo and said, "Flank them from the right and light up the altar area until we can clear the others."

Bravo nodded and hurried away.

Echo ran back to the path. Seconds later, he heard Bravo firing hard and fast into the altar area. He saw Alpha take a last couple of shots in that direction and then crawl toward Charlie and Delta. He also saw Sierra with Liah over one shoulder and Romeo over the other, staggering in his direction. Echo stopped where he stood, tears streaming down his face as Cristina ran up to him and jumped into his arms.

"Papi," she cried, and he hugged her fiercely. "Stay here," he said. "I'll be right back."

Alpha dragged Charlie and Delta up the cave path toward Echo, who stepped forward to help. He looked beyond and he saw Sierra struggling with Liah and Romeo and he jumped forward and ran to take Liah.

Outside the tunnel, Mike roared up and Juliet jumped from the vehicle and hugged Angelic fiercely. "Get in the dune buggy!" he shouted and began pushing the women toward it. Keno ran to Mike and jumped into his arms. Each couple hugged for a moment, Gina standing silently and watching, tears running down her face. "Where's Dee?" she sobbed.

"He's inside. He'll be along. He's too ornery to die," said Mike. "We got specific orders. We got to go." He carried Keno and pulled Gina to the vehicle. Angelic had climbed in and Mike and Juliet forcibly put Gina in the middle between Keno and Angelic.

"He'll be okay. They're right behind us," added Juliet.

Mike jumped into the driver's seat, and the dune buggy roared away.

Back inside, Bravo had ceased firing and worked his way back around to the tunnel entrance. Echo had Liah over his shoulder and was holding Cristina by the hand. Sierra had Romeo. Alpha, with his leg oozing blood, had Charlie over his shoulder.

Echo spoke while pointing to Bravo, "Put an RPG into that altar."

Bravo glanced at him. "It may bring the whole cave down," replied Bravo.

"What's your point?" answered Echo turning away. "When you're done, grab Delta, and let's go home."

19

THE YUCATAN (LAST PLANE OUT)

They stumbled out of the tunnel and staggered to the remaining dune buggy. It was going to be tight. Bravo drove, with Echo and Cristina in the passenger seat. Alpha and Sierra strapped Charlie and Delta to the roll bar roof and then loaded Liah and Romeo between them in the back. They each basically had a dead body in their lap.

Bravo raced down the rise and toward the Campeche road. It was well after midnight now, and there was no traffic or any other sign of life. There was a lingering scent of dust in the air and they knew Mike and Juliet and the women weren't too far ahead of them.

Alpha and Sierra kept a sharp eye on anyone tailing them, but saw nothing. They appeared alone in the world, under a full moon and a star-filled sky.

A couple of miles further and Echo called out where Bravo, Alpha, and Sierra could hear him. "We'll have to stop for the truck. I told Mike to leave it. We can't go into town like this. We'll have to split up and put the bodies in the bed of the truck and drive it back to the hangar."

Bravo nodded from the driver's seat.

"How's the leg?" Echo called out to Alpha.

Alpha shook his head while he worked on it. He had laid Liah against Romeo and forced both of them toward Sierra, who was penned on the far side, while he pulled off his pack and dug for the first aid kit. He slapped a pack of anti-clot on the wound and fashioned a tourniquet to slow the bleeding. "I can move it, but it hurts like the devil. I think it may have been a ricochet which tore out a chunk of my thigh on its way past. I'm feeling a little woozy, but I can get to the plane."

Echo nodded his head in appreciation. Then he turned to the other side of the rear seat. "Sierra, you making it?" he called out.

Sierra was pretty well covered up, but grunted and waved a hand that stuck out, toward the front seat.

Cristina looked up at Echo and tugged on his arm. "Papi, what's wrong with Mommy and Daddy?"

Echo squeezed the little girl and held her for a minute. Then, his voice came, thick, "They're sleeping. Let's not wake them right now. You'll be okay with me, won't you?"

Cristina looked back at her parents and then turned her head into his chest. "You won't leave me, will you?"

Echo squeezed her tightly again. "Never," he said.

Bravo, who was gripping the wheel tightly and trying for every bit of speed he could get out of the dune buggy, called out, "Sierra, shout out when we're getting close to the truck."

Sierra grunted again.

Echo turned to Bravo, who dipped his head and said, "I feel like the driver for the taxi of the dead."

Echo grunted in acknowledgement. "Yeah, that wasn't much of a plan we had. I never could tell what happened, what tripped the lights. It might have been a motion detector buried in the ground, or maybe they were seen? I never saw anyone."

Bravo responded, "Could have been the guards didn't check in on time, or someone in the main party tried to reach them."

"Like you said, that RPG seemed to pretty well bring the cave down, hopefully destroyed them all." He glanced backward, quickly. Alpha was leaning against the seat, his eyes closed. He couldn't see Sierra. "Nobody seems to be following us."

"There didn't seem to be that many of them, but they handled their weapons well. They must have been armed forces, ex-military, something other than drug runners and gangbangers," added Bravo.

"Agreed," said Echo. "I should have figured Miguelito for the best. I thought we'd have more of an element of surprise."

They heard Sierra shouting out, and Bravo slowed the vehicle. He saw a turn just ahead and eased off the road into a ravine.

Bravo saw the old truck and stopped beside it.

Echo looked down at Christina and said, "Stay here for now, little one. I'll be right back."

He and Bravo jumped out. Alpha's eyes fluttered open, and he went to get up. Echo and Bravo were already pulling Liah and Romeo off of the two men in the back. Sierra struggled out and unstrapped Charlie and Delta. Alpha had made it to his feet but was leaning against the side of the dune buggy.

Echo touched Alpha on the shoulder. "Can you make it to the truck?"

Alpha nodded and staggered toward the door of the truck.

Bravo opened the tailgate and he and Echo laid Liah and Romeo in the bed, face down.

By then Sierra had Charlie and Delta unstrapped and

the three of them carried the two men over to the truck and placed them face down on top of the other two.

"Bravo, can you drive the truck, monitor Alpha? We'll be right behind you," called out Echo.

Bravo nodded and hopped in the truck, starting it quickly.

Echo looked at Sierra. "Can you drive the dune buggy?" he said.

Sierra jumped behind the wheel while Echo climbed in and adjusted Cristina in his lap. They rolled out after Bravo, who had pulled back onto the road and was accelerating away.

Shortly afterward, they were back in the city. Most of it looked sound asleep, with only a few revelers about as they moved through the more touristy area on their way to the airport. They came in through the backside of the terminals and approached their hangar. They made it to the plane. The others were already loaded, and Papa had the motors running.

He came running up to them. "I got everyone boarded, all the gear, the hangar is empty, we going to leave the vehicles?"

Echo nodded to him as he got out of the dune buggy. He placed Cristina's hand in Papa's and said, "Please put her on the plane, with the other women." Papa nodded in response and hurried away with the girl.

Alpha remained in the front seat while Bravo, Echo and Sierra loaded the bodies of Charlie, Delta, Liah, and Romeo onto the plane.

Papa came back and led Alpha aboard where he seated him, strapped him in, and gave him an injection of painkiller.

Echo, Bravo, and Sierra struggled aboard and took seats. Gina unbuckled, jumped up, and ran to Dee, where she hugged him tightly and he leaned against her, smiling, his arm wrapped around her shoulder. They sat down together and buckled up.

Papa came on the PA. "Hold on tight, we're out of here. Shut your eyes and the next time you open them, we'll be looking at the bright lights of Panama."

They taxied down the runway and lifted into the air, and as the night faded away, they turned into another bright light streaking across the sky.

PART II

COZUMEL 2 THE CANARY ISLANDS

20

PANAMA CITY (THE RETURN)

They arrived in Panama City in the early afternoon. Papa said they were running on fumes, but they were home.

Alicia, and a couple of other older men, met them at their hangar.

Echo, now Ernie again, spoke to the group before they de-boarded the plane.

"These gentlemen are friends of mine, and they will help us with the bodies. The rest of you, please go with Alicia, and I will meet you at the B&B. I need to have a quick discussion with customs and immigration. We sometimes help them with unique opportunities and we can come and go, and anyone with us. It's efficient. I'll see you soon."

And he turned and walked away from the plane toward the terminal.

Alicia gathered everyone up, with Cristina sticking to her like glue, and loaded them all into the Excursion. She motored slowly through the city toward the Palace Panama. It was just like before, with Liah driving. Only it wasn't. Alicia had little to say other than to squeeze each of them as they climbed into the vehicle. They were all silent on the drive across town.

When they arrived at the B&B and parked, Alicia turned to them and said, "You can stay in the same rooms. If you need to go out, you can use the Excursion. We do not have any guests for the next several days. I am going to take Cristina and go inside. We'll wait for Ernie."

The group nodded and watched as Alicia and Cristina walked toward the house. Cristina turned and looked back at them.

They had slept on the plane, all of them tired, but they were still exhausted. It had been a hard couple of days and seemed far away from them docking in Cozumel.

"Who's going to use the shower first?" asked Dee. "I think I'll swim and then shower."

Gina was standing next to him and holding his hand. "You'll have to do it in your underwear or nothing at all. I don't see you swimming well in those camo pants."

Dee, Jamal, and Mike were still wearing what was left of their uniforms.

The others broke into grins. Jamal said, "Angelic and I want to lie back down. Mike, you and Keno can go first, if you like."

Keno nodded first, and then Mike. The group split up, and each couple went in their own direction for the moment.

Dee and Gina made their way to the pool. Dee slipped out of his camo pants and boots and slid into the water. Gina watched him from the side of the pool. When he was in the water, she slipped completely out of what she was wearing—an outfit she had put on two days before to go to the ruins—and swam up beside him.

"It's not really polite to wear your underwear in somebody's pool," she said.

He looked at her for a moment and then slipped off the wet underwear and tossed it over to his pants.

"That better?" he asked.

She wrapped herself around him. "So much better, so happy that you're here, and so am I."

He held her tightly for several moments. "I'll tell you about it, someday, and you can tell me your story. But right now, I'm just glad to be here, too."

They stood, wrapped about one another, in the corner of the pool, for several more minutes. The sky was cloud-free above them, and the breeze moved lightly across the water. There were birds chirping in the trees. They could hear every sound, and leaning back, they noted how blue and green the world was around them.

"We'd better go up and clean up," he said.

Gina nodded and stepped from the pool. "I'll get us a towel."

Dee watched her walk away, overwhelmed by her beauty and grace.

Back upstairs Mike, Keno, Jamal, and Angelic were in the sitting room of Jamal's and Angelic's bedroom.

"We probably used all the hot water," called Jamal.

Gina grinned at him. "We'll just stand close together."

"I bet you will," Jamal replied playfully.

"Jam, leave them alone," giggled Angelic.

A short time later Alicia brought Mike, Keno, Jamal, and Angelic's clothes up the stairs.

"I didn't see you," she said to Gina and Dee, "when I gathered up the others' clothes. I bet I can find you something for the short term." She disappeared and returned shortly with two pairs of shorts and two tee shirts. "These were Liah's and Roberto's. They may not fit well but hopefully they will be okay while I wash your other clothes."

They thanked her, and she went back down the steps.

Slipping into the clothing, Dee's shorts and tee shirt fit pretty well. Gina had on shorts longer than anyone had ever seen her in, which she rolled up, and a tee shirt that was tight enough that the others could see the pattern on her bra.

"It'll do," she said, "Don't y'all be staring."

THEY SAT FOR A FEW MINUTES AS A GROUP, SILENT IN THEIR thoughts.

"Would you tell us what happened?" Dee asked the women.

The three women looked at one another. Angelic spoke first. "We were at the Mayan ruins, near the end of the tour. We foolishly let ourselves get separated from the group, by our own decision. We wanted to take a longer look at the sacrificial temple of the fertility goddess. We were standing there looking at it and then when we turned to rejoin the tour, Cortes and four of his men were standing in front of us. I don't know where they came from. I assume out of the jungle as that's where they took us, out beyond the ruins and eventually to the beach."

She paused, and Keno began. "I had come out of the temple with Cristina first and we had gone down the steps and turned to wait on the others. Suddenly they were behind and beside me. There were four big men with rifles, and pistols. The one man, the biggest one in the middle, with the birthmark, he put his hand over Cristina's mouth and put a pistol to her head. Then he said, 'anyone screams or makes a sound, she dies.' It was the most chilling thing I've ever heard."

Gina added, "Liah went toward the man holding Cristina and one of the other men punched her in the stomach with his rifle butt. She fell to her knees, and he put the rifle to her head. At the point, the big one with Cristina said 'come with us' and waved ahead to one of the other men. We followed them around to the back of the ruins and started into the jungle. They stopped us a few feet after we got through the brush and took all our phones. They turned them off and pitched them into the dirt and brush."

Jamal nodded. "But they didn't get them all," he said.

Angelic picked back up. "We didn't know it at the time but Liah kept her phone by handing them Cristina's play phone, which was an actual phone but one of her old ones. They didn't notice."

Keno started again. "They tied our hands together at the wrists with zip ties, but they left them in front of us. Then they put us on the back of four ATVs and we had to use our hands to hold on to the belts of each of the drivers while they transported us to the ocean. It was rough, and they went fast. I thought for sure that one of us would fall off. They put Cristina inside Liah's arms and she had to hold the girl and the belt of the driver. I was most worried about them. But it was petrifying."

Gina resumed. "I was thinking they're taking us to a boat on the beach. And yeah, it was the beach. But then this helicopter flies in and they load us up. They were putting the ATVs up against this rock structure and they took Cristina away from Liah, who screamed and they slapped her, and she fell to the ground. That's when she tried to send Roberto a text, as she was lying there. But one guard saw her and ripped the phone out of her hands and cracked her over the head with his rifle. He threw the phone against the rock."

"But it still had the message on it," said Mike. "Roberto found the phone. That's how we knew where to look."

Gina continued again. "Liah was out until we were almost ashore. I think she had a headache the rest of the time. It must have been a concussion."

"They flew us ashore," said Angelic. "I saw some signs that said Cancun, so we were somewhere in the city. They took us to a warehouse in an industrial area, dropped us off, and flew away. There were new guards, but we saw no one else. They locked us in a room, fed us once a day, and marched us to a bathroom twice a day. They never bothered us physically, other than the beating they gave Liah."

Keno began. "Then they loaded us into a truck and we drove for an hour. It was hard to tell what was happening. We were blindfolded and gagged. It was hot and smelly. When they led us from the truck, we were taken inside to the pen where you found us. There were new guards, not the same guys who took us from the ruins or at the building."

"That's where it got really weird," said Gina. "The guards didn't talk to us, but they talked to one another. They started telling about how Cortes was going to sacrifice us. That they would have to walk each one of us up the steps to the altar and then he, Cortes, would have a ceremony, and then behead us. They seemed to know there was something Cortes wanted to learn from each of us, some piece of information. But that no matter what we told him, he was going to kill us. They said he planned to start with the virgin, with Cristina."

"Until then we were scared but still kind of hopeful," said Keno. We thought maybe you guys could find us. But it was looking pretty bleak. The guards by the pen were trying to call one guard at the entrance and couldn't reach him. They wanted one more guard to walk us up the steps. That's when the lights came on and the shooting started. We didn't know who anybody was until we saw Dee. Roberto ran by so fast we weren't sure it was him."

"And then that guy in the costume grabbed Cristina, and Liah went ballistic and ran up the steps. It was out of control. We all thought we were going to die," concluded Angelic.

"We want to hear what happened to you guys, how you found us," said Gina.

BUT BEFORE ANYONE COULD RELAY WHAT HAPPENED, THEY heard the front door and Ernie called out, "Alicia?"

"We should probably give them a minute," said Angelic. Everyone nodded. "I can't imagine what that must be like, to lose your daughter and son-in-law."

"But at least they have Cristina," added Gina. "She's so much like them."

"Probably a joy and a pain," said Keno.

The men sat silently.

They heard Ernie at the bottom of the stairs. "Can we come up?" he asked.

"Please," replied Dee and Jamal almost simultaneously.

Ernie, Alicia, and Cristina came slowly up the steps and joined the group in the sitting room.

Ernie stood before them while Alicia and Cristina took a seat between Angelic and Gina.

"I want to thank you for all that you did," he said. Dee, Jamal, and Mike all looked at one another, and then at Ernie.

"We wouldn't have gotten out of there if each of you hadn't been so strong and done your job. It is tragic, how and what happened, but we are grateful for you. You are family to us now. And in that, we'd like to ask you to come back often, to help us with Cristina. You knew her parents, and they were very fond of you all. You can help by sharing your memories of them with Cristina so that she may have memories of her own. Alicia and I," he reached across and took Alicia's hand, "we'd like for you all to be aunts and uncles and to help us with Cristina." He paused, choked on emotion.

"We'd be happy to help you. We are indebted to you and your family and friends. Anything that we can do, we will," replied Dee.

"The funeral will be in a couple of days. If you could assist us with that and, please, stay as long as you like, you are always welcome here."

"We'll stay as long as you need us," replied Angelic.

Alicia, sitting on the couch with Cristina beside her, sobbed and took her hands to her face. Angelic went to her, and Gina and Keno went to Cristina.

Mike rose and approached Ernie. "Tell us what you need done," he said.

Two days later, they assembled in a large Catholic cathedral in the downtown area. It was an enormous structure, artfully and intricately crafted. There was an enormous crowd, as many of the people knew or knew of Liah from her Olympic days, and much of the Panamanian Special Forces knew Roberto. The church was overflowing.

Alicia had shared that she had several conversations with Cristina and while the little girl still wanted her parents back, she was happy with her grandmother and grandfather. Cristina had told Alicia of how she had bit the hand of the man that was carrying her up the steps and, when he dropped her, she ran for her daddy.

"How difficult that will be for her," noted Angelic.

Jamal shook his head. "In a few years it will be like Ernie and Alicia have always been her parents. She'll wonder about them, but she'll know she is loved."

"We promised to help," said Dee.

"And we will," said Gina, taking his hand. Mike and Keno nodded in agreement.

Angelic and Jamal returned the nod.

THE SERVICE BEGAN, AND THE CROWDS GREW SILENT. IT WAS over too soon for some, and perhaps not soon enough for others. Alicia was in tears and Ernie stood holding her by the shoulder with Cristina grasping his other hand. The crowds pressed in on them.

Dee, Jamal, and Mike were pallbearers on one side of Liah's casket, and Bravo, Papa, and Alpha—who was in a leg brace—were on the other side. Members of the Special Forces, in full uniforms, manned Roberto's casket.

As they moved Liah, Alpha spoke, "We start together, we stay together, until the journey is over."

BACK AT THE B&B, THE GROUP PACKED UP WHAT LITTLE THEY had acquired since returning to Panama.

Ernie came up the steps a few minutes later. "It looks like you're off to somewhere," he said. "Might I ask and remind you, you are welcome to stay."

"We appreciate that," replied Dee. "But we feel you and Alicia, and Cristina, need some time. We should try to catch up with our luggage."

Ernie grinned. "I understand."

Angelic stepped forward. "It was a beautiful ceremony. Liah and Roberto were such wonderful people."

Ernie looked down for just a second and then back up. He smiled genuinely. "Thank you."

Mike shook his hand, and Gina and Keno hugged him.

"We should probably leave for Key West in the morning," said Dee.

"Shouldn't we go to Vera Cruz?" replied Jamal. "One of the last things Liah told me was that Cortes founded the city, set himself up as governor, and cast aside his ties to Velasquez, the governor of Cuba, who sent him to discover Mexico. It was the same thing Velasquez had done to Columbus when Velasquez was sent from Hispaniola and discovered Cuba. Apparently it was a common thing among the Spanish, basically every man for himself."

Ernie chuckled. "That sounds like something Liah would say."

Jamal nodded in agreement. "She also said Cortes established a training facility, record keeping, a library, and many other city functions. She thought it would be a good place to dig around for information on the bell."

"I don't know," said Mike. "We should probably just get rid of that thing. It's bad news."

Ernie raised a hand. "It's not my place to say, but I agree with Jamal. You have come this far. Good people have died, bad people, too, but there was something about the bell that was important to Miguelito, and to Liah. She would want to know the truth."

"Alright then," said Dee, "If everyone agrees, I'll verify with my friend Ike and have him pick up our gear in Key West and store it for a few days, until we can get there. How long do you think this might take, Jamal?"

"Man, I got no idea," he replied.

"Was Liah specific?" asked Ernie.

"She said to look in the library," he replied.

"Sounds like a smart girl to me," added Gina, and she and Keno and Angelic giggled at the men.

Ernie put out his hand and the other men placed there's on top of his and one another's.

"Good luck to you, be safe, be successful, and come back to us."

21

PANAMA CITY 2 VERA CRUZ

Ernie arose early the next morning and drove them to the airport. There was only one flight from Panama City to Vera Cruz and it left early. He hugged each of them, kissed the women on the cheek, and shook hands with the men.

"Call me if anything comes up, or you need something," he said.

They all nodded and smiled and then waved to him as they entered the terminal.

Alicia had fixed them breakfast, and Cristina had run in to see them before they left. They were sad for many reasons, but they were excited to be going on and pursuing the origin of the bell. It was dear to them now, and they wanted answers.

The flight was approximately four hours and there was a point where the pilot told them they were flying over the Yucatan.

"Better up here, than down there," said Keno.

They landed in Vera Cruz in the late morning. Before leaving the air-conditioned comfort of the terminal, they decided on some lunch.

"Let's research a little before we leave," said Mike. Dee grinned and nodded.

"It'll be hot and humid," he added.

"We're going to the library, is that right?" asked Keno.

Jamal nodded. "Yes, Cortes founded the city and set up much of the original infrastructure. The Spanish keep everything. If we can find the oldest material, perhaps we can find something about the bell."

"Who will interpret for us?" asked Gina.

No one spoke up, and then Jamal sighed. "My Spanish is pretty weak. I worked on it a little with Liah. I'll do the best I can."

"This is going to be difficult," added Mike.

"I'm hoping we can find someone in the library that will help. It may be like it was in Cozumel where we find something that adds to the puzzle rather than an absolute answer. We'll go in and say that we are curious about his founding of the city and since my degree is in history, I wondered what inception documents they might have."

"Sounds suspicious," said Keno.

Jamal grinned. "Yeah, it does. If we can't make any headway we'll go on to Key West."

"You really mean that?" asked Dee.

Jamal took a second before he said, "Not really, I want to know about the bell."

"Then we'll just have to keep digging," Dee replied.

They finished lunch and took a taxi to the library, which was downtown, in the older part of the city. There was much colonial architecture and the downtown area was quite scenic. They didn't see many tourists, just people going about their business.

"This isn't really a tourist town, is it?" asked Mike.

"It's mostly around the seaport," replied Jamal.

They entered the library from the heat and humidity of the street and were relieved to find it cool and comfortable.

"Maybe Dee and I should ask," said Jamal. "Can the rest of you play tourist for a few minutes?"

"This building is beautiful inside. We can look busy," replied Angelic.

"I'll stay with and keep an eye on the ladies," added Mike.

Jamal and Dee agreed and wandered off toward the reference area. The others began a slow exploration of the lobby.

Jamal found a middle-aged, heavyset woman with dark hair and glasses. She looked up at him with a stern expression. Her name tag said Conchita Alvarez.

"Ms. Alvarez," Jamal began.

"You're a long way from the beach," she replied.

"Yes, ma'am," he answered, and she looked up, surprised perhaps at his courtesy.

"My friend and I," he said, pointing to himself and then Dee, "are interested in the early days of Vera Cruz. I studied Cortes and some of his history. I was hoping we might get a better understanding of what he accomplished here in Vera Cruz."

Ms. Alvarez studied him for a moment.

"Most Mexicans think of Cortes as quite the scoundrel. It wasn't always that way. Change, some call progress, comes to everything in time. There's no stopping it. Cortes was no different. If the Aztecs didn't like him, they should have killed him. Just like in your country with the native Americans and the white men, yes?"

"That's one way to look at it," said Jamal, grinning.

"You find me humorous?" she asked.

"No, ma'am, I find you refreshing," he replied.

That brought a big smile to her face.

"What exactly is it you and your friend want to know?" she asked.

Jamal shrugged. "We're just curious about the early days, what Cortes set up, how it happened, if there are records that survive."

"What *specifically* are you after?" she asked, looking over the top of her glasses.

Jamal was taken aback.

She chuckled. "You see, much of the early writings are in more of a colloquial Spanish, and unless you have some understanding of it, or speak fluently, you probably won't know what you're reading."

Jamal looked at Dee, who grinned at him, and then at Ms. Alvarez. Then Dee spoke. "Ma'am, we're curious about what Cortes did in his time here. There's an exhibit in Key West where a ship from 1715 was discovered in the Florida Straits that was full of Spanish gold. Some of it was rumored to be Aztec in origin, reforged into the Spanish idea of gifts. We wondered if Cortes had a role in that."

"1715 was long after Cortes, you're treasure hunters," she said with a smirk.

"Not really," replied Jamal. "It's more like treasure confirmers. We saw a bell, commemorative, and there was no confirmed origin. I just had this idea that maybe Cortes had something to do with it. There were swirls in the design that made me think of Aztec. It's just a hunch, we're curious. You may not be able to help us."

She looked at the two men for a moment, and then said, "Nonsense. If there's something here, we can find it. Follow me." She called out as she turned, "Estella, I'm going back in the stacks with these two gentlemen, I may be a few minutes."

They followed her down a long hall, her heels clicking on

the marble. She turned and went into a large room with floor-to-ceiling shelves on all four walls. Windows let light into the center of the room from well up near the interior gables and roofline of the room.

"This is our special collections," she said. "These are many of the earliest records of the city of Vera Cruz. Where should we start?"

Jamal shrugged. "Any personal correspondence of Cortes?" he asked.

"What about business that he did, shipping records, anything like that?" asked Dee.

She smiled. "You're looking for manifests. Cortes sent ships back to Spain with a twenty percent tribute to the king. Those contents are listed in extensive detail. Would that help?"

Jamal looked at Dee, who returned his glance, and then to Ms. Alvarez he said, "Possibly."

"I know what you're thinking," she replied. "You're fixated on locations, but you have to understand, things moved around, the Spanish were always moving their treasure, and not everything got reported or listed on the manifests. You need to broaden your scope of thought."

"How?" asked Jamal.

"We'll look at the manifests, but let's also look at the documents around the same time periods. There may not be direct references to specific things. We may have to interpret."

THEY SEARCHED THE STACKS, FROM THE LATEST OF CORTES' records to the earliest. There were lots of manifests and Jamal and Dee were flabbergasted at the volume of gold and treasure that was sent back to the king.

"It just goes to show you how wealthy in resources the

new world was," Ms. Alvarez stated. "And that's just the tip. I doubt seriously that the manifests represent any twenty percent probably more like two percent. Greed is a powerful thing to behold."

Nowhere was there a mention of a bell, any bell. But there were many gifts, and Cortes' correspondence showed that he had Spanish craftsmen recast the Aztec gold into many different objects.

Ms. Alvarez was thumbing through some related correspondence when she paused. "This may not have a bearing on what you're looking for, but I see something I don't think I've been aware of before." She held up a letter. "It's a casual reference from one of the last manifests, but it says that the ships on the way from the new world, back to Spain, stop in the Canary Islands. That's near to Seville, which was home to Cortes. Why would they stop there, unless of course it was to offload a little more of the so called twenty percent tribute? Perhaps Cortes kept a little gold in the new world and a little gold in the old world, just to be safe. Gold in the Canary Islands could have been a great boon to him after the Spanish brought him back and he was stuck in Seville for the balance of his life. It's just a thought."

Dee watched Jamal processing that information and wondered what would come next.

They continued looking, and then Ms. Alvarez paused again. "You know, we may be going about this wrong. At the end of Cortes' time in Mexico, he led an expedition to the north, where he discovered northern modern day Mexico and the Sea of Cortes. He was attempting to flee the Spanish by sailing south on the sea when he was captured and his ship went down. What if he had treasure with him?"

"He was on the wrong coast to sail to Spain on his own," replied Dee.

"I doubt he tried that. I think perhaps he thought sailing

might get him away from pursuit more quickly and then he could turn inland in southern Mexico and cross back to the east coast or to his capital, which is now modern day Mexico City."

All that information seemed to fit to Jamal and Dee, but where was the bell? How did it come into play?

"Why would you think he had treasure with him?" asked Jamal.

This time, Ms. Alvarez shrugged. "He probably felt like it wasn't worth the risk to leave it in the capital. I doubt he trusted anyone. In the worst case, he might have used it to barter for his own life, but apparently his captors were so eager to return him that it didn't work."

"Or he lost the treasure," added Dee.

Ms. Alvarez looked up and smiled. "That's possible, which meant that he had nothing to barter with."

"Was the Aztec woman with him when he was captured?" asked Jamal.

"Not that I'm aware of," Ms. Alvarez replied. "I think she was back at the capital."

"Which supports your theory of Cortes going back?" asked Dee.

"Cortes christened her as Marina. She learned Spanish and bore him a son. Her people, the Aztec, looked upon her as a traitor. She probably would have wanted to go with him wherever he went."

Shortly after, they reached the end of the material. There was nothing about the bell.

"So, what we learned is that Cortes made a stop on his way to Spain, at the Canary Islands," stated Jamal.

Ms. Alvarez nodded. "Those islands would have been the closest to Spain, under Spanish control. Other nearby islands were primarily Portuguese, and Cortes wouldn't have wanted to store gold there. Also, geographically, there is some argument for stopping in the Canary Islands. Coming up from Mexico, once you leave the Caribbean, you've just sailed open ocean for some time and that is your first chance to port. If anyone inquired, he'd have a valid reason."

"So, it wouldn't have just been the logical stopping point?" asked Dee.

"It could have been, but on a slightly different heading he would have nearly been to Cadiz on the mainland in approximately the same time. Perhaps there were weather or wind issues. It just seems odd to me," she concluded.

Dee now understood what Jamal was thinking.

22

VERA CRUZ (BY NIGHT)

The library was closing as Ms. Alvarez, Jamal, and Dee made their way back to the reference desk.

"We can't thank you enough," said Jamal.

Ms. Alvarez looked over her glasses and said, "Did you find what you were looking for?"

Jamal was thoughtful for a moment. "We helped clarify what we were thinking, and we added another piece to the puzzle. You were very helpful."

Ms. Alvarez flashed her biggest smile of the day. "It was a pleasure and I hope you find what you are looking for, perhaps in the Canary Islands," she said and she winked at them and turned away.

They strolled toward the library and saw the others sitting in heavy, overstuffed leather chairs.

"Took you long enough," Angelic teased.

"There was a lot to learn," replied Dee.

"So, what's the answer?" asked Keno.

"We have to keep looking," replied Jamal and he saw faces fall. "But first, let's get some dinner and something to drink. I'm thirsty."

. . .

They found a place to stay in the harbor area. Angelic and Gina had looked for something while Jamal and Dee had worked. Keno had found a restaurant nearby and everybody settled in at a large, round wooden table that looked out over the water for dinner.

It was the first moment since early in Cozumel that they could relax. Everyone was still weary, but the women had found a couple of shopfronts near the hotel and changed into colorful local or beach garb. They felt festive and wanted to celebrate.

The men were just tired but tried their best to comply. A couple of hours later, after eating a massive meal and several cold cerveza, they got to talking.

"So, we're bound for Key West now?" asked Mike.

"Yeah, I got a text from Ike when we were in Panama City that said he picked up our luggage and gear. I told him we might be a few more days. He said he had a tournament in Bermuda, the Bermuda Open, that he would leave for shortly, but he thought he might be around a few more days."

"How do we get there?" asked Keno.

"Fly, I should hope," replied Angelic.

Gina was already on her phone. Each of the men had saved their partner's phone when Roberto had found them behind the Mayan ruins. They had thought to return them to the women when they got back to Panama City.

Gina had the airline site and said, "We can leave early tomorrow or later."

"Later," everyone sang out.

"Done," she replied, and booked six slots on the afternoon flight.

She sat her phone aside and said, "Now, that it's decided, let's have another cerveza."

THEY HAD ANOTHER ROUND OR TWO AND MADE THEIR WAY TO the hotel. It was a beautiful night with a sky full of stars, their light reflecting off the water.

"Goodnight all," called Angelic.

There was a chorus of goodnights as each couple headed for their respective room.

Dee and Gina got inside, and Dee walked across the room and opened the balcony door to look out on the sea. He sat in a chair near the railing.

Gina followed along behind and then turned and sat in his lap.

She whispered in his ear, "I'm ready to go to bed, but I'm not really sleepy, you?"

23

VERA CRUZ 2 KEY WEST

They slept in the next morning and ate a late breakfast at the hotel. Then they strolled the waterfront area and admired the beaches and the tourists. It was unfortunate they didn't have more time.

Back at the hotel, they spent a few hours by the pool to relax. The time passed quickly, and they checked out and caught a taxi to the airport.

Strolling through the terminal they looked like six tourists headed home after a restful vacation—rousing perhaps, but not restful.

It would be late in the evening by the time the flight arrived. Dee texted Ike before they boarded with the estimated time of arrival. Ike texted back he would be there to pick them up.

They tried sleeping on the plane but weren't successful. They fidgeted and monitored their watches and phones.

Late that evening they touched down. As the plane emptied, it looked like the small airport was mostly shut down. There were only a handful of people waiting to pick up. Most of the travelers wandered out to taxis or vehicles in the lot.

Ike leaned against the wall and saw Dee before Dee saw him. Ike pushed off and strolled out into the aisle.

"Dee, about time you got here. You're going to keep me up all night," Ike lamented. Then he waved at everybody else and said, "I'm Ike, an old friend of Dee's. Glad you all made it safe. I want to hear all about it, in the morning," he finished with a laugh. They all laughed with him, yawned, and rubbed their eyes. "See what I mean," he said.

He turned and started out the doors. "Come on, let's go, it's not far, it's a small island, but I live on the other side, down beyond the old town. I hope you don't mind riding in the back of a truck? Ladies, ride up front with me, men in the back. This is my Conch wagon, a 1953 Ford F-100 Custom pick up, in baby blue. Welcome to Key West."

Ike's house was only six hundred square feet and had one big open room on the ground floor with a kitchen and bathroom at the back and a half loft overhead which served as the bedroom. It wasn't air conditioned but had multiple ceiling fans and openings around the house that let the air flow through. The air wasn't cool, but the temperature wasn't unpleasant with the moving breeze.

Ike had a pile of sheets and pillows laid on one couch. "I'm sorry there aren't more beds," he said. "There is a full bed upstairs that one couple can have. There are two couches that don't fold out, but they recline."

"What about you?" asked Angelic.

Ike grinned. "I've got my trusty backpacking pad and pillow. I'm good. I actually sleep in the hammock out on the back porch about half the time. No worries."

In a quick discussion Jamal and Angelic got the loft, and Mike and Keno, and Dee and Gina, took a couch each.

"Let's get to bed," said Ike. "Get up when you wake up. No alarm clocks here. The sun will wake you. Goodnight all."

IT HAD BEEN LIGHT FOR A WHILE BEFORE THEY ALL STIRRED. It was the smell of breakfast that did it. As their heads popped up and they crawled to their feet, Ike sang out, "Breakfast will be ready shortly. After a B&B in Panama City and a four-star hotel in Vera Cruz, this may not compare, but it won't kill you. This is high season on the island and everything is crowded. There's no going out for a meal with a group this size. Sorry!"

Gina and Keno wandered back to the kitchen to see if Ike could use any help. He directed them to dishes and silverware.

"It's buffet style, come and get it," Ike called out.

They stood around the kitchen area and polished off everything Ike had fixed. He talked while they ate.

"This house is really just where I keep my stuff. I'm not here a lot," he said. "I got a deal on it, $600,000 for 600 square feet. It's the going rate in this part of Key West. My former doubles partner is a realtor in Miami, he heard about it and hooked me up. It's an excellent investment and a good stop off point for traveling with the tour."

"You still play?" asked Keno.

Ike shook his head. "I retired last year after a decade as a player. Now I work for one of the racquet companies as a distributor. I was trying to catch a job doing some commentary on the networks, but no luck so far. I may coach a little. I've had some interest from a couple of players."

"We appreciate you hooking us up," said Dee.

"It's good to see you, all of you. Dee told me some of

what you've been through. It's unbelievable, you couldn't make that stuff up," he said.

"Dee said you were about to travel to…Bermuda?" asked Mike.

"Yeah, the Bermuda Open, it's my first appearance as a racquet distributor for a new company out of Australia. We'll see how it goes," he replied.

"The bed was comfortable," added Angelic. "We really appreciate it."

Ike smiled. "You guys can stay as long as you like. I'm in Bermuda for a week and then I circle back to the states for the Challenger circuit through the south-Knoxville, Charlottesville, Savanah, Jacksonville, Austin, and a couple of others. It's about eight weeks. Shouldn't be as hot as here," he said and laughed. "I'll be flying out later today. I can show you around a bit if you like, although Dee and I have been here a few times when we were younger. I expect he still remembers his way around. It's more crowded, though, more tourists, more cruise ships."

Dee nodded to Ike. "We appreciate that. Do what you need. We may just rest up a couple days if that's okay."

"Absolutely, there's the beach and the pool at the resort you can use. Grocery store is down the street on the left. They have most everything. I have a few things to do this morning before I go, so make yourselves comfortable and I'll see you soon." He paused for a moment.

"I almost forgot," he grinned, "and you didn't ask, but your luggage is in the closet on the back porch and your gear, I parked at the treasure museum in the old customs house. I know a couple of security guys that work there, and I just thought it might be safer until you decide what to do."

"Treasure museum," said Jamal. "That wreck you were talking about in Vera Cruz," he said, pointing at Dee.

Dee nodded.

"They have excellent security, as you might imagine," said Ike. "You can pick it up when you want." He grinned and left for his errands.

THEY SAT ON THE COUCHES AND ON THE FLOOR AND discussed what to do and how to do it.

"We need to go to the Canary Islands," said Jamal.

"Why?" asked Keno.

"It's where the clues lead," replied Jamal.

"What do you really expect to find?" asked Mike.

"Probably just the next piece of the puzzle," answered Gina. Jamal grinned at her.

"I don't know what we'll find," replied Jamal.

"What do we do with the bell?" asked Angelic.

"I think we leave it here," answered Dee. "I think it will be as safe here as with us. They have a lot of gold in the museum. It won't seem out of place, at least until we figure out who it belongs to. I mean, at this moment, that Cortes had something to do with it, is only a guess."

"It could have been from anywhere," added Gina.

"Or been commissioned by anyone," said Angelic.

"Alright, people," exclaimed Jamal, "I know we're all tired. We can do this leisurely and rest up. Could we take another cruise? I can continue my research and you guys can rest up, work out, swim, shop, whatever you want to do."

"You don't want to just fly over there and get it over with?" asked Angelic.

"Like Dee said, it being commissioned by Cortes is a guess, and like you and Gina said, it could be from anywhere and from anyone. I can broaden my research while we travel. We get to Gibraltar or wherever, maybe we tour the

Mediterranean. When we get back, we give the bell to the Mexican historical group or whomever, if we figure out anything different."

Everyone sat quietly for a moment. Jamal pulled his tablet out of his backpack.

"Let me see if there is a cruise from here to Europe," he said. A few minutes of research gave him a couple of options.

"There are several cruises departing from here over the next week," he said. "The best one leaves in two days and it's from here to Gibraltar and it stops in the Canary Islands. Let me check something."

The group sat quietly for a moment while Jamal worked. Then Angelic asked, "What are we going to do for the next couple of days?"

"Shop," said Keno.

"Spend some time at the pool," said Gina.

"Rest," said Dee.

"Get some exercise," said Mike.

"Hey," called out Jamal, "It says here that the Canary Islands were a common stopping point for ships traveling from the new world back to the old, something about trade winds."

"So, Ms. Alvarez may have been mistaken," replied Dee.

"Maybe," answered Jamal.

"Why does it matter?" asked Mike.

"Ms. Alvarez thought Cortes may have offloaded gold in the Canary Islands, and he could have, especially if he was expected to stop there. She thought that perhaps the Canary Islands were out of the way of the most direct route back to Spain and that Cortes was taking a detour. It sounds like he needed to stop, which made it even easier for him to offload something."

"Does that mean the bell?" asked Keno.

"We don't know," replied Jamal. "I'm afraid Gina's probably right, and the stop in the Canary Islands will hopefully add another piece to the puzzle. We just have one day and then we're on to Gibraltar. We'll have to be quick."

24

KEY WEST 2 THE CANARY ISLANDS

Ike came back late that first afternoon and gathered up his stuff. Dee and Mike drove him to the airport in Ike's truck. He had shaken hands with the men and hugged the women before wishing them luck and asking them to do the same for him on his adventure.

As they dropped him at the terminal, Dee said again, "Thanks for having us and looking out for our gear."

"Anytime, you and your friends are always welcome here," Ike replied and then waved as he headed for the terminal door.

Dee and Mike got back to the house to find the rest of the group sitting on the back porch in the shade, having a cold drink.

"Nice guy," said Keno, "Not married?" Dee and Jamal looked at Mike, who rolled his eyes.

"He was, to a player on the women's tour. He was once ranked as high as number eight in the world on the men's side, and she was ranked number three on the women's side. They had two young children, a boy and a girl," replied Dee.

"What happened?" asked Angelic.

"They had some issues, it's a complicated story. I'll let him tell it to you sometime. But he's divorced now."

FOR THE FOLLOWING TWO DAYS THEY TOOLED AROUND KEY West, trying to avoid the tourists while they laid by the pool, shopped and worked out. They got little rest, but they watched the sunsets on Mallory Square and laughed at the jugglers, hustlers, and clowns that worked the tourist crowds.

Jamal continued his research on Cortes, and more broadly on bells, but he also spent some time looking at the path of the cruise.

"We'll sail out of here to the Bahamas, skirt the south edge of the Sargasso Sea, and then make for the Canary Islands, which are off the coast of Africa, specifically the coasts of Morocco and Western Sahara. It will take a week to get there and then a few days along the Moroccan coast, with a stop in Casablanca, and then we slip into Gibraltar."

"What is the Sargasso Sea?" asked Mike.

"Best I can tell, it's a body of water that is heavily affected by seaweed and marine life," replied Jamal. "It doesn't influence modern day shipping, but it was probably a hazard to sailing ships in Cortes' time."

"That might explain it, if Cortes' ships had to sail south around it, or for the trade winds, and then come up the African coast, the Canary Islands would be the first stop," said Dee.

Jamal nodded. "Yeah, it looks that way. Fortunately for us we stop at Las Palmas on Gran Canaria, which was the major city at the time of Cortes. It mostly likely would have been where he had his ships dock."

"Any idea what we'll look for?" asked Mike.

"Not a clue," sighed Jamal. "But I'll keep working."

. . .

They cleaned up the house, locked the doors, and took a taxi to the dock.

"That was fun," said Keno. "I miss it already."

Gina nodded in agreement. "I could stay there awhile."

Dee looked at Mike, who nodded. "Ike offered it to us at any time. We'll have to come back."

"So we can hear his story," said a grinning Angelic.

They checked in and were assigned state rooms next to one another. The ship sailed in the late afternoon for Nassau, from where they would depart in the morning.

Gathering for dinner, they sat at one of the outside bars and watched the sunset. It had gotten to be a habit for them.

After a quiet night, they gathered on the deck in the morning as the ship pulled away from Nassau.

"Once we pass Eleuthera, it will be a few days before we see land again," said Dee.

"Is that part of the Bahamas?" asked Keno.

"It's one of the outer Bahamian islands, moving into the Atlantic," answered Jamal. "Then it's five or six days to the Canary Islands."

"No pirates, but maybe Bermuda Triangle," laughed Mike.

"That's not funny," said Keno.

"Really, it isn't," laughed Angelic. "Come on, Keno, let's go shopping."

"I'm going to the pool," said Gina.

"Researching," said Jamal.

"Let's find a gym," said Mike to Dee, who nodded in agreement.

. . .

SEVERAL HOURS LATER, THEY MET FOR LUNCH. AFTER A quick bite, Jamal announced, "I might have a place for us to begin in Las Palmas. There's a church, Cathedral of Santa Ana, which has a museum with an immense collection of historical art, gold and silver, much of it from the time of Cortes and somewhat later, roughly from 1500 to 1700. Some of his gold or gifts might be there. We have a day in port, we can check it out."

"Sounds…boring," teased Angelic.

"You guys can do something else. They're supposed to have a great beach as well."

THAT NIGHT THEY MET FOR DINNER IN ONE OF THE FORMAL dining rooms. They all dressed for the occasion.

"This is kind of like the night we met on the Hawaiian cruise," said Keno.

"That seems so long ago," replied Angelic.

"I saw you all across the dining room," added Gina.

"Why didn't you come and join us?" asked Mike.

"I was being hit on by a billionaire, so he said," replied Gina.

"And you'd rather have been with us?" asked Jamal.

"I thought Dee was cuter," she replied, squeezing Dee's hand.

"And he turned out to have some money," chuckled Angelic.

"Just with an 'M' and not a 'B,'" added Mike.

Gina smiled at them all. "Sometimes you just have to make do," she said, then she turned and smiled at Dee.

"Wasn't I lucky," replied Dee.

"You most certainly were," answered Angelic. Then she and Keno giggled and smiled at Gina.

.   .   .

AND SO, THEY PASSED THE NEXT COUPLE OF DAYS, TAKING IT easy, cutting up with one another and trying to decide what to do after they reached Gibraltar. They sat on the deck one afternoon in a strong breeze and looked at the water.

"The Atlantic isn't as blue as the Pacific or the Caribbean," noted Angelic.

"At least it's calmer than the Pacific," added Keno.

"The Mediterranean will be even bluer than the Caribbean," added Dee.

"Hardly seems possible," replied Keno.

"We'll be there in two more days?" asked Gina.

"Yes, we should be there day after tomorrow," answered Jamal. He looked up at the group from his tablet. "I've been researching the painter, Castillo, and it's on record that he painted a portrait of Cortes prior to Cortes leaving Spain. Also, that Cortes commissioned him to paint several historical, biblical works, which is mostly what he painted. He was somewhat renowned in his time for extremely detailed biblical settings and renderings. It was odd that he painted a portrait, although he would have had the skill for it. I don't know what all that means except he and Cortes seemed to have a close relationship. Especially since the bell has what appears to be his name cast in it. It has to be part of that relationship."

"Castillo isn't that uncommon a name. It could just be a coincidence," added Dee.

Jamal looked up at him. "Maybe, but that doesn't feel right. Not based on where we found the bell and in the type of ship we found it."

Dee nodded. "I don't disagree, but we're just not finding much else to go on."

"I'm really hoping we find something at Las Palmas, we're just about out of clues," replied Jamal.

. . .

LATE THE FOLLOWING DAY, THEY COULD SEE THE AFRICAN coastline. They were moving more slowly than they had for the previous couple of days.

"We must be approaching the islands," said Dee.

"That would make the coastline, the state of Western Sahara, headed toward Morocco," replied Jamal.

"We dock in the morning and we have all day?" asked Dee.

"That's my understanding," answered Jamal.

"Just you and I going to the church?" asked Dee.

"I think so. From what I can tell, the coastal area will be much like the beaches in Mexico, with more desert terrain inland. It should be very similar. Las Palmas is an old city, founded in 1458 or somewhere thereabouts. It had been around fifty years before Cortes would have shown up. Columbus used it as a base on his way to the new world. It was an established trade center. I think it's our last best chance to find something."

"Sometimes you get lucky," replied Dee.

THE FOLLOWING MORNING THE SHIP WAS DOCKED AT THE LAS Palmas harbor with excursions going to the beach, the city, and the cathedral. Mike went with the women to stroll through the city in the morning and hit the beach in the afternoon. Jamal and Dee would catch up with them if they found anything quickly. They expected and hoped to be all day.

25

THE CANARY ISLANDS (CATHEDRAL OF SANTA ANA)

They boarded the tender in the morning and rode to shore. There, they split up for the bus and walking tour of the city, except for Jamal and Dee, who caught a tram to the cathedral.

"Let us know when you head for the beach," called Dee. "We'll see where we're at and maybe join you."

Jamal punched him in the shoulder. "Man, we'll just be getting started to uncovering the truth," he said, laughing.

They waved at the others and mounted the tram. The cathedral was only a few minutes away and shortly afterwards they were deposited at the steps of the plaza.

There, a tour guide met them and the handful of others from the ship, along with a few curious tourists.

Looking up toward the plaza, there were a few short sets of steps and a palm tree and building lined walkway that lead to the cathedral. It was majestic looking.

As they walked, "It was originally built in the 15th century and then rehabbed in the 17th century," said the guide. "It is the oldest church and was the only church in the islands until the early 1800s."

They walked slowly along, a slight breeze blowing across them and bringing the smell of the nearby ocean.

"This better be good," said Dee.

"I'd rather be lucky than good, or maybe both," laughed Jamal.

THEY REACHED THE ENTRANCE, AND THE TOUR BEGAN. AN hour later, they had seen and heard far more than they thought possible for them to absorb. So much of the history of the new world had passed through the islands.

The tour reached the section of the cathedral housing the museum, where the guide pointed out the contents—art, objects of gold and silver, and artifacts from the 15th and 16th centuries. She suggested they come back at the end of the tour for further examination, then she went to move the group on to the next area.

Jamal and Dee watched the group walk away and then slipped into the museum. This is what they came for. They strolled around the rooms, looking at items, trying to find anything that might be related to Cortes.

Dee stood in a long narrow room lined with paintings. Jamal was around the corner. Dee stopped in front of a large canvas. It was an intense biblical depiction of the virgin and child surrounded by saints and onlookers, in an outdoor setting. Dee looked to the plaque identifying the painting and artist and there it was: Juan Bautista Castillo.

"Jamal," he called out. There was the sound of footsteps.

Jamal had come into the room. "Yeah?" he said, looking back the way he came.

"Here he is, your painter, Castillo, doing biblical, like you said."

Jamal stopped and stared for a moment. "Yeah, that's him. In fact, I think I've seen a picture of that painting."

"As well you should have," announced a third voice. "Although he did primarily biblical work and often painted similar themes and settings. That one is popular."

Dee and Jamal turned and there was a lovely young woman with light brown skin and green eyes, her hair piled atop her head. She had on a sharp looking and fitting suit and sensible shoes. Before they could read her name tag, she said, "I'm Elizabeth Adassa, the curator for the museum. I see you noticed our Castillo."

"Yes," stammered Jamal. "I'd been reviewing his work while we've been on vacation, but this is the first chance I've had to see one in person."

Ms. Adassa held a hand out toward the painting. "It's really quite lovely. Castillo isn't as well known in contemporary times as some other Spanish artists. How did you come across him?"

"I was fascinated by the 1500s and I was looking through painters, when I saw his work and I didn't recognize the name," Jamal replied.

"You have a background in art?" she queried.

Jamal smiled at her and said, "I have a degree in art history, so it surprised me I didn't know the name, or have at least heard of him."

"He had a successful but relatively short-lived career. He was good friends with the explorer Cortes."

Jamal couldn't help himself and grinned broadly.

"You have some interest in Cortes then, as well?" she asked. "Tell me more."

Jamal was silent for a second, and Dee started to speak, but then Jamal interjected.

"I saw in my research that Castillo had painted a portrait of Cortes and the article suggested they were friends. We were in Mexico recently and heard a great deal about Cortes."

Ms. Adassa smiled. "Vera Cruz, Cozumel, Mexico City?"

"Cozumel and Vera Cruz," answered Dee.

"Cortes' beginnings are in New Spain or Old Mexico, if you don't mind my play on words," she replied.

Jamal grinned and then replied, "I was curious about their relationship when I saw they were acquainted. You just don't normally think of people from other era's knowing one another, everything gets compartmentalized."

Ms. Adassa smiled again. "I absolutely agree. If you're interested in both men, we have a couple of smaller Castillo's and we have some items from Cortes." She waved a finger at them. "Let me show you those and we can come back to the Madonna."

She stepped through a carved set of double doors and led them into a larger room that they had not yet entered. The room had an intricately tiled floor and was lined around the perimeter with other large oil paintings. At the front of the room a life-size marble crucifix was mounted on the wall. But the items she pointed to were a series of velvet covered pedestals with acrylic cases on top of them. Inside each case was an item that appeared to be made of gold. A quick glance revealed a miniature crucifix, an amphora, a set of knives, a figurine, and several other intricate looking objects.

Ms. Adassa pointed at the cases. "These are reportedly from the personal collection of Hernando Cortes."

Jamal and Dee were stunned. Perhaps she saw it in their faces.

"Yes, they are gold. Cortes or his representatives passed through the Canary Islands on their way back to Spain. They had to sail south from Mexico and then come up the coast of Africa to benefit from the trade winds. The Canary Islands were under Spanish control and it was the ship's first opportunity to port after potentially weeks at sea."

"How did the museum..." Jamal couldn't finish the thought.

It seemed to be her nature, and Ms. Adassa smiled again. "Apparently Cortes maintained property or some type of relationship on the island. Whether he deposited these items knowingly or whether they were a secret he was trying to hide away is unknown. But what we know is that after the Spanish authorities returned Cortes to Spain, he or his representatives collected many of the items that were on hand here on the island. Some of them, however," she paused, "managed to escape and found their way into the local business trade. The church bought them. Cortes at one point supposedly heard about the items and demanded them back."

"And...?" said Dee.

"The church ignored his requests and his petitions to the king were also ignored. It is suspected that Cortes himself liberated the items from one of the king's royalty payments."

"That's an amazing story," said Jamal.

"History indicates that Cortes was a colorful and ambitious fellow," Ms. Adassa replied.

"Could this be Aztec gold?" asked Dee.

Ms. Adassa didn't blink an eye. "Most likely, the source material. All these shapes would have been common elements for the Spanish from that time period. We don't have anything Aztec in nature, but they may have existed. It's unlikely the church, at that point in time, would have purchased any 'pagan' items. But the gold had to come from somewhere and most schools of thought believe these items came from the new world and were headed back to Spain. Not from the old world headed to the new. That's an interesting question. What made you think of it?"

Jamal stepped back in and answered. "In studying Cortes, it appeared he had access to quite a bit of Aztec gold," Ms. Adassa rolled her eyes and grinned, "and we just wondered what he did with it."

She held a hand up, finger extended. "I just had a thought," she said. "Let's move back to the outer room by the window, where I can get better reception. I want to call a friend, actually just an acquaintance, who might shed some light."

She put the call through, and after some brief pleasantries, she set the bait. "Would you by chance have any of the Cortes' items?" she asked.

There was a muted reply that neither Jamal nor Dee could understand.

She resumed, "What I'm looking for is any item that appears as though it might be Aztec in nature?"

This time, Dee and Jamal heard the cackle from the other end.

"You have a figurine of Quetzalcoatl, the feathered serpent?" she replied.

The men saw her nod her head in agreement, followed by, "Can you send me a picture? Yes, that will be sufficient for now." And then she hung up.

She turned to the two men. "That's an antiquities dealer that I know." She rolled her eyes again as she spoke. "He often has access to or knowledge of …things," she concluded.

"He's sending you a picture?" asked Jamal.

"He said he would," she said, and then her phone chimed.

She brought the picture up on screen and then enlarged it with her fingers. "Looks like it to me," she said.

Jamal and Dee both took a quick look.

"Do you think it's real?" asked Jamal.

"He showed it to me without asking why I wanted to know. I'd say he is comfortable that it's real. There have always been rumors that there were Aztec treasures as well as the items the church bought. I'd just never checked it out before now," she replied.

They went back into the larger room.

"So, there's some correlation that the church treasures are made from Aztec gold recast into items the Spanish wanted or desired?" asked Jamal.

"I would say so. Cortes spent most of his career in Cuba and Mexico. I don't think he would have had much in the way of gold from elsewhere," she replied.

"It's amazing you have all these pieces of information and no one has pulled them together and told the story," said Dee.

Ms. Adassa smiled again. "You know there are lots of pieces of information of all kinds scattered around. You see things, you hear things, there's something on the news, but people are busy with their lives, who has time to pull all these different things together from around the world? How do you substantiate something from five hundred years ago? At the end of the day, it's just an opinion. Maybe it's an informed one, maybe not, but it's still just an opinion."

They stood looking at the items for a moment.

"History gets rewritten every twenty years. After a couple of generations, an opinion, any opinion, is relegated to the dustbin of time," she continued.

"You said there were a couple of other Castillo's? Could we see them?" Jamal asked.

Ms. Adassa nodded and led the way back into the smaller room and then further down the wall from the large painting Dee had seen earlier.

"These two," she said, "which are variations on the larger one."

She paused for a moment. "Going back to Cortes for a moment, he did commission a portrait, but he also had

Castillo paint several biblical scenes for him. Those are in the fine arts museum in Seville, Spain, along with many others of Castillo's work. Seville was the original area of Cortes' home and where he eventually died. It was also Castillo's home."

"Are the paintings worth the trip?" Jamal asked.

"If you like Castillo," murmured Ms. Adassa. "Actually, the collection is quite good. You'd probably enjoy it. But there is one unusual note. Most of Castillo's biblical work is of the Madonna and child in a natural or outdoor setting. Castillo did one painting where the Madonna and child are in front of what appears to be a curtain or a tapestry, or backdrop of some kind, and they are against a field of numbers and letters. It's called the 'Numeric Madonna.' But it disappeared about thirty years ago, supposedly stolen, and has never reappeared. I believe I might have a photograph. Since Castillo isn't well remembered, the lost painting got little press and so much time has passed that it's all but forgotten. If you want to follow me back to my desk, I'll see if I can find that picture."

They followed her down the hall and into a small alcove that served as her office. She sat while they stood, and she dug through her files.

"It's in my Castillo folder somewhere," she said.

After a couple of minutes, she flipped through a folder titled 'related' and found a newspaper article and then a blowup of the painting. It was the Madonna holding the child in front of what looked like a scroll, or a curtain covered with numbers and letters. They filled the entire background, almost as if the Madonna had been painted on top of them. Many of the rows were completely visible, others only partially so. There were numbers, then letters, then more numbers, more letters. There didn't seem to be any rhyme or reason to them, just a meaningless backdrop.

"What's the story about it?" asked Jamal.

"It was in the collection in Seville and it disappeared about thirty years ago," Ms. Adassa explained.

"No, I meant, what is the story of the background, the numbers and letters?" Jamal asked.

"There's never been an answer to that. Castillo never said why he did it at the time it was painted and questions later in his life regarding the painting went unanswered. If there was a reason, it probably died with him. Nothing was every related to it or subsequently discovered," she added.

Jamal and Dee stood and looked at one another.

Ms. Adassa looked up at them and laughed. "You should see your faces," she said. "Was there something life altering in that bit of news?"

Jamal and Dee both broke into grins. "No," replied Jamal. "It's just that we've looked a couple of places for information, and you just overloaded us with it. We're just appreciating your knowledge, and your willingness to share. Thank you so much. May I take a picture?"

Ms. Adassa nodded, and Jamal snapped a quick shot with his phone.

Dee looked at his watch, and saw it was nearly lunchtime. It felt like it had been longer. "We want to sit down and talk about all this. Could we take you to lunch?" he asked.

Ms. Adassa looked at both of them quickly and smiled again. "We're not really supposed to eat with patrons, but by now, you feel like friends. And how could a girl say no to two good-looking men like you?"

She rose from her chair. "There's a small café down the plaza that should suit us, and I can get back quickly, if that works for you."

They both nodded and held out a hand to her. She smiled, took each of their hands in one of hers, and led the way out the door.

26

THE CANARY ISLANDS (AFTER CHURCH)

They strolled the short distance to the café. Ms. Adassa—she asked them to call her Elizabeth—walked between the two men, turning her head back and forth, listening to each of them as they all conversed.

The maitre d seated them just inside the window and they could see out on the plaza as those passing by made their way along.

"Both of you are married?" she asked. "Where are your wives? Do they not like history?" They were all very rapid questions.

Jamal nodded and held up his ring finger. "Yes, I'm married." Pointing at Dee, he said, "He has a very steady girlfriend. They are doing the walking tour with a couple of other friends of ours. There are six of us traveling together. Then they are headed for the beach."

She smiled. "I saw your ring," she said, looking at Jamal, "and I could tell from the way you didn't look at me," she had turned and spoke to Dee, "that there was someone in your life that has your attention."

Both men blushed.

"Girl, you're pretty direct," said Jamal.

"Not really," she replied. "You both look happy when you don't look surprised." She paused to smile. "I'm envious. It's a small island and there aren't that many opportunities, especially if you count out the tourists."

Jamal leaned back. "You're a smart woman, attractive, personable, you have a good job, I'd think men would be lined up down the street."

She leaned back in her chair. "Not any that I'd want."

"Why don't you leave, then? You should have lots of opportunities?" asked Dee.

"I wake up every morning and I think that, but then my apartment overlooks the ocean, the sky is so blue and the water so inviting, the beach and the city are beautiful, the people are gracious and kind, my job pays well, for the island, where could I go that I could match all those things?" she said. "Plus, I love the museum."

"That's easy to see," said Dee, and she smiled full on at him so that he turned away.

A couple walked by in tennis clothes, carrying racquets. Jamal saw Elizabeth take notice.

"Do you play tennis?" he asked.

"I did in secondary school, and for a couple of years in college. I double majored and my studies got really intense, so I dropped off the team. But I still like to get out when I can. We have an old established club here on the island. I'm a member. It hosts a Challenger event every year. Are you familiar with those?" she replied.

Dee nodded to her. "Do you know the name 'Ike Mann?'" asked Dee, and Jamal grinned as he had been about to say the same thing.

"I follow the men's and women's tours, somewhat, so yeah, I've heard that name. In fact, he played in the

Challenger here some years ago. He's a tall, good-looking guy, right, big serve and forehand?" she replied.

"That sounds like him, although that description fits a lot of tour players," replied Dee.

"Why do you ask?" she inquired.

"He was my roommate in college," replied Dee.

"You play?" She leaned forward, more eager now.

"No, I'm a swimmer," he answered.

She turned and looked at Jamal.

"No, I'm football," he replied.

"I thought you were both athletic," she stated.

Dee spoke, "Ike is a good friend of ours and we were staying at his place in Key West until we left on the cruise. He's single and recently retired. Sometime we'd like to introduce you. In fact, I'll give him your contact information. Maybe you can hook up on social media, if you're interested?"

She pulled out her phone and searched for Ike's profile and picture. "I'm sure that seems awfully shallow, but I wanted to be sure I remembered him correctly. I'd love to chat with him," she said, smiling.

"Done," replied Dee. "Here's my number, text me what you're willing to share with him."

She finished, sat her phone down, and looked at them both. "Shall we return to the topic that was at hand? What else can I tell you about Cortes or Castillo?"

"Do you think they ever worked together?" asked Jamal.

"How do you mean? One's a painter, one's an explorer. Castillo was commissioned by Cortes." she replied.

"Right," replied Jamal. "I just meant do you think they might ever have had dealings outside of the commissions, were they friends or partners of any kind or anything, did they go bar hopping together?"

That last comment brought a smile to her face, and she laughed.

"That's the thing about history. It's so hard to know because no one ever wrote that kind of thing down. Plus, it was five hundred years ago. What did people in that era really do?"

She continued, "The evidence suggests that Cortes commissioned quite a few paintings over several years, so yeah, they were strongly acquainted and probably friends. It's also written that Cortes was very self-centered and standoffish, not very trusting, but how much of that is based on any fact and not just modern day conjecture, extrapolated from circumstances? Castillo might have been his only friend."

She paused for a moment and looked at the two of them. "What is it you really want to know?"

Jamal hesitated and looked over at Dee, who said, "We read Cortes funded many of his own expeditions. We wondered if maybe some of his friends might have 'chipped in,' maybe someone like Castillo, who was at the height of his popularity and probably his wealth around the same time."

"That's an interesting thought," she replied. "I'd say it might be possible. Anyone that backed an expedition had expectations of being rewarded. You know about the king's royalty. Also, that Velasquez, governor of Cuba, financed the first expedition, before Cortes founded Vera Cruz and made himself governor or New Spain, throwing off Velasquez."

"Yeah, same thing Velasquez did to Columbus," replied Jamal.

Elizabeth grinned. "And modern day historians think the Spaniards were paranoid, with good reason, I'd say. So yeah, Castillo could have been a partner, but what would have been his reward? There's no historical record that I'm familiar with, which doesn't mean it isn't out there. I could research it a bit and let you know. Once Cortes was brought back to Spain, he probably didn't have access to much of the gold or treasures he may have amassed."

"So, Castillo may have lost out?" asked Dee.

"Possibly, or maybe just nobody ever knew," she added.

"Could the numeric painting be related as you said earlier, there was never an explanation?" asked Jamal.

"It most certainly served some purpose," she replied.

Glancing at her watch, Elizabeth noted, "It's about time for me to go. This has been fun. Most tourists are not this interesting," she said, smiling. "I'll do a little research. If there's anything I find, I'll let you know." She shook hands with each man and then hugged them lightly and headed for the door. She turned and waved as she exited.

They watched her go. "Nice girl," said Jamal.

"Yeah, she was a big help. I bet Ike will like her, too."

Jamal just grinned.

They sat for a while longer and continued to chat about the possibilities. The crowd outside thinned down as lunch passed and the plaza was empty in the afternoon sun. Then Dee's phoned chimed. He checked it and there was a text from Gina saying they had arrived at the beach, it was beautiful and to hurry on down before they need to go back to the ship.

Dee read the text to Jamal, and with a quick nod they rose and stepped outside. At the bottom of the plaza, they caught a cab for the beach.

A few minutes later, they were lying in the sand and relaxing with the rest of the group.

"How was it?" asked Angelic.

"Exhausting, but rewarding," replied Jamal. "We learned a lot, filled in some gaps, but still we don't know for sure. We made a new friend who is going to research a few things and forward anything she finds."

"She," said Keno.

"The curator," replied Jamal, "an ancient woman, nearly as old as Cortes." He rolled over to his side to look away. Dee sat across from him, grinning.

"What are you grinning at?" asked Gina.

Dee paused for a moment. "You," he replied, and pulled her closer to him.

LATER THAT NIGHT, THEY ALL CLEANED UP AND DRESSED FOR dinner with the captain.

"This is the most formal we've been in a while," said Gina to Dee as they dressed in their room.

"Yeah," he responded, "I prefer you in less clothes."

"Do you now?" She grinned at him and took his hand, pulling him toward the door. "Too bad for you, for now."

They met the others and made their way to the captain's table.

He was in full uniform, a short man with a head full of hair and a big mustache. He talked and talked and then talked some more. They heard all about shipping routes, timetables, pirates off other parts of the African coast, his time at sea, and his family. Some two hours later, they were returning to their rooms.

"Let's stop for a drink," said Jamal. "I need to catch my breath and get some air."

"He was so talky," added Keno.

Mike sighed audibly.

"You know, some of these captains, apparently they talk all the time, while others, never talk at all," added Angelic.

They all laughed at that thought and settled into the outdoor bar to catch a fresh breeze.

27

THE CANARY ISLANDS 2 GIBRALTAR

They woke the next morning to find themselves at sea. Yes, they were off the coast of Africa, and if they squinted through Dee's scope, they could prove it. Around lunch of the following day, they would port in Casablanca for a half day. As they sat around breakfast, there was much discussion about what they could do.

"Just keep in mind, the movie was shot on a sound stage in Hollywood, a really long time ago," said Jamal. "There's not much we can see in half a day."

"Don't we have a full day in Tangier?" asked Mike.

"Yes, we sail overnight from Casablanca and dock in Tangier for a day while we wait for our approach to Gibraltar. We'll have a little more time there," replied Dee.

"I think I'm for staying on the ship in Casablanca and maybe going ashore in Tangier, do some shopping," added Gina.

"I'm for that," chimed in Angelic.

"Me too," added Keno.

"In Tangier, we could rock on over to the 'Kasbah,'" said Jamal.

"Do what?" asked Keno.

"Jam, that was really bad," said Angelic.

"What exactly is the 'Kasbah?'" asked Gina.

"It's the palace of the sultan, when he stayed in the city, from back in the day, 17th century," replied Dee.

"Anything to do with Cortes?" asked Gina.

"Not likely," replied Dee, laughing. "There is a museum of Moroccan history that includes a café that was famous back in the 1960s for being the hangout of a bunch of American literary types and hippies."

"Doesn't that sound exciting," replied Keno, in a deadpan tone.

"You can always go shopping," replied Dee, and Keno's face brightened.

"I think we should try it," said Angelic, "just to give Jamal a break for a day, something other than Cortes."

Jamal looked up from his tablet and replied, "Might not be a bad idea, although we'll probably take a little time in Gibraltar before we head to Seville."

Angelic hit him with a pillow from her chair. "You definitely need a break," she said, laughing at him.

And so, it was decided, they'd rest on the ship in Casablanca and then they'd take in the Kasbah for some history and some lunch and then they'd go shopping and exploring in the Medina (old city).

The two days passed quickly, and they ported to Gibraltar on the third day. It was the official end of the cruise, and they prepared to disembark from the ship. They hadn't decided how long to stay in Gibraltar or how to get to Seville. Jamal had mentioned nothing about the bell or Cortes in the last couple of days. They were almost like tourists on vacation.

They left the ship and caught a taxi to a small boutique hotel in the harbor area that Keno had found online. It was a brief ride, and they checked in without incident. Again, they had adjacent rooms and basically occupied an entire floor of the small hotel.

After unpacking, they got suggestions from the concierge for lunch and hopped back in the same taxi and he drove them away.

The driver dropped them off at the local seaside establishment that had been recommended. They got a table on the deck under an awning with a spectacular view of the harbor. In the distance they could see a cable car trudging slowly up the mountain.

Jamal pointed in the distance and said, "That's something I think we should do."

"What's that?" replied Mike.

"The cable car," replied Jamal.

"I don't know," answered Keno, "I'm a little afraid of heights."

"Then we definitely should do the skywalk and suspension bridge at the top," answered Jamal.

Keno stuck her tongue out at him.

"Jamal, don't be so cruel," said Angelic, and Gina nodded.

Dee laughed and then said, "The cable car ride is probably not that far off the ground, and you just rise up in the air. The skywalk might have some height to it. But the views should be spectacular."

They ate a long lunch and took the cable car to the top. Keno decided she'd just close her eyes or hold on to Mike until they got there.

Riding up in the early afternoon, the ocean, and the harbor, and the surrounding landscape of Spain just fell away, although they were never over thirty feet off the ground. They just went up.

On top, they could see for miles in every direction. The

wind blew across them and the city and harbor spread out before them.

They meandered through the reserve, taking in the sights, stopping often to look in each direction.

They approached the Skywalk and realized that while it was seventy-five yards across, the gorge it spanned was only about fifty yards deep.

"If I hold on to the rail and look at the horizon, it shouldn't be a big deal," said Keno.

She took the rail in one hand and Mike's hand in the other, and they all strolled slowly along the skywalk. After a few minutes, she shifted her view to the trees on the far side of the gorge as the rock outcropping fell away and the skyline opened.

They got to the far side, and Keno sighed.

"Well done, girl," said Angelic. "I didn't know you had an issue with heights."

"Yeah, when we were on the island, I just always looked at the ground whenever we went up to the top, until we got situated, and then I could look out," Keno replied.

They had paused on the far side of the gorge and looked out across the water. "I'm fine here, it's just when I'm moving and the ground falls away, that I get a little queasy," Keno added.

"You did well," added Gina.

They moved along and hiked toward a site called the 'Top of the Rock,' the highest point on the island. They stopped for a break at a small café that had views of both Spain and Africa. It was the juncture of two worlds, both plain to see.

As they sat in the shade and talked, their next destination came up.

"Are we still going to Seville?" asked Mike.

Jamal looked thoughtful for a moment. "Yeah, I think so.

I don't have any other clues, and this looks like the end of the journey. If we can't find anything, we can turn the bell over to the Mexican authorities when we get back."

Angelic ran a hand across Jamal's shoulder. "It's okay, Jam, you'll find it or you won't. Either way, it's been an adventure we won't soon forget."

"Where will we go from there?" asked Keno.

Gina shrugged and Dee held up both hands, palms up.

"Let's see what we find first," answered Dee. "How are we going to get there?"

"I've been looking and there are a couple of choices, but only one that seems to make sense," replied Jamal. "It's too short of a distance to fly. There is no train, and to take a bus we have to hike or take a taxi across the border into Spain to catch the bus line. It looks like the easiest and quickest way is to drive."

"Drive?" asked Mike.

"In a car?" asked Keno.

"Are we allowed to do that, is it safe?" asked Gina.

Jamal held his hands up and grinned. "Driving is the most direct route. It'll take us a little over three hours. They drive on the right side of the road, just like at home, and the roads look good, there's just one highway change, so it seems easy enough. If we see signs that say Welcome to Portugal we've gone too far. We can rent an SUV or something larger so we have enough room."

"We can see the countryside," added Dee.

"I've never been to Spain, but I've been to Oklahoma," said Gina.

Everyone looked at her with blank faces. "Never mind," she said.

"I can check with the car rental, see if we can rent here and drop off there, and then we can move on wherever we want," added Jamal.

"Is everyone in agreement?" asked Dee.

There were nods all around.

"We've come this far, let's finish it," added Mike.

THE SUN WAS SINKING IN THE SKY.

"Let's head back to the skywalk," said Gina. "The view should be amazing."

They rose and strolled back the way they had come. When they got to the skywalk, there was a crowd, but they found a spot where Keno felt comfortable and they could see the sun sinking in the west. The harbor, the city, and the ocean beyond lit up below them and shimmered as the sun settled into the water. The crowd murmured their approval. That seemed to be a universal gesture, no matter where they found themselves in the world.

Making their way to the cable car, they returned to the base of the rock and caught a cab back to the hotel. They'd clean up for a late dinner where they'd decide what else they wanted to see in Gibraltar while Jamal made arrangements for the rental.

28

GIBRALTAR 2 SEVILLE

They spent another day in Gibraltar seeing a few more sights while Jamal made arrangements. They couldn't pick up the vehicle until the following day, so they spent the afternoon resting and lay by the rooftop pool of their hotel.

"The only vehicle that I could find that could seat all of us comfortably and our luggage is a 2016 Ford Flex, it's silver with tinted windows. One person will have to sit in the third row with the luggage," said Jamal.

"I'll do it," said Keno, "I'm the smallest."

"I'll trade with you some," added Gina. Keno nodded her thanks.

"All right," answered Jamal, "We'll leave in the morning."

The following day, the rental facility dropped off the vehicle. Jamal signed all the papers, the group checked out of the hotel, and got on the road. An hour later they had left Gibraltar, entered Spain, had no problems at the border crossing, and were motoring up the N-4 (N-IV) highway toward Seville.

"This was the most direct route. There were two others that circled out to the west, but they were mostly in flat lands or plains rolling down to the ocean. This way we get mountains to the east and plains to the west. It should be more scenic. The route is pretty much due north," said Jamal to the others.

The group had eaten at the hotel that morning and planned to drive straight through to Seville or until they needed gas. Arrival should be just after lunch and then they could get checked into the hotel they had booked.

The highway was smooth, and they made good time. They rolled into the outskirts of Seville around noon.

"We're staying in the 'Casco Antiguo,' which is the old part of the city near the museum," said Dee as they closed in on the downtown area. He and Jamal had found a four-star with three small suites for them. They had discussed how long the group might stay and came up with no conclusive idea. So, they thought, at least let's be comfortable and centrally located.

Dee parked the Flex, and they checked into the hotel. After getting settled in their rooms, they met on a rooftop lounge and sat under shaded umbrellas while they looked out upon the city.

"Is the museum far?" asked Keno.

"It's a couple of blocks that way," replied Jamal, pointing down the street from which they had just traveled.

"Is that all we plan to do?" asked Angelic.

Jamal shook his head. "No, let's stay a couple of days. I'll turn the car in, and we can figure out what we want to do next and where we want to go from here."

"Maybe Jamal and I should go look at the museum while you guys tour the city," said Dee.

"You want to keep it all to yourself," teased Gina.

Dee shook his head. "No, I just thought you all might be bored. There may be nothing to see."

"I'll keep an eye on the ladies," grinned Mike. He turned to them. "Where do we want to go?"

"Let's go see the 'Real Alcazar,' which is a palace of the Spanish royalty, and see how it compares to the 'Kasbah' in Morocco. Who's got the best digs?" said Angelic, grinning. "Then we can follow up with some Flamenco later on tonight."

She put a hand on Jamal's shoulder. "Maybe you guys can join us tomorrow evening?"

Jamal squeezed her hand and nodded.

Gina had come over and sat on Dee's leg. He squeezed her at the waist.

"We'll run through the museum and see what there is and then hook up with you guys for a night out," said Dee.

"Good," added Keno, "But tonight, I'd like to just take it easy and stay in the room or sit here and watch the sky and the city," she said as she leaned back in her lounge.

29

SEVILLE (MUSEUM OF FINE ARTS)

The following morning, rested and feeling better, the group got up for early breakfast in the inner plaza and courtyard of the hotel. The hotel itself was made up of two older, former residences and had multiple interior and exterior balconies, atriums, courtyards, walkways, and gardens. It was almost a maze.

The sun streamed down from the opening in the roof and a bright, natural, and peaceful light surrounded them.

"I hate to get up and leave this," said Jamal, looking around the atrium approvingly.

"You can go with us, babe," replied Angelic.

Jamal paused for a moment and looked at Dee, who sat quietly without responding.

"Let us go get this done. Then we can move on," he answered. "You guys going to the palace?"

Angelic nodded and said, "And then to the 'Plaza de Espana' and a walk along the river, maybe the Cathedral later. But tonight, we want a big dinner and Flamenco dancing, so you'd better be back in time."

Gina waved a finger under Dee's nose and grinned at him. "You hear that?" she giggled.

Jamal and Dee both nodded as they rose, waved, and walked away.

"There's a drop site for the vehicle a few blocks over. Let's get rid of the car and then head for the museum," said Jamal.

AN HOUR LATER, JAMAL AND DEE STOOD IN FRONT OF A multistory building designed in a highly ornate Baroque style, surrounded by elaborate landscaping and gardens.

"The building is as much a work of art as its contents," said Jamal as he stood and took in the many architectural details.

"I'll leave that observation to you, as you're the qualified one," replied Dee, "but, it is stunning to look at. It must have taken years to build, and the craftsmanship is almost unimaginable in today's world."

Jamal nodded in agreement. "I think it may have originally been a convent built in the 17th century, and then converted to a museum in the 1800s. Let's go look."

THEY STOOD AT THE ENTRANCE OF THE GRAND HALLWAY. IT was multiple stories high and domed in an elaborate stained-glass pattern. The walls were painted in a light color and dominated by massive canvases from the middle ages to the 20th century.

"Where do we start?" asked Dee.

"This could take days," replied Jamal. "Elizabeth said it was an enormous collection."

They wandered down the long entrance, glancing at the painting names as they made their way toward a reception desk. It sat in front of a wall covered in smaller paintings, almost too numerous to look at individually.

There was a line to the receptionist and Jamal saw a flyer on the desk that he stepped forward and retrieved. He walked back to Dee, who was trying to sort through all the paintings behind the desk.

Jamal held up the flyer. "This is the museum layout. There is likely a room dedicated to 16th century painters. We just need to determine its location and go have a look," he said.

"Couldn't we just ask the museum personnel?" said Dee.

"We could," replied Jamal, "but we don't know what we're looking for."

Glancing at the map, Jamal said, "It looks like there are a couple of interior courtyards as well, if we need to take a break and get some air. Hopefully, there's one near the room we're looking for."

Dee followed along behind Jamal as they made their way through the museum. One room after another was chock full of paintings and sculptures.

"I wish I had more time just to look," said Jamal.

"You, or we, could spend a lot of time here," added Dee.

"This is an amazing collection," replied Jamal.

And then he stopped. They had entered a sizeable marble floored room with a vaulted ceiling. Painted in a very pale green, it was an interior room with no natural light, and each painting hung with its own display light detailing its shapes and colors.

"This is supposed to be the 16th century collection," said Jamal.

"What do we do?" asked Dee.

Jamal grinned. "Spread out, look, like we did in the Canary Islands. Shout out if you see something," he replied.

It was a big room. There were a lot of paintings. Dee

went left. Jamal went right. They made their way slowly around the room, studying each painting, each artist's name, not really knowing what they were looking for, but hopefully they'd recognize it if they saw it.

The room was empty but for the two of them. They looked, they took a few steps, and they looked again. They were beautiful pieces of art and it tempted both men to stay longer at each piece, but they forced themselves to keep moving. They were thirty yards apart before Dee waved at Jamal and called, "Hey, I found Castillo."

It was a moment before Jamal replied, "Yeah, I did, too. Biblical?"

"Yeah, Madonna and child, outdoors," replied Dee.

"Same," responded Jamal.

"What am I looking for?" called Dee.

"Insight," replied Jamal.

"You're asking a lot," answered Dee.

"Just keep looking," replied Jamal.

And for the next several hours, they did. There were quite a few Castillo's, all that they saw, biblical, mostly Madonna and child.

Dee heard footsteps and looked up. He had moved into an adjacent room. Apparently, the museum's collection of 16th century painting was quite extensive.

"I need to rest my eyes, and my brain," said Jamal, waving at him. "Let's take a break and go outside."

They made their way to an exit and stepped out onto a marble terraced balcony that ran around a courtyard of intricately cut hedges. Had they not been just waist height, the hedges would have formed a maze, but it was more of a formal garden.

"There has to be some serious maintenance to keep this place going," commented Dee as they leaned on the balcony and took in the garden below.

"Don't know how they do it. They must have an extensive budget," replied Jamal.

Dee pointed below. A series of Roman arches lined the walkway. Behind them on the lower walls were friezes in designs that reflected the pattern cut into the hedges. "See how the walls reflect the hedge," he said.

Jamal leaned forward and took note. "Or the hedge reflects the wall. I've seen floors and ceilings mirror each other but never garden hedges and wall murals, unbelievable. I can't imagine to what purpose."

They stood and admired the intricacy for a moment.

Turning toward Jamal, Dee asked, "Have you seen anything?"

"A lot of fine painting, great composition, good color, and use of light, but nothing that tells me anything about Cortes or the bell," Jamal replied.

"Yeah, the same for me," answered Dee.

As they stood on the balcony, a light breeze picked up.

"Let's walk down to the end of the terrace and back, just to move around a little," said Dee.

They started out and glanced back as they got closer to their turning point.

"This place must have been something, back in the day, full of nuns," said Dee.

Jamal grinned. "Hard to imagine, hundreds of years between us and them, but the building remains unchanged."

"Do you think we're going to find anything?" asked Dee.

"I don't know, I really don't," answered Jamal.

They returned to the door where they had exited.

"Let's go keep looking, it's all we got for now," said Jamal.

Dee nodded, and they went back inside.

"Let's get some lunch," said Dee. "I saw a café on the

first floor, right after we started looking for the 16th century collection."

Jamal nodded. "Yeah, I'm hungry, could use some caffeine."

They found the café and ate sandwiches and sweet Spanish pastries, then started back to resume their search. Before leaving, Dee pointed to the exit, and they stepped outside, below where they'd stood on the upstairs balcony, to be on the lower terrace where the arches and the murals and the hedge stood silently in the sun. They looked around for a moment.

"You don't notice the reflection of the pattern down here, like you did upstairs," said Dee.

"Not at all," replied Jamal. "No one would ever know."

THEY RETURNED INSIDE AND STARTED THEIR WALK BACK TO the 16th century collection.

"I'm going to have to swim a few extra laps after eating that dessert," said Dee. "Yeah," replied Jamal. "Or I could just pick up the pace," he added and started walking faster toward the room.

"You can slow down," called Dee. "I'd rather swim."

They got back to the room and split up again to resume their search. More time passed. They moved less quickly than in the morning as their concentration and effort slowly wore them down. They had seen a lot of Castillo's work, but nothing registered. It was growing late in the day and the museum would close shortly. Dee turned another corner and saw the name plate showing the artist as Castillo. When he turned to the painting, he stopped, refocused, and then looked again. All afternoon he had been looking at biblical scenes. Before him now was a portrait. He looked again at the title, 'Portrait of Hernando Cortes' by Juan Bautista Castillo.

Dee took a step back and refocused. The portrait captured a man from the chest up. He was in formal clothing for the time period, but the man's face dominated the painting. He had pale skin, hard eyes, and a firm chin with the wisp of a beard. He looked capable, confident, and almost cruel. Dee noted that this was clearly a younger man. He had seen Jamal's pictures of other portraits of Cortes. They were always of an older man with tired eyes and a full beard, as if he were hiding behind something. This was very different. He called out for Jamal.

Jamal stood, studying the portrait.

"This is a man who would cast a gold bell from the fortunes of his enemies," Jamal noted.

Dee could only nod.

"Impregnate his enemies' daughter, steal their gold, kill them all, flee with the woman and child, this is a man whose only conviction is his own self-interest," continued Jamal. "He had to have commissioned the bell."

The museum was about to close, and Jamal and Dee slowly and almost sadly made their way to the door.

"We'll have to come back tomorrow," said Jamal.

"Yeah," replied Dee. "Although I'm not sure what else the painting can tell us, nor what else we might find."

Jamal nodded his agreement. "But we have to look, we have to try," he said.

30

SEVILLE (MUSEUM OF FINE ARTS-DAY 2)

They took a cab back to the hotel and found everyone sitting by the pool in the early evening light.

"You guys need to get cleaned up," said Angelic. "We have a short 'tapas tour' that finishes near the cathedral at a tablao where we'll watch a Flamenco show or demonstration."

"'Tapas Tour?'" said Jamal.

"Yes," replied Angelic. "We'll go to four different restaurants and try each of their specialties, its small plate, like an hors d'oeuvres."

Jamal nodded his head. "How long is all this?" he asked.

"The tour is about two to three hours, and the show starts after that. It's about ninety minutes," answered Keno.

Jamal and Dee looked at Mike.

"I'm just the bodyguard. They did the planning," he replied, grinning.

"Get moving," added Gina. "we'll wait here."

Dee and Jamal hustled up to their rooms to get ready for the big evening.

. . .

THE NEXT MORNING, DEE AND JAMAL LEFT THE OTHERS
sleeping and headed for the museum. As they rode in the taxi
Dee stretched his arms and covered his mouth to yawn while
thinking to himself, *I wish I had some of the energy those Flamenco
dancers had last night.* The dancers, women in bright red, form
fitting dresses, and the men, all in black, had hardly stopped
for the ninety minutes of the program. It made Dee tired just
to think about it.

Jamal, noticing Dee's predicament, said, "We'll get some
more of those pastries, that'll energize you, and me, too."

"Tell me again why we had to start so early?" asked Dee.

"No reason, really, I just wanted to get back to it. I feel
like we're close to finding something. I just don't know what,"
replied Jamal.

Dee laughed at him as the taxi pulled up. "Let's go find
it, great explorer and discoverer of sunken stuff," he said.

A COUPLE OF HOURS LATER THEY HAD REVIEWED THE
painting again and came to the same conclusion about
Cortes casting the bell, looked around the balance of the 16th
century paintings, and several other rooms in the museum,
and had come up with nothing.

The museum didn't have any Cortes artifacts, and the
balance of the Castillo paintings had all been biblical. There
was nothing left for them to look at.

Angelic had texted Jamal about mid-morning and asked
how it was going. Jamal had replied 'slowly' and asked if the
group wanted to come over for lunch at the café and to see
the Cortes portrait. They were on their way over as Dee and
Jamal found their way to the first-floor outdoor grill.

While they waited for the others, Dee sat at one of the
nearby tables and Jamal studied the frieze behind them. He

ran his fingers across the ridges of the hedge depicted on the wall. It was textured, just like the real hedge. Jamal's fingers followed the patterns and pushed occasionally as the forms curved and flowed, extended from the wall.

"These are amazingly detailed," he said to Dee.

"Incredible artistry," replied Dee, "but I still wonder why?"

"Maybe because they could," whispered Jamal.

"Hey, you guys," called Angelic, waving at them as the group came through the door from the inside of the museum.

"Nice," said Mike, looking around the courtyard while the others gathered.

Gina slid beside Dee and hugged him, and he wrapped his arm around her shoulder.

"Let's order and grab a seat," said Dee, moving toward the café.

The others fell in behind, and they lined up to make their selections.

"Dee recommends the pastries," called out Jamal.

Gina patted Dee's stomach. "I thought he was getting softer," she said, laughing.

They gathered their food and moved down the walkway toward the empty tables that intersected the next wall of the courtyard. They sat and ate and enjoyed the sunshine.

After a moment, Dee pointed to the frieze behind them. "If you look hard, you can see the pattern in the hedges in the garden, reflected in the wall mural," he said.

They all turned and looked at the hedges and then at the wall.

"What?" asked Keno.

"Not sure I see it," said Mike.

"When we go up to the second floor to see the portrait,

I'll show you from the balcony up there. It's easier to see," Dee replied.

"Is this how you guys spent your time?" giggled Angelic, "staring at the bushes?"

Gina whispered in Dee's ear, "I didn't think you liked bushes."

He whispered back, "I'm not into grooming."

"Look," said Jamal, who stood and approached the frieze. He ran his hand along the design, turning and following the curves of it. "This follows the same pattern as the hedge, and it's even textured." He pointed to the hedges in the center of the courtyard. "See here, it works right into the center, just like the hedge." His hand rested on the center of the frieze, and as he went to turn and sit back down, he pressed lightly against the wall.

There was a click and a small groan, and the frieze swung slightly outward toward Keno, who sat closest to the wall. She jumped up and scrambled out of the way. The frieze hung slightly ajar from the wall.

Everyone sat there, staring and silent. There were no sirens or bells, no one came running.

Dee rose and said to Jamal, "Let's take a look." They stepped closer, and Dee swung the door a little further open while Jamal peered inside.

"There is a package wrapped in brown paper," called out Jamal. "It's roughly three feet by four feet and three or four inches thick. I'm guessing a painting."

He went to reach for the package. "Should you touch it?" said Angelic. Jamal stopped his hand.

"Let me go get the desk person or a guard," said Dee. "Everybody, stay here. Jamal, be ready to explain."

· · ·

SEVERAL MINUTES LATER, DEE CAME BACK WITH A GUARD AND an older man, who turned out to be the museum director. He had overhead Dee asking the guard what to do.

Mike and the women moved the table out of the way and the man opened the frieze door further. He and Jamal got on each side of the painting and lifted by the edge.

"Hold it by the frame," the man said, and Jamal nodded. "Let's take it inside," he continued.

Mike grabbed the door, and the director and Jamal made their way through, followed by Dee and the rest of the group.

The man quickly directed them to a large conference room. They gingerly set the painting on the table. There was a twine string wrapped around the outside of the paper. The director pulled out a small pocketknife and cut the string. Jamal lifted the painting up on its frame and the man unwrapped it.

When he got the last stretch of paper removed, his breath did a sharp intake.

"It's Castillo's 'Numeric Madonna,'" said Jamal.

The man turned quickly. "You know this piece?" he asked.

"Only by reputation," said Dee.

"We'd seen a picture," added Jamal.

"Few people know this work," the director added.

"I was looking at some of his biblical work and this piece was mentioned," replied Jamal.

"How did you know where to look? This piece was thought to be stolen thirty years or more ago," the man asked, and then quickly paused.

"Forgive me," he continued, "I am Diego Schwartz, the director of the museum. I overheard this man," he pointed at Dee, "telling the guard the story, and I'll be honest, I thought, what nonsense, but I must see for myself. I cannot thank you enough. All this time the museum had thought this painting stolen, yet it never reappeared in any of the black markets."

"What happened, I mean, how did it happen?" asked Keno.

DIEGO PAUSED FOR A MOMENT, AS IF THINKING BACK. "I HAD just started here at the museum, so it's closer to thirty-five years ago, and there was a break-in on a long weekend. There were several paintings being taken. There was an anonymous call to the police, and they came to investigate. Apparently, there were two groups of thieves working together, although the thought has always been that one turned on the other and made the call, perhaps as a diversion so that the caller might get away. At any rate, a couple of the paintings went missing but turned up shortly afterward and the museum was able to reclaim them. This one, though, it never reappeared. It was the least known, valuable mostly for its unusual setting and curious history."

"Curious history?" asked Gina.

"Castillo, the artist who painted this, never explained his reasoning or the purpose for the backdrop of letters and numbers in the painting. All of his other work is biblical with outdoor settings, other than his portrait of Cortes," replied Diego.

"We just spent the last day and a half looking through his work," added Jamal. "Particularly the portrait."

Diego nodded. "You are an art historian?" he asked.

"Art history degree," replied Jamal. "Just curious about Castillo while we were on vacation here."

"Well, you've certainly made a big find. The art world will take notice. There are so many mysteries, so many unsolved thefts, and unknown locations. It will make a great story. Tell me how you found it," answered Diego.

"It was really by accident," stated Jamal. He pointed at Dee. "We were here yesterday, looking at Castillo's work, and we took a break out on the upper balcony. Dee noticed that the pattern on the frieze was the same as the pattern of the hedge. We thought that was odd, and we came down at lunch to look closer. You couldn't really tell it from down here. Today, we brought our friends to show them, and I was pointing out the similarity when I hit something in the middle of the frieze, and it clicked and popped open. It was a surprise and was totally unrelated to anything other than admiring the building and the grounds."

Diego shook his head. "That's incredible," he sighed. "I need to call my friend at the newspaper, 'El Pais,' and have her come out for a photograph. This will be a headline generator for them."

"I didn't think Castillo was that well known," said Gina.

"Outside of Spain, not as much, but he is popular in the country. It will start out as a big local story and get smaller as it moves around the world. It is a significant find and people deserve to know how your friend," he said, pointing at Jamal," found it."

Jamal pointed at Dee. "He helped me find it. If he hadn't pointed out the hedges, I'd never have found it."

"The hedges were just a clue. You punched the button or whatever it was in the door. You found it," said Dee as he nodded at Diego, who returned the nod.

Diego pulled out his phone and dialed. As the connection made, he stepped a few paces away and spoke in rapid Spanish.

Everyone looked at Jamal. "I got no idea what he is saying," said Jamal.

They went back to the courtyard and finished lunch while waiting for Diego's friend to arrive.

DIEGO AND THE PHOTOGRAPHER CAME BUSTLING UP A FEW minutes later. The frieze door still stood partially open.

"Everyone, stand around the door," she said. She took a couple of quick pictures and then had Diego and Jamal stand on the threshold of the door and she got some close-ups.

"Where does that door lead?" asked Mike.

Diego stepped down while brushing off his hands. "I remember it now. There is an inner door as well. We renovated one of the shipping rooms a few years after the theft and I'm guessing it got covered up. We also had a turnover in maintenance staff around that time, several retirements, and I'm guessing the new people, who've been with us ever since, weren't aware of the door's existence. It's amazing."

"Did the police ever capture any of the thieves?" asked Gina.

Diego paused for a minute. "It's been a while but what I vividly remember is that the paintings we recovered were because of the police cornering a van and having a shoot-out, which is unusual for typical art thieves. They were later identified as belonging to a European crime gang, which might explain why they fought to the death. The whole thing was kind of strange. I was new, but I remember the former director pondering over what had happened. It differed from most art heists, so he said. It was much more violent and visible.

"They chased the other thieves down along the river, but they escaped. That is what we always thought happened to the 'Numeric Madonna,' the one that got away. "

The photographer had been busy snapping pictures and making notes.

"Let's go back to the conference room," she said. "I'd like to get a photo of Diego, Jamal, and the painting. It should get picked up by the national and international papers. You'll be famous," she said, pointing at Jamal. "For a few minutes."

31

SEVILLE (THE PAINTING)

The photographer snapped a few pictures and promised that the news would be in tomorrow's paper. She bagged up her equipment and left.

Jamal and Diego stood looking at the painting while the rest of the group stood back and admired them and the painting.

"What will you do with it now?" asked Jamal.

Diego ran a finger lightly over the canvas and replied, "We'll clean it up a little and design a layout in the 16th century room to feature it and tell the surrounding story. It's a delightful piece, unusual, visitors will like it. We'll do some promotional material and put it online, maybe a tee shirt."

Then he turned to Jamal and said, "You said you weren't looking for it specifically, but you seem to have some curiosity about the piece, beyond finding it. I see how you keep looking at it."

Jamal smiled and nodded at Diego. "I'm just curious about the nature of the painting. Why did Castillo do that? What does it mean? As an art historian, sort of, I'm curious."

"Most definitely," replied Diego. "You are certainly an art historian now. People will know your name."

"Would it be okay if my friends and I came back by to see the painting over the next few days?" Jamal asked.

Diego looked up at him.

"We have pictures, and we can take some more now, but there's something about seeing the painting on canvas that prompts the mind. We're just curious," Jamal continued.

Diego did not hesitate. "Absolutely. You can come by. It will eventually be on display. It's not an important piece, but it is an interesting piece. There is no reason you shouldn't see it."

"Thank you," replied Jamal. Dee and Mike both moved forward and took several more pictures of the painting.

They left the museum, again with Diego's express thanks, and returned to the hotel. They lay by the pool, as it was one of their favorite things to do, and talked about the discovery.

"What do you think this can tell us?" asked Mike.

Jamal shook his head. "I don't know, although I think somehow it is related," he replied.

"Was Castillo trying to tell Cortes something?" asked Angelic.

"Possibly, probably. There had to be some reason for it. And it was so unlike any of his other work," replied Jamal.

"Like he was giving him directions, maybe," added Gina.

"Directions to what?" asked Keno.

Dee pulled his phone out and was looking at the pictures. "It makes little sense, unless they were hiding something. Castillo would have explained it otherwise."

"It's a riddle, that I don't know how to solve," added Jamal.

"What would an accountant do to solve the problem?" asked Gina, turning to look at Dee.

"I'd follow the money, but I don't see a trail," replied Dee.

They cleaned up and ate dinner at a five-star restaurant that wasn't really as good as the tapas bars they'd been to the night before. They caught more Flamenco, and it was just as good, just as energetic and exciting, as the night before. Then they went back to their rooms feeling tired. They talked as they walked.

"Where we headed next?" asked Keno.

"Where's everybody want to go?" asked Dee.

"We're here," replied Angelic, "let's tour the Mediterranean."

There were murmurs of ascent.

"But first, we go back and look at the painting in the morning," answered Jamal.

32

SEVILLE (THE DISCOVERY)

They rose the next morning and, after a quick breakfast, rode as a group to the museum.

"Do you think it's about over?" Angelic asked Jamal.

"I don't know, doesn't feel it, but I don't know where to go next," he replied.

"It's been amazing," said Keno, "and I don't even like adventure."

Mike laughed at her and said, "Sure you do, you just don't want to admit it."

Keno made a face at him. Dee and Gina silently watched them and smiled at their antics.

The taxi pulled up, and the group made their way inside. Although it had only been a couple of days, Jamal and Dee felt that so much had happened since they'd arrived. Something ingrained them in the museum, as if it were a second home, a place where they belonged.

They made their way to the conference room, and Diego waved at them from his office.

"There you are, happy to see you again. You were serious

about coming by." He stepped toward them and continued, "Let's go look."

Inside the conference room, the painting sat unadorned on the table, yet it still had a glow about it. The letters and numbers jumped out at the viewer and nearly overpowered the Madonna and child.

Diego watched them study the painting for a moment and then stepped forward and said "Art historians over the years have thought that the key to this painting," he stopped speaking and pointed at a specific set of letters, "was the word *SEWN*. It's the only complete word that exists from all the combinations of letters. The word is somehow a link to the remaining body of Castillo's religious work and ties it all together. The joke has always been that this word is the thread to unraveling the mystery." Diego chuckled at his own joke.

THEY SAT AS A GROUP AND STUDIED THE PAINTING. DIEGO watched them as much as he did the painting.

"What happens when you pull a thread?" asked Keno.

"It unravels," answered Angelic.

"The same letters as *SEWN* also form the word *NEWS*," added Gina.

"But that word doesn't appear in any combination on the painting," answered Diego, pointing at the canvas. "There's NE over here and WS over there, but nowhere together."

After a moment, Dee spoke. "Are we making this too difficult? What if we aren't looking for a word? What if they are individual letters that standalone? It could be direction, like NSEW—north, south, east, and west, since those are the only letters on the painting, which makes the numbers longitude and latitude or maybe latitude and speed. I don't think Columbus had longitude, that's how he ended up in the

Caribbean, instead of Virginia. He was over twenty degrees off course from his original heading."

"Are these directions from Castillo to Cortes?" asked Mike.

"That might explain why he never explained the painting," added Angelic.

"Directions to where or what?" asked Diego.

"The location of something," answered Dee.

"The location of the bell, with the name 'Castillo,'" said Jamal.

"Or the treasure perhaps, that included the bell?" asked Gina.

"What treasure?" asked Diego.

"When Cortes was captured by the Spanish, he was fleeing in a ship. Ms. Alvarez, a librarian we spoke with in Vera Cruz, said the ship was sunk, and she made it sound like the Spanish that were pursuing Cortes were responsible. But what if they weren't? What if Cortes sank the ship himself?"

"That would explain why he had no gold or treasure to barter with, or that no record of any treasure being captured with him exists," said Dee.

Diego jumped in, "In a capture like that, treasure may not have been reported, if they found it."

"Why not?" asked Keno.

"The captors kept it for themselves. Their job was to capture Cortes. Anything else would have been secondary. But, with no treasure, Cortes couldn't barter with them," replied Diego.

There was silence for a moment as each of them struggled through the possibilities.

Then Jamal spoke. "I think Cortes sank the ship because he didn't want the treasure captured. He planned to escape and return for it. Could this be the location where he sank it?

Could Castillo have been recording this so that he and Cortes would always know the location if something happened to either of them? Hidden in plain sight, so to speak?"

"That would explain a lot about the painting," said Diego. Now that he'd seen the letters and numbers in the light of indicating direction, he couldn't look at the painting and not see it. "For hundreds of years, we've looked at this wrong," he sighed. "Oh, by the way, have you seen today's paper?"

When they all shook their heads, Diego said, "Let me go get it." He stepped away toward his office.

"So where is it, the ship, I mean?" asked Keno. She looked at Jamal and then at Dee.

They looked at each other.

"There is still some randomness to the arrangement," answered Dee. "There had to be, in order to make the location less apparent. Look at the letters followed immediately by numbers. It should be one of them."

Each of the others looked at the painting and murmured. There were numerous letters, followed immediately by numbers.

"What are we looking for, exactly?" asked Angelic.

"A location," replied Jamal.

"Location to what?" asked Diego, as he returned to the room.

"We're speculating on which line is the one that tells where the ship might be," replied Jamal.

"Do you really think so?" asked Diego.

"Seen in this light, I think it has to be the directions to or location of something," replied Jamal.

"What we know is that Cortes was fleeing, probably south toward the Pacific Ocean or southern Mexico." Dee said. "He'd been on an expedition into northern Mexico and discovered the Sea of Cortez. He was returning to the capital in Mexico City or making a run for it. But he was still in the northern hemisphere at that point, so his latitude would be north so many degrees, or N and a number, possibly followed by a speed. There was no longitude at that time. Sailors used a couple of different methods, celestial or by the stars, if they could, or 'dead reckoning' or 'deduced reckoning' where they determined their speed in knots, which were literally from a knotted line with the knots set at predetermined intervals. The number of actual knots, let out in a predetermined period of time, gave you the speed the ship was traveling. In that manner, captains could track how far they had traveled with their ship."

As they looked back at the painting, Diego held the paper up for Jamal. "Look," he said, "You're famous."

The entire group stopped for a moment and glanced at the paper. It was a large picture with the story opposite. It was the featured article in the arts and entertainment section of the paper, prominently above the fold.

"Look at you, dog," said Mike to Jamal. "You're grinning from ear to ear."

"It's a big moment," said Diego. "This painting has been missing for thirty-five years. While I admit the find doesn't make the museum look very good, actually quite stupid, I'm happy for the recovery."

"You're a star, Jam," said Angelic.

"I don't feel like one. I still don't know about the bell," he replied.

"Bell?" said Diego.

The entire group looked at one another.

Jamal looked at Diego, paused for a moment, and then said, "We were diving in the Sea of Cortez, and we found a bell. Maybe gold, maybe Aztec gold. It has the name 'Castillo' stamped into it. We have this theory that Castillo the painter had a relationship with Cortes the explorer and that they are somehow connected, through the bell, and perhaps through this painting."

Diego stood, his mouth open, but no sound coming out. "Unbelievable," he finally murmured. "The pieces seem to fit, at least on the surface. You have this bell?"

"It's in a safe place," answered Dee quickly.

"A wise answer, my friend," replied Diego. "Should what you suggest be true, there are many who will be interested, officially and unofficially."

The group stood silent for a moment.

Diego pressed on. "If you found the bell in Mexican waters, and it belonged to Cortes or even Castillo, and was made of Aztec gold, I would say Mexico has the right to it. Not everyone in Spain might agree with that, but it is my feeling. I will help you if I can. I am grateful for what you have done for the museum. Your theory makes sense, whether or not it is true. But do not tell me anymore. Just ask me if you need something or tell me if you find the answer."

Jamal reached out a hand to Diego. "Thank you," he said.

"Don't thank me just yet," replied Diego. "I had no idea there was more when I asked for the picture. I was only thinking of the painting and some credit for you, to advance your name in the art world. But, if others know of this bell, or when they find out, you may be subjected to some, shall we say, persistent inquiries," concluded Diego.

Jamal and Dee looked at one another as the rest of the group looked at the two men.

Diego was quick to notice. "Someone else knows about the bell?" he asked, then held up a hand. "Don't tell me, just be cautious." He paused for a moment. "Going back to the painting, can you determine anything about location?"

"We're looking for an N with some numbers following it, probably latitude and speed," answered Dee.

The group turned to the painting and searched. Keno was the first to point out an N, but the number following it was a larger one, and Dee shook her off.

"I don't think so," he said. "See how the numbers immediately following the letters range from zero to ninety. That is the span of latitude. Zero is the equator and ninety is the North Pole or the South Pole."

"It makes more and more sense," murmured Diego. "It's hard to believe no one saw this."

"They weren't looking for it, "replied Dee. "It's easy to not see something. Hold on a minute." He reached for his phone. Scrolling through the phone to a map he said, "The Sea of Cortez is not that far north, even at its origin, the numbers should be smaller." He continued. "'34 degrees N' is the northernmost point. If Cortes was sailing south, the numbers would get smaller."

"Look," said Gina, "Right there, two lines."

They all turned to where she pointed. There was a line with an N, then another directly below. The top line read N 27 5 and the line below it read N 25 5.

"That's it," called out Dee. Holding up his phone, he exclaimed, "Those numbers coincide with the approximate latitude of La Paz, Mexico. He sank the ship somewhere between those two points."

33

SEVILLE (THE SURPRISE)

They celebrated that night, and they took Diego with them. He knew a small local restaurant, and it was the best food they'd eaten yet. They sat for a long time after, drinking slowly and talking rapidly.

"I am so happy for you. When will you return to Mexico and pursue the wreck?" Diego asked.

"I'm not sure when or if we'll go back," answered Dee. "We found the wreck already, or at least a small part of it. It was five hundred years ago. There wasn't a lot of it left. "

"What we're really trying to figure out is how to tie the bell to Cortes and or Castillo," added Jamal. "That's the missing piece. The rest of it seems plausible now, but we need confirmation that Cortes made the bell, had the bell, or however Castillo was involved. We'd also like to know if it is in fact Aztec gold."

"It's not likely it'd be anything else, is it?" asked Diego. "I mean Cortes spent his entire career, prior to his death, in the new world, in Mexico."

"We've heard that speculated," replied Dee, "but we wish

we could substantiate that fact or at least that Cortes had the bell made for Castillo."

Diego looked at his watch. "My friends, it is getting late, even for a Spaniard. My wife will expect me. If there is any way that I can help, I will. I wish you all success. I think your best hope is in Mexico, since that is likely where the bell originated. Raising questions in Spain will only cause turmoil over ownership. That is something to think about, no?" he added. "I must be going." He rose, hugged each of the men, kissed the women on both cheeks, and waved farewell.

The group sat a while longer and had one last round.

"He may be right," said Jamal. "Maybe we should go back to Mexico?"

"Possibly," replied Dee and then turned to address the group. "What do you all think?"

"I don't have any ideas," replied Mike.

"If we go back, I want to fly," said Angelic.

"I agree," added Keno.

"What other choice do we have?" asked Gina.

"Let's take a day or two and rest, relax a bit, and think about it. Maybe something else will turn up, or Diego will have an idea," replied Dee.

There was some murmuring, but then agreement. They rose and started back to the hotel.

TWO DAYS LATER AND A TRIP ACROSS THE OCEAN AWAY, a large man, on a large white yacht with a large birthmark running up his arm, across his shoulder and onto his face, sat on the deck, in the shade, and ate his breakfast. In front of him was a copy of the New York Times. As he ate, he flipped casually through the paper. Then he saw it. There on a back page, in a single column, was the picture of a man that he had been looking for a short time. Beside the man in the picture was a painting that the man on the ship had been looking for a very long time. The man skimmed the article and then picked up the phone. "Call the pilots, scramble the jet, we're going to Seville."

PART III

CORTES' REVENGE

34

SEVILLE (THE DECISION)

They had enjoyed two days in Seville seeing the sights. Nothing had been said about the bell or what the group planned to do next.

Diego had checked in with them, and the painting was about to be put on display. He asked if they were still in town, if Jamal would like to be a part of the opening ceremony with the rest of them included as guests. Jamal quickly agreed.

The ceremony was scheduled for the following morning. After touristing for two days the group was content to sit around the hotel and by the pool.

"We about ready to move on?" asked Mike.

Dee and Jamal both nodded. "I haven't turned up anything else and seem to be at a dead end," replied Jamal.

"We've been looking at tours," said Keno pointing to herself, Angelic and Gina. "There's a nice one that circles the Mediterranean, leaves from Gibraltar in a couple of days."

"We could head back there and see some sights before we go," added Mike.

"Soon as we wrap up the opening ceremony tomorrow," said Jamal, looking at Dee.

"Okay, by me, but I hate to give up," replied Dee. "We'll have to turn the bell over to the Mexican authorities. Maybe you and I should fly back and take care of that."

Gina had been listening and spoke up. "The bell has been lost for five hundred years. Ten more days won't hurt. We can fly back to Mexico after we finish in the Mediterranean. We can check on Ernie and Cristina."

Jamal, Mike, and Dee all nodded. The women had a plan.

At an airport outside of Mexico City, six men were boarding a private jet, a Gulfstream G650. They were big, strong men, former military. They accompanied Miguelito Cortes.

The plane taxied down the runway and was soon aloft and headed for Seville, Spain. The passengers were looking at an eight hour plus nonstop flight. They were traveling over 5500 miles, but one advantage of being employed by a billionaire was having access to the fastest means of travel.

Miguelito sat back in his seat and admired the surrounding circumstances. *The plane was beautiful and had cost him a small fortune, which meant that it was good he had an enormous fortune. The men he had hired were professionals, not inexpensive. But they should be more than enough to take away from these tourists whatever it was they had found on the Cortes wreck. And what they had found would be worth a fortune.* Even though Miguelito had no plans to sell the Aztec gold, he felt it was rightfully his, his inheritance from his Aztec and Spanish ancestors. Miguelito was still furious that the tourists had gotten to the wreck before his team of divers. *How had they known? Could it have been just an accident, a curiosity for them, a blind hog that found an acorn, a golden acorn? The boys that had told Miguelito about the wreck had been free divers. They hadn't been able to stay down long enough to determine anything. All they had known was they dived into the spot regularly and there was a wreck on the shelf where there hadn't been one the week before.* Miguelito regularly paid for tips about anything anyone had seen while diving in the Sea of Cortez. He'd been looking for the wreck for twenty-five years. *When he sent divers down the day after the tourists, and after unsuccessfully finding anything in their vehicle in La Paz, his divers had come up empty-handed. There was only a fragment of the hull remaining. There had been no gold, nothing. Where was the balance of the ship? What had the tourists found? He knew it was something because he'd seen them throw a towel over it as his yacht had motored past them. Soon he would know what it was.*

Miguelito paused in his thoughts for a moment, then resumed. *Really, he was lucky to be alive. Perhaps he should show some mercy on these tourists for stumbling into something with which they had no business being involved. No, they nearly killed me. I was lucky to have survived the blast when they took out that cave. Had I not exited seconds before to the truck, to call for more backup, I'd have been killed too, just like all the others I had with me. And I didn't learn what I needed to know, making this trip necessary. Plus, the sacrifices weren't made, and that made the gods angry. The Aztec gods Miguelito wanted on his side, which he was descended from. No, the tourists would have to answer for their intrusion.*

The following morning, the group readied and then taxied to the museum. They were a few minutes early and sat and watched as Diego scurried around, making sure all the final arrangements were in place for the unveiling of the painting.

There was a fair-sized crowd, mostly older people who remembered the theft and had seen the painting years before.

The ceremony went quickly and smoothly, and the crowd

responded to it with a large round of applause. Jamal took a bow.

Afterwards, Diego took them all to lunch.

"What now, my friends?" he asked.

"We'll catch a tour of the Mediterranean out of Gibraltar in a couple of days," replied Jamal.

Diego clasped his hands together. "That sounds like fun. You can forget all this business and enjoy yourselves for a week. Were I not so old, I'd wish I could go with you."

"You're welcome to," added Dee, "bring the wife."

Diego smiled as he said, "That might be too much togetherness. My wife is a busy woman." Then he winked at them. "I must be going. I am a slave to the museum."

They sat a while longer, enjoying the patio of the restaurant. As the sun moved across the sky, a shadow fell across their table, and they went back to the hotel.

Miguelito and his men landed late in the evening of the day they departed. By the following morning, he had rented a house in an affluent area of Seville to serve as their base of operations. During the flight, Miguelito had been on the phone with several of his operatives, researching the group and the museum. He wanted to get into town, get what he needed, resolve the issue with the tourist, and get back to Mexico and the ship, the treasure.

NOT LONG AFTER THE GROUP GOT BACK TO THE HOTEL, Dee's phone rang. Before he could pick it up, the call ended. Dee went to the 'recent calls' screen but saw nothing other than where he'd talked to Diego that morning. *Odd*, he thought.

The group assembled by the pool for the afternoon.

"We can pick the car up this evening," said Jamal, "for the drive back to Gibraltar."

"How long do we have there?" asked Mike.

"Just a day," answered Angelic, "before we board for the cruise."

Dee had pulled his phone out and left it in the chair next to Gina when he had gone for a short swim. She saw it vibrate and waved to Dee, holding the phone aloft as he swam past.

A moment later, he was standing beside her, drying off.

"I think it may have been a text," she said.

Dee checked the phone quickly.

"What's wrong?" Gina asked. "Your face just turned pale."

Dee glanced up at her and shook his head. "Jamal," he called.

Jamal saw him, stood up, and came over by Dee's side.

They looked at the screen together. There was a single word, 'RUN.' it said.

Dee's head shot up, and he looked around the pool quickly.

"Who is that from?" asked Jamal.

Dee fumbled with the phone and saw only the number at the top of the screen. "I think it might be Diego," whispered Dee.

Gina moved closer to them. "What is it?"

Dee looked up. "Not sure yet, need to verify, maybe Diego."

"Mike," called Jamal.

Mike looked up, and Dee waved him over.

"Take the women and go pack up. Don't check out. We got an odd message, maybe from Diego. Take the luggage and go to the rental car place and pick up, wait for the car if you need. We'll call you if we need to be picked up. Just be alert. This may be nothing. Jamal and I will go check on Diego," said Dee.

"What's going on?" asked Mike.

Dee held up the phone with the message 'RUN.' Mike swallowed hard.

Dee replied, "If somebody's chasing us, we'll make it look like we're still at the hotel. Maybe buy some time. The hotel has a credit card on file. They'll charge us an extra day or so, but that might allow us to get away."

Mike nodded and turned away toward the women.

"Ladies, change of plans, let's go get packed up. We're going to leave for Gibraltar this afternoon, have dinner on the ocean tonight. Let's move it," said Mike and he started for the rooms.

The women scrambled around, looking confused, but followed him. Angelic and Gina waved at Jamal and Dee.

"We'll be right back and join you," called Jamal.

They caught a taxi, still in their swim trunks and tee shirts, and headed for the museum.

"Let's go in one of the side doors," said Dee. "We don't know what this is about."

"Are we smart to do this?" asked Jamal. "Why don't you call him?"

Dee nodded and dialed while the taxi approached the museum. The phone went straight to voicemail with Diego, telling them to leave a message. Jamal could overhear the voice and shook his head, to which Dee nodded.

"Something is definitely not right," Jamal added.

"Why would he tell us to run? It feels more like something has happened to him," replied Dee.

"This is all very strange," added Jamal.

They exited the taxi and looked for the side entrances to the museum. They scanned the sidewalks and grounds while moving at a normal pace. They wanted to break into a run but were afraid of the attention it might bring.

Slipping inside, they made their way around to Diego's office. They strolled through a couple of galleries in an indirect line, just to see if anyone noticed them. They saw nothing.

Diego's office was a mostly glass structure that, for the first time, had the shades drawn.

Dee slipped around to the door and knocked softly. He heard nothing. He knocked again, and he thought he might have heard a shuffling sound. Dee tried the door, and it was unlocked. Glancing at the doorknob, he noted there was no lock.

He pushed the door open slowly and entered on his hands and knees. Nothing happened. He rose slowly, and then he saw Diego on the other side of the desk. He was tied to his chair, gagged, and bleeding. Diego was trying to bounce the chair to make a noise. Dee held up a hand and moved toward him.

"Jamal," Dee called, and Jamal popped in beside him. Jamal closed the door quickly after glancing around the office.

Dee looked around for something to cut Diego's bonds. Diego nodded his head toward the desk, and Dee opened the top drawer and pulled out a pair of scissors. He cut the zip ties that bound Diego and then went to work on the gag. Jamal was looking around the room. Some files were scattered, and someone knocked a table to its side, but the room was mostly intact.

Diego rubbed his wrists as the gag came free. "You must go, leave the city quickly," he cried.

"Wait." Dee held up a hand. "What happened?"

Diego, still rubbing his wrists, sighed. "There was a group of men, four total, led by a big man with a birthmark on his face. I tried to call you, but they took the phone away."

Jamal and Dee both stepped back, a look of astonishment on their faces.

"What?" said Diego.

"A big man with a birthmark on his face, neck, and shoulder?" asked Jamal.

"I didn't see all that. It happened so fast. I was sitting at my desk and suddenly they all burst in and wanted to know about the painting, and about you."

"Go on," said Dee.

"They asked if you and your group were still around. That's when the first one hit me. I told them you were leaving town, and they hit me again." He paused. "I'm not a violent man. They said they would kill me right then unless I told them everything I knew about you. Which I did. That's why I told you not to tell me anything. I'm so sorry. One small thing, they didn't ask about the painting, or the numbers, and I didn't tell them you may have figured out the location of the ship. They didn't ask, I didn't tell."

"The man with the birthmark, did he hit you?" asked Dee.

"No," replied Diego. "He seemed in charge, one of the others, and then a second man, like they were taking turns. They searched the office, and one of them pushed me aside. I retrieved the phone and texted you before they grabbed me again."

"What did you tell them?" asked Jamal.

"Everything that I knew. That I thought you discovered the painting by accident, that you were interested in Cortes and Castillo," he said, "and that you had found a bell, possibly gold, possibly Aztec." Diego flinched. "I am so sorry. I'm not a brave man. You must run, hide. Those were evil men. I was lucky that a group came by on their way to see the painting and they tied me up instead of killing me."

"Did they take the painting?" asked Jamal.

"I don't know, let's go look," replied Diego.

The three men ran from the office to the conference room. The podium the painting had been sitting on was still there, and the placard with the story of the painting, but the painting itself was gone.

Jamal pointed. "How did they do that, take it, I mean?"

Diego visibly gulped. "We didn't have it attached to the security system. It's not a valuable piece, just a curiosity. It was easier to see out here in the middle of the room, bigger crowds, and more space."

They walked back to his office.

"Should you call the police?" asked Jamal.

Diego shook his head. "They warned me that if I did, I'd be dead before morning. I'll issue a press release and say we've temporarily withdrawn the painting in order to stabilize it. The colors are fading or something like that. People won't think much about it. Those curious have already seen it."

"That lets the men think you comply, so hopefully they won't bother you again," said Dee.

"But they will come for you," added Diego.

Dee texted Mike. "Did you get the car?"

Dee's phone chimed back in a moment." Yes, we have it," Mike replied.

"Come and get us at the museum, park on the back side, down the street, we'll come to you," replied Dee.

Diego had been dabbing at his mouth with a handkerchief.

"Are you hurt?" asked Dee.

"Mostly my pride," replied Diego. "I had the painting less than a week and I've already lost it again."

Jamal and Dee couldn't help but smile at him, and he smiled back.

"You have to go. They want the bell, whether or not you prove ownership. You can't let them catch you," said Diego.

"Was the birthmark man, possibly Miguelito Cortes, injured in any way?" asked Dee.

"Mexican billionaire, dad was a crime lord or a drug boss, or something I read about, that guy? That's who that was?" asked Diego.

Dee nodded.

Diego shook his head. "Not injured that I could see, but again, it all happened quickly. Why would he be injured?"

"We thought he was dead," replied Jamal.

Diego shook his head. "No, he was very much alive and looking for you. Let me walk you to the back door."

They arrived, and Diego shook hands with both of them, but then held a finger up. "Don't tell me where or when or how, just go. Do call me if I can help. Again, I am so sorry for what happened. Be safe, my friends." Then he turned and reentered the museum, leaving them alone.

35

SEVILLE (ON THE RUN)

They had found the museum director in his office. The little man hadn't taken much convincing before he told all he knew. It wasn't much, but what it was made Miguelito's head swim. *The tourists had the bell.* The director hadn't known where. He begged them to believe him, and he told them everything else they asked. What a poor excuse for a man. He wasn't even worthy of a sacrifice. Besides, they'd been on a timetable to get the information, grab the painting, and get out. Miguelito looked over at the painting and it brought an enormous smile to his face. His father had labored for years trying to find and gain the painting. In fact, he'd nearly gotten himself killed, just down the street from the museum in Seville. He'd escaped to the river and got away. That was more than most of the Europeans he had been working with, who had all gotten themselves killed. All these years each group had thought the other had gotten away with the painting. *But now he had it. What did it mean? Had the tourists solved the riddle? He was going to have to ask them and no, it wouldn't be politely.*

. . .

Jamal and Dee slipped down the street, away from the museum. They glanced back periodically to see if anyone was following them, or if anything looked unusual. There was no sign.

"They've got the Ford Flex again," said Dee. "Apparently no one else wanted to rent it."

"It was comfortable," replied Jamal, "and sturdy. We may need that. How much should we tell the women?"

Dee paused a moment in thought as they made their way closer to the Flex. "Everything, I guess. I mean, this could get dangerous. They have a right to know," he replied.

They spotted the car on the next block and made their way toward it. Jamal jumped into the passenger seat in front and Dee sat in the middle with Angelic and Gina. Keno waved from the back.

"Gibraltar?" asked Mike. Dee nodded.

They rolled through town to catch the N-4 and head south. After only a moment Angelic spoke up, "Okay, what's going on?"

Dee caught Mike's eyes in the rearview mirror.

"I only told them there appeared to be a problem with Diego and that dinner on the ocean, in Gibraltar, was a surprise from us, the men." He glanced around the car. "I don't think they believed me."

Dee had to grin and saw all the women turning toward him for an explanation.

"I got a text from Diego," Dee said and leaned toward Gina, "the one that came in when we were by the pool."

She nodded. "Go on," she said.

"I showed Jamal, and we thought something was wrong with Diego, and possibly that something might be wrong for us, too. That's why we had you all pack up and Mike get the car. We went to check. Diego had been attacked in his office."

There were 'ahs' from the women.

"But he wasn't hurt badly. They slapped him around a little, but he seemed okay. The men that attacked him wanted to know about Jamal and the rest of us and to verify that the painting was on hand. Diego was warning us with the text."

"Who would do that? Why?" asked Angelic.

"Diego said the painting wasn't valuable," added Gina.

Dee paused a moment, looking at the women. "Diego said it was a large man with a birthmark on his face, and three other large, strong men. They questioned him, tied him up and took the painting."

"That Cortes guy," said Keno. "Are you telling us he's alive? How is that possible?"

Dee shook his head. "I don't know. Diego described him pretty well, with no help from Jamal or me. It certainly sounds like him. The man and the others with him took the painting."

"It's got to be him," said Angelic.

"How could he have survived?" added Gina.

"It makes little sense," said Jamal, "but what does, is that he or whoever this is must have known about the painting as well, maybe about the connection between Cortes and Castillo, if there is one, and been looking for the painting. It was supposedly stolen all those years ago. Maybe Miguelito or his group had something to do with that?"

They rode on in silence for a few moments.

"What are we going to do?" asked Keno from the back of the vehicle.

"Get to Gibraltar. Hope they get slowed down looking for us, that's why we didn't check out. Get on the ship, sail away," answered Dee.

"Ship doesn't leave until day after tomorrow, in the morning," added Angelic.

"We'll have to lie low," replied Dee. "From Gibraltar, we could go anywhere. It should take a little while to find us."

"On the Mediterranean, we're just going around in a circle," said Angelic.

"Maybe we should get on a plane, fly someplace far away," added Keno.

"A plane is probably the easiest thing to trace. This guy, if it's him, is a billionaire, he has resources," answered Dee.

"Then there's probably nowhere to hide," replied Angelic.

"Fly back to Key West, turn the bell over to the authorities, hopefully then we're out of it," said Gina.

"I doubt it," said Jamal. "From talking to Diego, I think this man carries a grudge. We kept him from getting the bell. He'll go hard on us."

"Give it to him then," said Keno. "Let's get away from that crazy fool."

Dee looked at Jamal and then answered Keno. "Might not be a bad idea. He looks like a hard man to kill."

Jamal sighed. "Let's get to Gibraltar and see if we can get to Key West."

"Most likely the flight will be to Miami with a connector," replied Gina.

Jamal nodded to her and sighed again. "We've been chasing this bell for over a month, maybe it is time to give it up."

MIGUELITO SUMMONED HIS MEN FROM AROUND THE HOUSE. He had a small package for each of them. It was an elaborately wrapped gift. Miguelito had commissioned small replicas of the Aztec god, Quetzalcoatl, in a gold-colored base metal. He used them as a calling card. He also had the small commemorative figures in solid gold, as gifts for his more intimate friends.

He handed each man a box. "I want you to go to every hotel in a six-block radius of the museum and present this at the desk for Jamal Jones." He had gathered the name from the New York Times story, and Diego had confirmed it. "I am going to presume they came to town for the museum and would stay nearby. Tell the desk clerk it is a gift from an admirer of the man who found the long-lost Castillo. When you find the correct hotel, let me know."

The leader of the group, aware of Miguelito's predispositions, politely asked a question, "Sir, with all your resources available, why wouldn't we summon an IT engineer and research hotel databases, it would likely be much quicker?"

Miguelito smiled at the man. He didn't mind inquisitiveness, as long as it was respectful.

"I'm old-fashioned. I am a hunter. I enjoy the hunt," he replied.

The man nodded and took the packages, handing them out to each of his men. He thought to himself, *I'm old-fashioned, too. I enjoy getting the job done quickly and getting paid.*

The leader and his men left the house to begin their task.

Miguelito watched them go and thought to himself, *This will be over soon. How do I want to resolve the tourists? Slowly would be nice. First, I must find the bell. But there is room on the plane. I could take them back to Mexico City. There I would have many options, full pageantry, and a lengthy and satisfying conclusion. I have just the facility, the grand Aztec sacrificial room, right outside the city.*

They drove on in silence, Mike making good time toward Gibraltar. No one had spoken for several minutes.

"How could he have escaped?" asked Angelic.

"Ernie blew up the whole cave," added Keno.

"Just lucky I guess, for him," replied Jamal, "and unlucky for us."

"Diego told him we found the bell," added Dee. "If anything should happen, just tell Miguelito where it is. If you're questioned, don't fight over it. Enough people have died."

"Do you think he's going to find us?" asked Gina.

"I don't know," answered Dee. "He got here pretty quick after that picture of the painting was posted."

"I'm sorry about that, guys," said Jamal.

"Nothing to be sorry about, Jam," said Angelic. "You and Dee put in the legwork to find it. Maybe you got lucky, but you still found it."

"She's right," said Mike. "Plus, we're in this together. We'll find a way."

Dee grinned at that. "How far?" he called out to Mike.

"About an hour and a half," Mike replied.

"Dinner on the ocean sounds good to me," Dee answered.

MIGUELITO'S MEN WORKED THEIR WAY OUT FROM THE HOTELS in the immediate area around the museum. About four blocks away, one man entered the former dual residence, now a hotel, and asked the question. He was rewarded with a 'yes,' and then told that the clerk would be happy to hold the package for Mr. Jones. The delivery man agreed, thanked the clerk, and moved away.

The man stepped outside and walked a short distance down the street to a café. He knew what Miguelito would want next. He texted the leader of his group and advised the name of the hotel and gave the address. He knew the others would converge for surveillance. In the meantime, he had an idea.

Seeing a flower stand nearby, he purchased the largest and brightest colored bouquet they had. A pretty, young woman took the money from him while an elderly man wrapped the flowers to be carried.

The man purchasing the flowers looked at the older man. "Do you think I could hire this young lady to deliver these flowers to the hotel down the street?" he asked. The man held up a hundred-dollar bill. The old man looked at the girl, who nodded anxiously.

"I suppose I could spare her for a few minutes," he replied.

The man handed the girl the money and said, "Wait about ten minutes and then deliver these to the hotel desk and say that they are for Mrs. Jamal Jones, from Mr. Jones, and that you would be happy to take them to the room. If he says he'll take them, let him. That's all you need to do."

The girl looked up at him and smiled. He smiled back at her, bowed his head slightly, and then walked away in the opposite direction. He blended into a crowd and disappeared at the next corner.

What he did was double back to the hotel and, stepping inside, he watched for cameras and for the desk clerk he had spoken to earlier. Seeing neither, he stepped briskly across the lobby and toward the elevators. He noted that this was only a four-story boutique hotel. Perching himself in a corner, he could see the door and the desk without being seen by the desk clerk. In a couple of minutes, the young girl appeared with the flowers. She approached the desk, and the clerk took the flowers from her. She nodded to the clerk and left.

The man continued to watch. In just a few moments, another clerk came to the desk and the clerk who had taken the flowers gave the new arrival some instructions and motioned to the flowers.

The second man picked them up and started toward the elevators.

The man watching dropped back and stood by the elevators. In a moment, the clerk with the flowers appeared.

"Lovely flowers," said the waiting man. The clerk nodded. The elevator arrived, and the man held the door back as the clerk got on board.

The man stepped aboard and asked, "What floor?"

The clerk replied, and the man pressed the button. Off they went. Having realized it was a small hotel, the man knew he wouldn't need much more than the floor. There were probably only four rooms to a floor and six people in three couples would take up most of those rooms, assuming they were all together. But then he really only wanted the Jones', anyway.

Admiring the flowers, the man said to the clerk, "Someone is very thoughtful."

The clerk replied, "I imagine so."

"I'm sure of it," said the man as he held the door for the clerk to depart.

As the doors closed, he pressed the lobby button and rode back down to meet his boss at the café.

His boss was sitting at a table facing the street. The man walked over and sat down in an adjacent chair.

"That was easy enough," said the man who just sat down.

"Would have been easier if we'd used a database," replied the seated man.

"Apparently we're doing this old school," replied the newly seated man.

"Apparently," answered the first man with some disgust.

"They're on the third floor, at least the Jones' are, and the others may be as well. It's a small hotel, multiple access points, shouldn't be a problem if we go that way."

"I'll check with Miguelito and see how he wants it to play," replied the seated man.

They eased into Gibraltar and stayed at a different hotel. Dee drove toward the beach and found a smaller roadside inn. They checked in individually and paid cash. The rooms were adequate and looked out on the ocean. They met on one of the room decks as they were scattered around the motel.

"Do we want to grab some dinner, or maybe get something to go?" asked Dee. "I think we should stay out of the Inn's restaurant and avoid the local places. One couple could go pick it up."

"This guy is making you paranoid, isn't he?" asked Mike.

"I'm afraid he's really dangerous and we're not clear of him yet," replied Dee. "I think we check out of here early and keep a low profile tomorrow. Get ready to board the ship."

"Is that what we're going to do?" asked Keno. "I thought maybe we were going to fly back and give the bell to the authorities or send this guy a message where he can find it."

"What do you want to do, Jamal?" asked Dee.

"I don't know," he replied.

"Miguelito wants us to observe the foot traffic around the hotel to see if we spot them. If we do, we'll move in and grab them. If we don't, we'll go into the rooms later tonight and grab them, then take them back to the safe house," said the leader to the group of men surrounding him.

They had assembled in a van down the street from the hotel and near the café. The leader gave each man a quadrant to watch. "Check in on the half hour. If we see no sign of them by midnight, we'll go in at 2am and get them."

They passed the evening watching the traffic, rotating shifts and locations, and drinking coffee from the café. No one saw anything. It was about 9pm.

The man who had found them strolled up to the leader of the group. "I'm getting a bad feeling," he said.

"Why is that?" the leader asked.

"We should have seen something, one or more of them, by the pool, in the lobby, coming or going," he replied.

"Why do you think that?" the leader asked.

"Nothing tangible, just doesn't feel right. Let me go back into the hotel and go up to their floor. Just to open the elevator and see what I see," he replied.

The leader thought for a moment and looked at his watch, then he nodded. "Go have a look, but no contact."

"Just a visual," he replied.

The man left the café and ambled toward the hotel, as if he was just another tourist returning to his room.

He strolled across the lobby, as there was now a new desk clerk who hadn't seen him before, nodding as he passed by the desk. He punched the button for the elevator, boarded, and waited as it slowly climbed to the third floor.

When the door opened, he saw the gift box and the flowers both sitting by the door. The elevator slowly closed, and he rode back to the lobby. He stood in the hallway and texted the leader. "Gift and flowers are still by the door. I'm betting no one is home, nor will they be."

Shortly afterward he got a return text. "Check the room."

He rode back up to the room and, after listening for a moment, he felt sure there was no one on the floor. Slipping a small card from his pocket, he finessed the door lock, and the door swung open into the room. With his hand to his shoulder holster, he entered the room.

The bed was unmade, but the closet stood empty, and so were the dresser drawers. There was no luggage. He sat down on the bed and texted the leader. "They're gone."

36

GIBRALTAR (THE CHASE)

The leader of the team withdrew them from the field and checked in with Miguelito.

"They're gone," he advised.

"How long?" asked Miguelito.

"Hard to say. They didn't check out, just grabbed their stuff and ran," he replied.

"It couldn't be much more than half a day. Someone must have found the director, and he warned them. We may have to pay him another visit before we go," continued Miguelito.

The man thought to himself, *I told you this morning we should have resolved that issue then.* Instead, he said, "I suggest we go to the databases and check the airport and other transportation."

Miguelito replied, "I'll get someone on it, but I think they're still in the area. We'll soon see," and he hung up the phone.

The leader held the phone for a moment. "In the van," he said, "Let's get back to the house and rest up. We're likely going to be mobile soon."

. . .

DEE AND THE GROUP SLEPT THROUGH THE NIGHT PEACEFULLY. In the early morning, they all felt a little better. The sun shone brightly on the water, and they'd have liked nothing more than to go to the beach and be tourists.

"Jamal and I will go find some breakfast and then we can decide what to do today," said Dee as he and Jamal headed out.

They returned an hour later after having made two stops. Dee went into one restaurant and made a purchase, and Jamal went into another and did the same. The nice thing about Gibraltar was that it was English, and while there was a wide range of people around the principality, the group didn't look as out of place as they had in Seville, and their accents weren't so pronounced. They wanted to be cautious and anonymous.

The group assembled in Jamal and Angelic's room and munched hungrily on the food.

"What's the decision?" asked Keno, chewing on her breakfast sandwich. "Breakfast at the hotel in Seville was so much nicer."

Dee gave her a dirty look and then grinned. She smiled back.

"Jamal," said Dee.

Jamal shook his head. "What's everyone want to do?"

"I'd say go home," replied Angelic, "but I don't know where that is, other than with you guys."

"So, you really think this guy is going to hunt us down?" asked Gina.

Dee nodded at her, and Jamal spoke." I think so. He's chased us across half the world. He's serious about the bell, the Aztec gold, the Cortes connection. I don't see him stopping, even if we give him the bell."

"As we've nearly seen up close, he believes in blood sacrifice. I'm surprised Diego survived," answered Dee.

"Where can we hide?" asked Mike.

"And for how long?" asked Gina.

"He'll expect us to run," replied Dee. "How can we do so and stay safe? Someplace public, maybe, in a direction he might not expect. Maybe we could misdirect him. Here's an idea, Gina, get on the internet and buy six airline tickets to Mexico City."

Keno interrupted Dee. "We're going to flee to his home base?"

"No," replied Dee, "we're going to make it look like we might go to him, while we go somewhere else. Angelic said it earlier. Touring the Mediterranean is going around in a circle. We'll end up back in Gibraltar. If he locates and trails us, we can jump off in a lot of different places. There's always a ready exit. If he doesn't find us, we end up back here and then we decide. See what Diego has learned or heard. We'll buy some time, lead him on a goose chase if needed."

"Are you sure about that?" asked Angelic. "I mean, he followed us from Mexico to Spain."

"No, I'm not sure, but I think he had lost us until the picture of the painting showed up. We need to slip away again," replied Dee.

IT WAS EARLY THE FOLLOWING MORNING FOR MIGUELITO. HE expected to hear from his IT people anytime. He'd gotten them started the night before on transportation—planes, trains, bus lines, rental cars. Short of the tourists stealing a vehicle, he felt like his people would turn up any information available.

His phone chirped, and he answered and listened. When

he hung up, there was a big smile on his face. He immediately contacted the leader of his support team by text, despite the man being in the same house.

"They have rented a car. I have the tag number and description. Better yet, there is a GPS tracker on the vehicle, and you can access it. I'm guessing Gibraltar."

The leader of the support team walked down from his bedroom to the living room—or command center, as Miguelito called it—and sat down opposite the man.

"It was a one-way rental from Seville to Gibraltar. It's a 2016 Ford Flex in silver with tinted windows. How American," Miguelito stated to the team leader. "Fortunately, the reservation was in Jones' name. The company installs GPS for tracking on all their units. Here are the coordinates. Find them, bring them to the plane, to me, alive, but compliant would be nice." Miguelito nodded slightly at the team leader.

"We're on it," replied the team leader, who rose from the table and began walking away.

"Keep me informed," growled Miguelito.

The leader nodded and threw up a hand but did not turn back around.

Miguelito watched the man walk away, thinking to himself, *When we are back in Mexico, I shall determine your fate and your teams as well.*

THEY AGREED TO DEE'S PLAN, PARTLY BECAUSE THEY DIDN'T have another one, but also because they felt the need to stick together.

"Let's go to the beach, hang out all day," said Dee. "Stay someplace closer to the docks tonight. We'll contact the cruise line and send our luggage on from here. That way there's less for us to keep up with. Keep your passport and whatever you need for an overnight in a carry bag. We'll get up and board in the morning and sail away."

They all agreed and broke up to pack and sort out what items they'd need. Gina called the cruise line and made arrangements.

Shortly afterwards, a porter from the cruise line picked up the luggage. They checked out and made ready for the beach. Everything was a go.

They drove to a nearby beach, parked the Flex in the shade of a tree, and took their remaining items down to the sand, where they made themselves comfortable. It was late morning, and they relaxed in the sun and the surf for several hours. They were in a much brighter mood.

HAVING ASSEMBLED HIS TEAM, THE LEADER RAN THE GPS information on the Flex. "It's in Gibraltar," said the leader.

"Wasn't that Miguelito's guess?" said one of the men.

"He got lucky," replied the leader, looking sharply at the man who had spoken. The man nodded and fell silent.

"The vehicle appears to be stationary and very near the water," added the leader.

"Abandoned?" asked one of the other men.

"Possibly, but I wouldn't have thought them smart enough for that," replied the leader. "Let's get to our van and get down there. I'll pass the word to Miguelito."

"I'M HUNGRY," SAID JAMAL.

"You're always hungry, Jam," teased Angelic.

"I'm feeling it myself," added Mike.

"He's another one," added Keno.

"I can jump in the Flex and snag some groceries for us?" offered Jamal.

Dee and Gina had been sitting and watching and smiling at their friends.

"There are a couple of food trucks and a café up by the boardwalk," said Dee. "Gina and I can stroll up and get us all something. What's everybody want?"

THE EX-MILITARY TEAM DROVE TOWARD GIBRALTAR WITH THE leader, periodically checking the location of the Flex. It hadn't moved. "It's still stationary, looks more like it might be abandoned," he told the group.

"What then?" asked one of the men.

"We keep looking, wrap this job up, I'm ready to go home. I've had enough of this goose chase, it's getting messy," the leader replied.

They drove another hour and entered Gibraltar. It was later in the afternoon. Nothing had changed with the tourist vehicle. They drove to the beach.

JAMAL HAD FLIPPED OVER IN THE SAND. "I'M GETTING TIRED," he said to no one in particular.

"There's still sun," said Gina, who had slipped mostly out of her suit.

"Girl, you are going to be roasted if you don't get in the shade," said Angelic.

Keno had complained of the brightness of the sun earlier in the day and the men had rented umbrellas for the afternoon. The couples, except Gina, were huddled under them in the shade.

Jamal held up a hand. "Quiet everybody," he hissed. He caught them off guard, but they fell silent.

"Dee, hand me your scope, slowly. Nobody else move, in fact, stay down." Jamal glanced around quickly and there were other people around them and a line of umbrellas stretching out down the beach.

"What is it?" whispered Dee.

"There're men over by the Flex, five of them, big guys, hired muscle. I recognize the type from my gym. They're looking around, feeling the hood," replied Jamal.

"Won't they think we're on the beach?" whispered Mike.

"Maybe," replied Dee. "We've been parked here all day, longer than most of these people. They must have tracked the Flex, GPS or something."

"They're looking toward the water," said Jamal, pulling his scope down. He could still see the men reasonably well. "Now they're gathering back together and getting in the van, all five of them." He raised the scope to watch them go. The van pulled onto the highway and raced away.

"What now?" asked Mike.

"We sit here for a while longer," replied Dee, "just in case they stopped and put the beach under surveillance. In a bit, we'll leave three at a time, just to break up the look of couples. Keno, you come with Gina and me. Mike, you go with Jamal and Angelic. You guys go to the far end of the boardwalk and in ten minutes we'll go to the near end. We'll head your way and look for an exit or call a cab, do something."

THE EX-MILITARY TEAM PULLED AWAY FROM THE BEACH, THE leader clearly frustrated. His men sat silently, waiting for his direction or for his mood to improve.

"'Tourists," the leader muttered to himself, "just gather them up and be done with it, a simple job."

"Where to?" asked the driver.

"Find us something to eat. I'll call Miguelito," the leader replied.

They pulled into a busy seafood place and the men entered in pairs. The leader stood outside and made the call.

"The vehicle was abandoned, no luggage. It has been sitting there all day. They are long gone. Have you checked transportation?" the leader asked.

"I anticipated that," replied Miguelito. There was silence for a moment. When the leader didn't press him, Miguelito continued. "There was a purchase of six tickets for Mexico City, scheduled to leave in the morning. You still have tonight to find them."

"Shouldn't we just let them go, I mean, that's much easier than us transporting them," added the leader.

"If that is what they were doing, then yes, but I don't think it is," answered Miguelito. "These tourists may be cleverer than they seem. I mean, why would they fly to Mexico City, to give themselves up, not likely. It's a diversion, they're headed elsewhere. Catch them."

"We can stake out the airport easy enough," added the leader.

"That's good, but I think I'd watch the docks as well," added Miguelito. "Need I remind you that if you don't catch them, you don't get paid."

The phone went dead, and the leader stood quietly for a moment thinking to himself, *If we don't get paid, there is going to be a sacrifice, and it won't be the tourists.*

DEE ASKED ONE OF THE BOARDWALK SHOP OWNERS IF THERE was a motel nearby that she'd recommend. The woman thought for a moment and gave him a location.

"Head down the beach, not the first one, but the second

one, with the pink shutters. It's clean and neat, not expensive," she said.

Dee thanked the woman and he and Gina and Keno made their way slowly down the boardwalk. They meet the others and explained the plan.

"We'll walk down the beach to the second hotel and check in for the night, take a cab to the dock in the morning," explained Dee.

"We caught a break there, Jamal seeing them," said Mike.

"And sending the luggage on," added Jamal. "If there'd been luggage, they'd have been all over that beach. We were lucky."

"They're good," added Dee.

"Yeah, but not that good," said Angelic.

"Or they would have caught us," finished Gina.

"Let's go get checked in. I'm tired," added Keno.

"Miguelito says they have booked six flights for Mexico City in the morning," the leader explained to his men after they had eaten and regrouped in the van. "He doesn't believe they are actually flying out, not to there, at least."

"What do you think?" asked one of the men.

"They are smarter than they look or they're lucky," he replied.

"Do we have any other information?" asked another man.

"Only that Miguelito says he wants them by the time the plane leaves in the morning or we don't get paid," the leader stated.

There were loud murmurs among the men.

"What do you think of that?" asked a third man.

"I think it's a crock," the leader replied. "We will find them, and we will get paid. Here's what we're going to do."

MIGUELITO WAS NOT HAPPY. HIS HIGH-PAID PROFESSIONALS had not made the capture. Yes, they had snatched the painting and found out about the bell. But still the tourists were loose, and the bell's location was unknown. Miguelito had made some calls to his cartel crew in Mexico City. When the team of ex-military professionals returned, there would be a special reception. Perhaps he could keep the leader alive and let him join the tourists at the sacrificial ceremonial altar. Miguelito was looking forward to that moment. It had been two moons, and he had missed the special 'Blue Moon' and the virgin girl. His gods demanded their bloodlust, and he would comply.

But first the tourists. They were on the run. That was a clever diversion, even humorous about the tickets to Mexico City, but they would in fact get to make the trip.

Miguelito felt sure they were still in Gibraltar and would make a run for it in the morning. The tourists liked the water, those idiots he had hired better watch the docks.

THE TEAM LEADER GATHERED THE MEN AROUND HIM AND said, "We're going to split up and watch the airport and the docks. Watch the general boarding areas. There are no other tickets shown on the airlines. The cruise ship passenger listings had no indication of them acquiring tickets in the last 24 hours. We'll send two to the airport and three to the docks. It's the only two ways out of here. I think it's water. Let's grab some caffeine and get started."

.   .   .

THEY HAD A RESTLESS NIGHT AT THE PINK SHUTTERED INN and awoke at daylight. It was several hours before they could board.

"Let's take two taxis with three in each," said Dee. "Mike and Gina and I will go first and check it out. You other three stay in the taxi, let the meter run, tell the driver you need a few minutes, tip him well. Keep moving around, we'll text you if it looks clear."

"What are you going to do?" asked Jamal.

Dee grinned. "If she's willing, I'm going to use Gina as a decoy with Mike and I as her bodyguards."

"How's that going to work?" asked Angelic.

"We'll have Gina walk up to the boarding gate and we'll watch her to see if anyone pays attention," replied Dee.

"Muscle heads like that are going to notice her, if they are around," added Jamal.

"I hope so," replied Dee.

"If they do and come for her, how does she get away?" asked Keno.

"Mike and I will have to deter them. Hopefully, they won't all five be there. Some will cover the airport and some the docks. If we're lucky, there won't be anyone and she can get on board. We'll follow her one at a time and then you guys do the same."

"I'll go last," said Jamal. Dee nodded to him.

"I don't really like it," said Angelic. "Gina's at risk. I don't know that you and Mike can stop those guys."

"I agree," added Keno.

"Well, Mike or I can go first," replied Dee. "I expect they are looking most closely for Jamal, since he was in the picture."

"I don't mind, if it will help us," added Gina. "I know how to attract a certain type of man, and fend for myself, if needed."

Dee nodded to her. "We'll be right there close, if you need us." She smiled at him and nodded back.

"Let's go check out," said Dee.

They made their way to the office and the woman who had checked them in the night before was behind the desk. She smiled at them. Dee noticed a gift shop area behind her.

"Could we look around?" said Dee, pointing to the shop. She smiled again and replied, "Certainly."

37

GIBRALTAR (THE CHASE-DAY 2)

Dee walked over to the gift shop and the others followed.

"What are we looking for?" asked Keno.

"Ideas," replied Dee.

"Oh!" said Angelic.

Gina reached across and picked up a tiny pink bikini top. She held it up to Dee. "I think this is what you have in mind?"

He shrugged.

"I've worn smaller things," she grinned and added, "This should work."

"You can wear my shirt over it, to cover up and then unleash the power of pink, if you need it?" asked Dee.

"That would be nice, to have some cover," she replied, holding the top to her chest.

Jamal picked up a hat with *Gibraltar* embroidered on it. "A little disguise or misdirection perhaps," he said.

"I think it's appropriate," replied Dee.

Jamal then picked up a blue pullover and tied it around his neck and slipped on a pair of wraparound sunglasses.

"Looking totally French, Jam," cooed Angelic.

Dee went with a white hat and Mike with a red. Angelic and Keno picked up pullovers in complimenting colors, and everyone was ready.

The woman at the desk was really smiling now.

They took two taxis to the dock. It was still early and there wasn't a lot of activity. Dee hoped that would help them spot the men pursuing them.

"We're early," said Dee to the driver. "Do you mind driving slowly around the area for a few minutes?"

"As long as the meter's running, mate," he replied. "What are you looking for?"

"Just taking in the sights," Dee replied.

"In a dock area," answered the driver. "You're buggars, but it's your money."

"Thanks," replied Dee.

They circled the area once and saw nothing. As they came back around, Dee had the driver stop beside a couple of small stores and a coffee shop. None of the businesses were open yet. Dee paid the man, and the driver pulled away. The other cab idled further down the street, continuing along the dock and out of sight.

There was a food truck with a short line of dock workers a little further down the street from where they stopped.

THE MEN ON THE EX-MILITARY TEAM HAD BEEN UP ALL NIGHT. There had been no one around, and they'd taken short power naps. Still, they were tired and on edge about the possibility of not being paid. The leader and two of the others took turns occasionally strolling the dock area and watching for anything. Their van was down beyond a food truck, and they gathered periodically to confer and check with the other two members they had dropped at the airport.

"We're out of coffee. How about the food truck?" said one of the men to the leader, who nodded in return.

"It's still early, shouldn't be a problem. Go ahead, grab us something to eat," he replied.

The man walked slowly toward the food truck.

Dee, Gina, and Mike stood in the recessed doorway of one of the shops, watching the dock area. All they saw was the food truck and a few workers.

"We don't know how many of us they will actually recognize. Certainly, Miguelito would know the women," said Dee.

"And Jamal," added Mike. "Do you think he's here?"

"He went to the museum, but they knew Diego and the painting were there. On a stakeout, I'd bet he'd stay away until they had something tangible," replied Dee.

"Then these guys may not know you and me or only have a general idea?" answered Mike.

Dee nodded.

Gina poked Dee in the shoulder. "Look," she said. He followed her finger, and she was pointing to a wheelchair by the door of the shop.

"They must use it to get the elderly on board or around the shopping," replied Dee.

"Could we use it?" Gina asked. "We could put Jamal in it and one of you guys rolls him on board."

Mike had resumed watching the dock. The ship staff was making ready to board people. "We're getting close," he said to Dee and Gina. "It's nearly time to board."

"When is departure?" asked Dee.

"Not until this afternoon," replied Gina.

"So even if we make it on board, we'll have to stay hidden for a while," answered Dee.

Gina nodded to him. "The rooms probably won't be ready for a while, although this is the origination point of the cruise and there shouldn't be anyone leaving."

Dee looked at the wheelchair for a moment. "Let me know when it looks ready to board. I got an idea. What if we put Gina in the wheelchair and you roll her toward the dock, and I'll assist her and keep a lookout?"

"Might work," replied Mike, while still watching the dock.

"Gina, pin your hair up and button your shirt to the neck," said Dee.

Gina reached back for her hair and grinned at Dee. "I didn't think that was the plan," she said as she finished her hair and brought her hands back around and buttoned her shirt. "We could put you in the chair and have Mike roll you up, while I assist and distract."

"Yeah," said Mike, "you could lean your head to the side and drool and make noises. People would stay clear of you. And," he paused and turned so they could see him grin, "Why does it always involve me pushing the wheelchair?"

"I could do that," said Dee, "but I'm afraid they'd come closer to recognizing Gina. I wouldn't be surprised if Miguelito didn't describe her and the other women in graphic detail."

"That is a thought," replied Mike, while Gina stood silently between them.

As the man moved further out into the street and away from the van, he saw the third member of the team in the far distance. That man had been making the rounds of the dock while the other two conversed. Heading for the food truck, he thought to himself, *I guess I'd better get three of everything.*

. . .

THEY PUT GINA IN THE WHEELCHAIR, AND MIKE LOANED HER his hat. After adjusting the band width, she put it on, bill backwards, and pulled the cap down low to her eyes, while slipping on her sunglasses. Dee's shirt even covered the top part of her legs and she brought one of them up under her to give the impression of impairment.

"They're not likely to recognize me now," she said.

Dee patted her on the shoulder. "Only your inner beauty shines through."

"You are so full of it," she replied, and grinned at him. Mike rolled his eyes.

"Let's roll," said Dee, and Mike pushed Gina onto the sidewalk. They moved slowly along, as if being cautious with someone quite frail. They had just emerged from the recessed opening to the store when Dee saw him. A man in a windbreaker, in the summer heat, long pants, broad shoulders, short hair. He was coming up from their right.

Then Gina whispered, "At the food truck, there's a big guy carrying food and coffee, doesn't look like a dock worker." Mike saw him as well.

"We might have something in front of us," he whispered.

Dee replied, "We may also have something behind us. Just keep moving toward the check-in."

"Why are they in jackets, it stands out?" whispered Gina.

"It covers their guns," replied Dee quietly.

THE THIRD MAN ON THE TEAM WAS WALKING SLOWLY BACK toward the van. It had been a long night, and he was tired. So far, they'd seen nothing. Therein lingered the promise of not being paid, and he needed the money. *A wife, two mistresses, a kid in private school. There just never was enough money or time.* He glanced up at three people who had appeared from somewhere. He was sure they weren't there a minute before. A one-legged person in a wheelchair and two guys, one of them pretty good size. They looked like tourists, no big deal, but then they were supposed to be pursuing tourists. He slowed another step just to have a look. There were supposed to be three young and attractive women and three ordinary guys. Looking more closely, the men were a possibility. He needed a better look at the person in the wheelchair. He changed directions slightly where he might intercept the group.

Dee felt the man as much as saw him. Not wanting to turn around, he whispered to the others, "I think he's coming our way."

"What do we do?" asked Gina.

"I'm thinking," replied Dee.

"Think faster," answered Mike.

The man was almost to them, and Dee turned quickly. One, to be sure of the man's approach, and two, to act surprised. The man stopped in mid-stride.

"Can we help you?" asked Dee in a mild voice.

The man shook his head after just a second. "I thought you were someone I know," he said and started to turn away.

Then he sprang back toward them quickly and went to grab Dee. Mike had seen him move and swung the wheelchair around, slinging Gina into the street. The chair blocked the man's path for a moment.

"Run!" cried out Dee. Gina jumped up and took off.

That attracted the man leaving the food truck, who then dropped his purchases and came running toward them. Mike turned to face him, holding his hands up to his sides. Dee grabbed the wheelchair and spun it back around, ramming the first man in the knees. When the man doubled over, Dee rammed him again and knocked him to the pavement.

"Follow Gina!" called out Mike. The other man was almost upon them.

Dee took off, spotted Gina, and looked back over his shoulder to see the second man running toward Mike as if to tackle him. Mike did a quick sidestep at the last second and, using the man's momentum, hurled him to the ground. He took off after Dee.

Dee looked back to see Mike coming and saw a third man stepping toward them. He was just beyond the food truck and was wearing a blue blazer and dress slacks. *More guns,* thought Dee as he turned to spot Gina and kept running.

They got a block off the docks and caught up with one another.

"Keep running, stay near the buildings, look for a taxi," called Dee.

They caught one at the next cross street. "Take us to the 'Great Siege Tunnels,'" panted Dee.

THE LEADER WALKED SLOWLY TOWARD HIS MEN, WHO WERE hobbling up from the pavement. He extended a hand and helped each man to his feet. "That was certainly embarrassing," said the leader.

"No one said anything about them evading or being clever enough for a disguise," said one of the men.

The leader nodded. "There's much about this job that wasn't made known. I'm tired of it."

"We could take what we got on the down payment and go," said the other man.

The leader looked at him for a moment. "I'd like to, but that would damage our reputation. We need to finish this in some fashion. Come on, I'll contact the others and get them over here. We'll spread out around the city. That was only three of them, wasn't it? The others can't be too far away." He walked back toward the van, leaving the men to follow.

"WHERE?" ASKED GINA.

Dee held up a finger and texted. "I'm telling the others what to do and where we're going," he said.

Then he turned back to Gina. "The Great Siege Tunnels are a fortification in the north face of the rock. They were built by the British in the 1700s and added to during World War II. They're about thirty-five miles in total length. There are lots of places to hide, plus they're located in the Gibraltar Reserve where we visited before. I wanted to see them then, but we ran out of time."

"Well, here we are. Sounds like we're going to see them now," replied Mike, grinning.

In only a few minutes, the driver dropped them at the entrance to the Reserve. They saw the others standing near the gate and joined them.

"You guys were supposed to go back to the ship and get on board while they were chasing us," said Dee.

"Not a chance," replied Jamal. "We got to stay together." The others nodded in agreement.

After standing in line for a few moments, they bought six tickets.

"This line, it's not a bad thing, we won't standout," said Dee. "Everybody pay for their own ticket, stand in different parts of the cable car. Walk toward the café by the bridge. We'll meet there."

A few minutes later they were at the top, starting toward the café, and looking for signs leading to the tunnels.

• • •

THE FIVE MEN STOOD AROUND THE VAN. "WHERE WOULD YOU go in four square miles?" the leader asked. "Where would you hide?"

"What makes you think they'll stay in Gibraltar?" asked one of the men.

"It's their way out. What are they going to do, drive back to Spain?" replied the leader.

"Somewhere in a sizeable crowd, or somewhere out of sight," responded another man.

"Big crowds would be in the square at the shopping plaza, 'Casemates Square' I think it's called," replied another man.

"Possibly," replied the leader, "but there's a bigger chance of being seen and of getting separated, than if you were hiding somewhere."

"One of the parks, possibly," said another man. "There's several around."

"What's the biggest, the Gibraltar Reserve?" asked the leader. "That's where I'd go."

He paused for a moment, looking at the men. "This is almost over. We'll collect our money and settle this. Mount up," he said, waving at the van.

MIGUELITO WAS NOT HAPPY TO HEAR THAT THE TOURISTS, AT least some of them, had been spotted and had gotten away. At least they were still in town. The team leader said they were in pursuit. Miguelito was wondering if they were something other than what they seemed. But then he dismissed it to them being lucky and being pursued by a bunch of clowns. He would deal with both groups soon enough.

. . .

THEY EACH MADE THEIR WAY TO THE CAFÉ NEAR THE suspension bridge. They sat for a moment and guzzled some water.

"So, you think hiding in these tunnels will keep us from being found?" asked Jamal.

"I think it'll help," answered Dee. "There's two tours, the older portion and the newer, from World War II. They're a couple hours each, plus we can wander around. We can spend most of the rest of the day there."

"Then what?" asked Angelic.

"We try to find a way out of the city. Maybe take a taxi to the Spanish border and catch a bus or a train," he answered. "I'm open to suggestion."

"These guys are persistent," added Mike.

"You should have seen him," Gina said, pointing at Mike, "He took one of those guys straight on."

Keno looked at Mike.

He grinned and looked at Jamal, and then at the others. "All those years of football, line blocking and hand drills, and they finally came in useful. The guy was out of control. I just helped him along and put in my best forty-yard sprint to catch up with those two," he said, pointing at Dee and Gina.

"Any other ideas?" asked Dee. There weren't, and so they moved on to the tunnels.

They spent the afternoon following along behind tour guides and other tourists, looking out the occasional opening toward the sea and admiring hundreds of years of old cannons. There were miles and miles of hallways carved from the rock. It was something you'd have to want to see.

THE TEAM PARKED THE VAN IN THE LOT AT THE BASE OF THE rock. They rode the cable car to the top.

The leader stopped to look at a map of the Reserve.

"There're several attractions or locations. Let's split up and see what we see." He pointed at one man. "Take the suspension bridge area, move around, see if there's any place off trail they could hide." He pointed to another man. "Take the Battery and Point and watch from the exit. There should only be one way out." He pointed to the last two. "Take the tunnels. One of you gets on one end, the other on the other, if they're inside they have to come out sometime. I'll walk the reserve and see if they could be moving about. Meet back here before the last car down."

They broke up and took off on their assignments.

MIGUELITO HAD A SECOND JET, JUST LIKE THE FIRST ONE. HE called them his fleet. He had called Mexico City when the ex-military team had left for Gibraltar. He ordered the jet to be loaded to capacity, eighteen men and the pilots, and commanded that they fly to Gibraltar as fast as possible. Miguelito rubbed his hands together in anticipation. Eighteen men should be plenty for what he had in mind.

AS IT GREW LATER IN THE AFTERNOON, DEE AND THE OTHERS wrapped up the last tour and milled about inside the area of the tunnel entrance.

"One of us should go outside and see if anyone is about," said Dee. "I don't mind doing it, if you guys want to stay here. I wish we could have remained at the other end of the tunnel, but the guide kept a close eye on the group. I guess they don't like stragglers."

Dee bought another hat and a tee shirt and slipped them on. Then he borrowed Jamal's wraparounds and ventured out into the sunshine. He looked for groups of people to stay near so that he might blend in and not be as visible.

He stood by the rail and looked back down the trail toward the cable car area. There he was, looking just like the two they had seen earlier, a big guy, broad shoulders, windbreaker, and high and tight hair. *You'd think these guys would try to blend in more*, thought Dee to himself, *maybe it's some kind of intimidation factor.*

Dee slipped behind a group of people heading toward the tunnel entrance and then back inside, where he rejoined the others.

"There's one out there. But he was the only one I saw. They stand out."

"What can we do?" asked Angelic.

"How far away is he?" asked Gina.

"Down at the bottom of the ramp," replied Dee.

"Was he one of the guys from this morning?" asked Gina.

"No," replied Dee.

Gina began unbuttoning her shirt, and when she finished, she tied it at the waist. There was a large expanse of stomach and breast visible.

"Girl," said Angelic, "you've been waiting for this all day."

Gina smiled. "If I distract him, can you guys get behind him or whatever you need to do?"

"Give me just a minute," said Dee.

He walked over to the gift shop and returned in a minute. In his hand he held a miniature cannon. It was a replica of one of the fortification guns. It was eight inches long and solid metal. Jamal took it from Dee and hefted it. "That'll make an impression," stated Jamal.

"A big one, a lasting one?" asked Mike.

"Let's go find out," replied Dee.

38

GIBRALTAR (ON THE RUN)

Gina led the way. She was about ten or twelve feet in front of the men. The other women watched from the tunnel entrance. Mike led the men, followed by Jamal and then by Dee. Each stood in front of the other in a single file so that at a quick glance there might appear to be only one man.

Dee noticed Gina had pulled her shorts up higher and that she walked with a bit more roll in the hips than he had seen before. She had her hands in front of her, holding the shirt together over the pink bikini top. She had grabbed Dee's white hat from the motel and pulled the brim down low over her eyes. Adding sunglasses, she strolled off toward the big man leaning on the rail.

He was looking out to sea and didn't see her until she was within ten feet of him. When he looked, she smiled broadly, and Dee noted that only the man's eyebrows shot up. *Maybe this isn't going to work*, he thought to himself.

As she walked by, the man's head did turn and she looked back at him, still smiling. He rotated his shoulders toward her, and she turned and flashed the shirt open, the pink bikini top dazzling in the sunlight. It was the last thing he saw.

Mike had slipped up from behind. Dee had passed the miniature cannon to Jamal while they walked, and Jamal had handed it to Mike right before Mike struck. Jamal and Dee stepped out from behind Mike and caught the man as he sagged. They turned him back to the rail and leaned him against it, his butt on the sidewalk. He had a bit of a gash and would probably have a nasty headache, but he was breathing regularly. They turned, waved to Angelic and Keno, and trotted down the ramp toward the trail beyond.

At the trailhead, they reconvened as a group. Knowing he had little time before the man recovered, Dee took a quick look and, with no one watching them, he slipped off the trail and into the foliage. The others followed silently behind him.

THE TEAM MEMBER WHO HAD BEEN AT THE FAR END OF THE tunnels had started back. He planned to catch up with his partner at the other end and head for the cable cars. As he came into view of the entrance, he didn't see his partner on the rail. *He must have gone on,* thought the man to himself.

He came around the trail and glanced back up the ramp to the entrance before he planned to move on. Then he saw his partner sprawled out on the sidewalk. He ran to the man and leaned him up by the shoulders.

The fallen man was coming around and thrashed for a moment, then swung his head around, looking, but finished by groaning loudly.

"What happened?" asked the upright man.

The seated man groaned again and put his hand to his head. "A woman walked by, and I thought she might be one of the tourists. I turned to look, and that's it."

"Was she alone?" the upright man asked.

The seated man paused for a moment. "Yeah, she was."

"Apparently not," replied the upright man. He struggled to help the seated man up, and said, "Got your gun and your money?" The seated man patted himself down and nodded. "Alright, so it wasn't a robbery attempt. Maybe it was the tourists. Come on, let's go report. He will not be happy. Get your story straight."

The two men shuffled away toward the cable car site.

Dee and the others looked down at the two men as they made their way along.

"We were lucky," said Jamal.

The others nodded and then Mike asked," What now?"

They all turned to Dee, who held his hands up in the air. Then he grinned. "You might not like this idea, but here it is. We need to make our way over to 'Highest Point and O'Hara's Battery.'"

"Haven't we done enough sightseeing?" asked Keno.

"Absolutely," replied Dee. "Near the Point, which is the highest spot in Gibraltar, are the 'Mediterranean Steps.'"

Looking at Dee, Keno asked, "How do you know all this stuff?"

Dee looked at her for a moment, then grinned and said, "I read a lot."

Keno looked to Gina, who had the slight of a smile on her face. "He studies things intensely," she added, and winked at Keno.

Keno glanced quickly at Mike, then back to Gina. "Intense, is good."

"I don't like the sound of this," added Mike. "'Mediterranean Steps.'"

Dee grinned again. "It's about five hundred yards to the bottom, to the highway, it's a lot of steps, but we can walk off and I don't think they'll expect it, plus it'll be night by the time we get to the bottom."

"You don't think they'll have a guard posted?" asked Jamal.

"Would you climb down all those steps if you didn't have to?" asked Dee.

"I have to, and I still don't want to," replied Mike.

Turning to the women, Dee said, "Ladies?"

"Let's get to walking," replied Angelic, Keno and Gina, standing beside her and nodding.

"Wish I'd worn my Fitbit," mumbled Jamal.

THE LEADER AND TWO OF HIS MEN STOOD NEAR THE CABLE car entry as the sun set and twilight appeared. They had seen nothing. Wondering where the other two men were, they saw them approaching, the one man still leaning on the other.

"What happened?" asked the leader.

"I got mugged," said the man with the bruise. The other man remained, supporting him, his face impassive.

"Mugged?" replied the leader.

"Yeah, I was standing watch and this one woman went by. She was young, and I thought she might be one of the tourists. She was alone but somebody caught me with a sap."

"Did they take your gun?" the leader asked.

The man shook his head.

"Short woman, dark hair, very shapely?" asked the leader.

The man nodded. "Short and shapely, she had on a cap."

"So, they're still up there," replied the leader.

"One woman that he may have seen. Are we sure?" asked another man.

The leader turned to the man that spoke.

The other man that had been waiting with the leader

then added, "We've been on our feet for several days. We're exhausted. There's no way off here if they aren't on this cable car run."

"There are steps on the back side," replied the leader.

The last man to speak continued, "They are five hundred yards up in the air. The steps are skinny, steep, and it's nearly dark. They'll hunker down somewhere if they are up there."

The leader looked around at his men. The one who had been hit was bleeding down the side of his face. The others stood slouched or inattentive. "Alright, let's check into a motel. Get some rest for a few hours. There should be someplace near the bottom where we can stay. I'll text Miguelito and tell him we're still in pursuit."

They looked around as darkness fell, then entered the cable car and the gate closed behind them.

It was nearly dark as Dee led the group to the entrance of the steps. It was a sheer, steep face of rock with a long view out to the water or down to the road.

"Use the flashlights on your phone. Stay several feet apart. Watch your feet and the rock face. Don't look out or down. Perhaps the darkness can help us," said Dee. He paused for a moment, then continued, "Can you do this, Keno?" He turned to look at her face in the fading light.

"The darkness is my friend. I'll follow Mike and all I'll see is the rock and his back," she replied.

Dee looked at Mike and then at Keno. They both nodded. "Lead the way," added Mike.

They started down the steps into the darkness, one small movement at a time. Five hundred yards were going to take a while. As darkness continued to fall, there was indirect light from the moon on the water below. It would have been beautiful to sit back and watch, but they had to keep moving.

．　．　．

MIGUELITO WAS ANGRY. THE LEADER OF THE EX-MILITARY team had texted him, hadn't bothered to call. They were still in pursuit. No details. Obviously, they'd lost them again, if they'd even seen them.

The only thing helping Miguelito control himself was that the flight from Mexico City had arrived. Eighteen of his best men, cartel men, were on hand. He could count on them. He thought to himself, *I should have had them do the job the first time. Now they can finish it.*

PROGRESS WAS SLOW, EACH STEP CAUTIOUSLY TAKEN. THE night had cooled, and they could see little beyond the range of their flashlights. Dee stopped the group every so often to rest.

"Call out if anyone needs to slow down or stop," whispered Dee.

"Why you whispering?" asked Jamal.

"Sound carries a long way, especially from this height," Dee replied.

"You mean just in case they have somebody down there," answered Jamal.

"Just in case," said Dee. "They'd probably see the flashlights anyway, although the moon has gotten brighter."

"What are we going to do when we get to the bottom?" asked Angelic.

"Rest," replied Dee.

AT A LOCAL MOTEL AT THE BOTTOM OF THE CABLE CAR LIFT, the ex-military team sacked out for a few hours. The leader, never a man that required much sleep, stood outside and looked up at the top of the rock. A steep, sheer surface reflected back at him. *Surely, they wouldn't try that in the dark,* he thought to himself.

Standing for another moment, he contemplated the options. They'd take another quick look in the morning, but if they found nothing, it was time to head back to Seville and have a chat with Miguelito. Nothing about this job had been as described, and it was dragging out way longer than needed. There was too much risk. These tourists were cleverer than they looked. He needed more information, not more cat and mouse.

Exhaling softly, he stepped back into his room to catch an hour of sleep.

As best Dee could tell, they were over halfway to the bottom. He could see just a touch of the road where it rounded the corner of the rock and caught a sliver of moonlight. The road grew bigger as they descended.

He could hear the heavy breathing of the group, as well as the sound of his own. He forced himself to move more slowly, trying to be cautious, getting more tired, and fearing that someone would slip.

Miguelito gathered the cartel men around him. "Get some transportation and drive toward Gibraltar. Find an appropriate place, where you can wait to intercept the ex-military team and the tourists. You can resolve a couple of things for me. I want the tourists alive."

"The others?" asked the leader of the cartel men.

Miguelito shrugged. "Here is the license number and color of the team van."

He paused for a moment, looking at his men. "Take care of this for me and I will handsomely reward you."

The men stamped their feet and nodded in approval.

DEE WAS CLOSE NOW. HE COULD HEAR THE WAVES LAPPING ON the shore, and he'd been able to smell the water for some time. His legs were screaming, the calves taunt from the exertion. He knew the others probably had it worse.

They'd only seen lights pass below them on the highway a couple of times. Apparently, the road wasn't heavily traveled at night. That was okay. Right now, all Dee wanted was to get to the bottom of the steps and walk out into the water and soak for a few minutes.

They trudged on, the heavy breathing turning to small gasps and sighs now. Dee reached the bottom without realizing and his knee nearly buckled as he went to take one more step, on a step that wasn't there, just a flat surface. They had reached the bottom.

"We made it," he called out. "Careful, these last few steps. We'll head for the water."

Dee collected everyone at the bottom and led them across the street onto a stretch of beach. They all held onto one another as they staggered toward the water. The moon was bright now and they could see each other clearly.

They settled into the water in a big circle and laid back.

THE TEAM LEADER WAS AWAKE AGAIN AND OUTSIDE THE room, pacing. He wanted to get the team up, but there really was no reason. The Reserve wouldn't open for several more hours. He just wanted to be mobile. He had a bad feeling about Miguelito. The man had not called or returned his text.

· · ·

They'd laid in the water for several minutes and began to move again.

"What now?" asked Jamal.

"Try to catch a ride, maybe start walking. I think town isn't too far around the bend," replied Dee.

"We're supposed to be on vacation," replied a weary Mike.

"I thought you liked to workout, that was one serious workout," replied Jamal. "I've run steps lots of times, but never like that."

"Would you guys quit commiserating and figure out what we're going to do," stated Keno.

"That was great, but I'm tired and hungry," added Angelic.

"Look," said Gina, "Lights coming this way." She scrambled up out of the water and ran for the highway.

Dee and the others started after her.

Gina was standing in the road waving down a truck that was approaching. The cab looked full as they eased to a stop, fishing poles sticking out of the bed in the back.

"Hey, guys," she called and waved. "We came out for a midnight swim and our taxi left us. Could we get a ride into town? In the back is fine."

The driver waved her around, and she stopped and called out to the rest of the group, "Come on, y'all."

They rolled into town and Gina banged on the rear window at a cross street with an old motel and some warehouses. They climbed down and thanked the men who pulled away toward the ocean.

"Should we check it out or check in?" asked Keno.

They all stood looking at the motel.

"Give me a minute," said Dee, and he crossed the street in the opposite direction.

There was a young man working on an old Monte Carlo

by lamplight. Dee walked up to within thirty feet and stopped. In a few seconds, the boy looked up.

"You look pretty handy," said Dee.

The boy nodded but didn't reply.

"Is there any place close by that I could purchase a vehicle?" Dee asked.

In a couple of seconds, the boy stopped working and got to his feet. He went to the warehouse door behind him and slid it open. He turned to Dee and waved.

Dee eased up to the warehouse and looked inside. There were about a half dozen vehicles, mostly mini-Coopers, Morris Minors, compact cars, except there was a Volkswagen Thing, bright yellow, no doors, and no roof, but roll bars, front and rear.

Dee pointed at the VW. "How old is that?"

The boy looked at him. "Old, but it runs good, big motor. You go fast," he replied.

"Is there a top?" asked Dee.

The boy stepped inside and rummaged around in one corner. He came out with a rolled-up piece of canvas. "You can tie this on for shade," he said. "It was part of a truck top, should be more than big enough."

"How much?" Dee asked.

The boy smiled for the first time and mumbled a number.

"That's too much, but I'll pay it," replied Dee. "Full tank of gas?"

The boy nodded and reached to a board mounted on the warehouse wall for a set of keys. He pitched them to Dee. "Drive safely," he said, and walked away.

"What are you thinking?" asked Jamal.

"It was the only thing he had that would carry us all," replied Dee.

"I can see that," answered Jamal.

"He's asking what's your plan," added Mike.

Dee looked at both of them. "They probably think we're still in the park. We drive back to Seville, catch a plane or a train. They'd be less likely to think we backtracked."

Keno had stepped up, along with the other women. "We're going to ride in that, to Seville?"

"Should be fun, now that we got some shade. Let's tie it on and get out of Gibraltar," he added.

THE TEAM LEADER HAD TURNED EVERYONE OUT OF THE motel and had them riding back up the cable car on the first run of the day.

"I don't think they're up here," said one of the men.

"Why not?" asked the leader.

"We'd have found them yesterday or," he said, looking at the man who had been hit over the head, "they're already gone."

The leader nodded. "We'll do a quick search." He pointed to one of the other men. "Get us some fresh transportation in a different color. We'll leave the van at the motel. If we don't find them in the first walk through, we'll head back to Seville."

"We going to get square with Miguelito?" asked another of the men.

"Yes, we are," replied the leader, "then we're going home."

THE MEN FROM THE CARTEL HAD RENTED TWO BIG TRUCKS. They weren't air conditioned, but these men were used to the deserts of Mexico and the temperatures in Spain were almost pleasant to them.

They rode down the N-4 toward Gibraltar. There was a

small bluff line as they swung east toward the mountains.

"That should work," said the leader, pointing at the bluff line.

The driver of the first truck looked over to the cartel group leader. "There were two other roads to the west they might have taken."

The leader looked back at him for a moment. "Maybe, but this one is the shortest and Miguelito said they told him they were going this way."

The leader lay back in the seat and thought to himself, *Coming in on their own plane. They had brought along some of their favorite toys. When they caught up to the ex-military team and the tourists, there would be fireworks.*

THE TEAM FINISHED THEIR WALK THROUGH OF THE Gibraltar Reserve and found nothing. They meet back at the cable car and returned to the bottom. The new van had been dropped at the motel parking lot. They checked their gear and got in for the ride to Seville.

"We taking the N-4?" asked the man driving.

The leader looked over at him. "No, swing east and take the E-5. Let's get a change of scenery."

39

ALONG THE ROAD

Dee got behind the wheel of the VW and fired it up. He pulled slowly out of the warehouse and Mike and Jamal tied on the canvas top after folding the material several times. Everyone scrambled for a seat, and then they took off. The boy, who had stood watching, threw up a hand as they pulled away.

"Friendly," said Jamal, who sat in the seat beside Dee.

"He should be, I paid him more than enough," replied Dee. "In fact, I'm about out of cash. You got some?"

Jamal stuck his hand in his pocket and felt his money clip. "Yeah, I'm still good."

Dee nodded. "We may need it. I'm thinking we go up the beach on the A-5, stay off the main road, take our time, and let them wonder about us."

Jamal nodded.

"I'm hungry," said Angelic.

"Sounds good, let's find a place to eat," replied Dee.

They drove for a time along the water and then stopped in a small town at a crossroads, where they would turn inland for an hour before reappearing on the coast. They ate a large breakfast in a small restaurant and got back on the road. Along the water they had a breeze and clung to their hats and glasses as they bounced around in the Thing. The other thing it didn't have was seatbelts. Moving inland, the breeze died, and the sun beat down on them. They huddled under the canopy and fanned themselves.

"How long are you thinking to get back to Seville?" asked Jamal, still seated next to Dee, who was still driving.

"I think it's around five hours on this road, but if we take our time and try to arrive in the evening, around sunset, it'll add several hours to the trip. Maybe we can stop somewhere along the beach or in one of the smaller towns we pass through."

Dee punched the accelerator for a couple of seconds and they both felt the vehicle surge.

"What's the hurry?" shouted out Mike from the backseat.

"No hurry, just testing. The kid said this thing had a big motor and would go fast. He wasn't kidding," replied Dee.

"Have Angelic and Gina look at train and bus routes from Seville," he said to Jamal. "I'd rather catch a plane, but that's too easy to track. If we go due east, we cross into Portugal. That might slow them down at a border crossing. If we can get to Faro, we can catch a plane."

"If this thing is that fast, why don't we just drive? What is the distance from Seville, a couple of hours?" asked Jamal. "Nothing to trace if we drive."

"You think they can stand it?" asked Dee, nodding to the passengers in the back.

Jamal grinned. "What choice do they have!"

THE EX-MILITARY TEAM WAS MOVING RAPIDLY ALONG THE E-5, making good time toward Seville.

"How we going to play this, when we get there?" asked the driver of the van to the team leader sitting beside him.

"Just like normal. We walk in, report, tell him we're done, and that we expect to be paid. He didn't deliver accurate information. We couldn't deliver the product," replied the leader.

"You think it'll be that simple?" asked the driver.

"No, I don't, but if he gives us an issue, we have a couple of options. We could just take the bell," said the leader.

The driver's head spun, and the van swerved slightly. "What bell?" he asked.

The leader glanced over at him and smiled. "I overheard Miguelito on a call. He doesn't know I'm fluent in Spanish. He and I have always spoken in English. He thinks these tourists have a solid gold bell stashed somewhere, and he wants it."

"So, if we found them, we could snatch it?" asked the driver.

"We could, but that information may not be any better than his information about their location," replied the leader.

From the back of the van came a shout, "Hey, I may have something helpful here."

"We'll see what time it is when we get back to the beach road, and we can decide about stopping or lunch or gas," called out Dee to Jamal.

The road was relatively smooth at this point and the landscape was all very similar, which had caused those in the back to try to nap a bit. But it was hot, and the seats were uncomfortable.

"Can we stop for a little while?" asked Keno, leaning

forward into the front. "I need to stretch my legs and get away from the vibration for a few minutes."

Dee nodded and looked for a place to pull over. Up ahead was a stand of trees along the road, and Dee could pull off far enough for them to exit the vehicle and have some shade.

As they stood in a group and stretched, Dee spoke, "We should be back nearer the beach shortly. There are a couple of small towns along the coast that we pass through before we make the turn north for Seville. I think we have to catch the E-5 at that point. We can go a little faster, but the wind, noise and vibration will probably increase."

"Let's get to one of those little towns, maybe by the beach, catch some shade, or maybe lunch and some air conditioning, and rest up through the hottest part of the day. Maybe driving a little later in the afternoon would be more comfortable," said Angelic.

The others looked at Dee, who nodded. "That's a good idea. Jamal and I talked about driving straight through to Faro, Portugal, which is about two to three hours beyond Seville. We can fly out from there. I don't think they'd look for us to fly out of Portugal."

"We going to touch base with Diego?" asked Gina.

"I wanted to, but I don't know that it helps us," replied Dee. "Finding the painting was great, but it didn't tell us anything about the bell. It told the location of the ship, which we already knew. I don't want to cause him any problems. I think we just need to catch a plane back to Mexico and see if there is anything else to learn about the bell or just hand it over and be done. I'm tired of running."

The others nodded their agreement.

They broke back on to the beach shortly afterwards and rolled along for another forty-five minutes before coming up on the last town before they turned inland and switched to the E-5 for Seville.

Dee called out, "Everyone for stopping here?" There were nods and shouts of agreement.

"Let's pull out on the beach and stop for a few hours," said Dee. "It's only late morning and we can grab some lunch when we start for the highway."

They slowed down and motored along until they found access to a beach road. Dee followed it until he ran into the sand. Pulling out a short way on the hard pack, he saw a stand of trees not far off the water. He stopped a car's length from the trees. They were close enough to the water for a pleasant breeze. He called out as he exited the VW, "Jamal, Mike, let's see if we can tie the tarp to the VW and then stretch it over and tie it off on the trees. It'll create a canopy that we can all sit under."

"Shade would be wonderful," called Angelic.

"The breeze is nice, too," added Keno.

"Let's take a nap," finished Gina.

They were set up in a few minutes and catching a breeze in the shade. They lay in the sand but were so tired they didn't care and slipped quietly off to sleep.

THE DRIVER MADE THE TURN ONTO THE NEW ROAD. THE EX-military team leader was as excited as he'd been since the job began. It didn't look like it would be too far now. The GPS tracking for the tourist's phones his man had found earlier changed the game. Maybe some of those things Miguelito said were true. He was a billionaire. Which would be worth more to them, the balance of the money owed or the gold bell? Anticipation was sitting in with the team leader.

· · ·

SITTING IN THE SHADE OF A BLUFF ON THE N-4, THE CARTEL team hadn't been very busy since they had stopped. The cartel leader had sent a man up on a rock ledge as a lookout. The man could see down the highway coming from Gibraltar. So far, he hadn't seen a single van in any color. An hour into it, the leader had sent up another man with two pairs of binoculars and told him to have both men look for passengers and not just the van. Miguelito had said the team would be easy to spot. Typical Americanos, big, dumb, short-haired, and maybe with the tourist, three couples, ordinary men with good-looking women. So far nothing.

One man signaled down to the leader, then shouted, "Maybe we should head that way? We see them, we can run them off the road, just like at home."

The cartel leader thought about it for a minute. "Let me call Miguelito," he shouted back. A quick phone call later, he was waving everyone back to the trucks.

"We're going to head on to Gibraltar. I want a man in each truck up front with binoculars scouting the oncoming traffic. They should have been here by now if they'd captured the tourists. Stay sharp."

They got in the trucks and pulled back onto the highway, headed south.

THE EX-MILITARY TEAM LEADER WAS WATCHING THE READOUT closely. They were on the A-5 and headed toward the water. It couldn't be far. When they reached the beach road, he hand signaled the driver who stopped the van.

Speaking softly, he gave the men their orders, "Everybody armed, rifles and handguns. We want these people alive, but we want to look forceful. Don't shoot unless you're shot at. I may have to fire a quick burst to convince them, but there doesn't seem to be much traffic and we'll be fast afterwards if I have to fire." He waved a hand for them to move out. "Perimeter line at twenty meters, no sound, move to the water."

JAMAL HAD WOKEN AND, GLANCING AROUND, SAW THAT THE others were still napping or resting quietly. He pulled out his phone to review the Cortes data. If they were going to fly back to Mexico, he really wanted to find something. He scrolled slowly through the screens.

THE TEAM MOVED SLOWLY TOWARD THE WATER, NOT MAKING a sound. Look, step, listen, repeat.

The sound of the surf was growing louder, and it was only a few dozen yards to the shoreline when the leader raised an arm and halted the group. He hand signaled a slight change in direction and the team saw a canopy flapping lightly just off the water. It was tied to trees and draped over a vehicle. The readout was almost perfectly aligned. They took a couple of steps closer and could make out six people laying on the sand in the shade of the canopy. Success at last.

JAMAL HEARD THE FAINTEST STRAY NOISE THAT DIDN'T SEEM to belong at the beach and looked up from his phone. He called out softly, "We have company."

The ex-military team leader sprang forward and shouted out, "Stay exactly where you are," which of course caused all the reclining figures to bolt upright. But there they stopped and saw five men surrounding them, automatic weapons in hand.

Dee noted the weapons looked like AK-47's, which the

group was familiar with from their time stranded on the island. They all knew what damage could be done with the weapon. No one moved.

"Slowly, rise to your feet," said the team leader.

Each of the group did so. Jamal still had his phone in his hand.

"We finally caught a break on you people," said the leader. "I don't know if you were clever or just lucky, avoiding us in Gibraltar. But we finally got phone data on you, and he," he pointed at Jamal," was on the line, that helped. We weren't far away."

Dee looked at Jamal, who shrugged and said, "I was reviewing the Cortes data, I didn't think it would hurt."

"Find anything?" asked Dee.

"Shut up," said the team leader.

Jamal shook his head at Dee.

"Miguelito says you have a gold bell that belongs to him," said the team leader.

Dee's head came up and Jamal's eyes flared even though neither spoke.

"I see that it's true," said the team leader. "Miguelito said the bell was on a list he has from a sunken Cortes ship, that you know the location of. We'll need that information too."

"We don't have the bell with us, obviously," said Dee. "You've been chasing us, we lost our luggage, and we've been on the run."

"But you know where it is?" replied the leader.

Dee shrugged.

The leader took a step closer and raised the barrel of the AK. "I'm sure more than one of you knows, one less to return to Miguelito won't matter," he said and he raised the gun higher.

"It's in Seville," whispered Dee.

"That's better," said the team leader. "You didn't really want to die."

"So, you'll tell us where, or better yet, you'll take us to it." Dee nodded.

"And just to show that we're good sports, if you tell us where the ship is, we'll let you all go free."

"You would do that?" asked Jamal.

"If we get the gold bell and the location of the ship, we don't care about you. Miguelito's list was extensive. That ship is full of Aztec gold. We'll be richer than he already is, it's only fair," he said with a laugh.

"So, you want to tell us, or you want to die? We'll just tell him you resisted, and we defended ourselves. That is, after one of you tells us where the bell is, and we'll still get paid. It's not the best deal, but it's not a bad one, either. It's up to you," he concluded.

"What assurances do we have?" asked Dee.

"None," replied the team leader. We've been running all over Spain chasing a bunch of lucky tourists who were supposed to be a simple pick up. We've wasted time and energy. But we'll let you live, because, again, you tell us everything, we don't care about you, dead or alive."

"Alright," replied Dee, "we'll lead you to it."

"Lead us to it," snorted the team leader.

"You're traveling in a single vehicle, aren't you?" asked Dee.

The team leader nodded.

"There's six of us, five of you, not going to fit in one vehicle. Besides. We're in this old beater." Dee pointed to the VW, covered mostly by the tarp. "We can't go anywhere."

The team leader pointed to one of his men and at the VW. The man pulled the tarp off and laughed. "My grandmother had one of these. It won't go fifty miles an hour."

The team leader laughed. "Then let's load up and go get the bell." He took a step closer to Dee and raised the AK again. "Where is the bell?" he snarled.

Dee paused for a second and then, in a soft voice, he said, "The museum."

The team leader nearly doubled over in laughter. "All this time, Miguelito's been sitting right down the street." He paused for a moment and pointed at the VW with the barrel of the AK.

"You just remember, we'll be right behind you. Any problem, we run you off the road, we shoot you on the spot, no second chances, understand?" he queried.

Dee nodded. He and the others moved toward the VW. Mike and Jamal quickly folded the tarp and tied it back to the roll bars. The team leader and one other man stood a few feet away while Dee and the others got ready and then settled into the VW.

"I'm going to walk right along beside you until we get to the van. Make a move, I'll shoot you," said the team leader.

Dee drove slowly back toward the beach road, the two men following along beside.

When they got to the van, Dee stopped.

"Shut it off," said the team leader. Dee did so.

The team leader and the other man climbed into the van. The team leader settled into his seat and then called out, "Go out the A-5 to the E-5 and straight into Seville and the museum. No deviations."

Dee nodded, started the Thing and pulled slowly away.

As soon as they were moving and the motor noise from both vehicles was audible, Jamal turned to Dee and said, "What are you thinking? The bell is thousands of miles away."

"Really," replied Dee, who winked at Jamal and said,

"Someone must have stolen it. Do you think Miguelito got to it first?"

"They'll kill us," replied Jamal.

"Maybe," answered Dee, "but we have to get to Seville first."

THE CARTEL LEADER SAT IN ONE OF THE TRUCKS IN THE motel parking lot at the bottom of the cable car incline in Gibraltar. He was looking at a van that matched the color and license number that Miguelito had given him. It looked very much abandoned.

He was frustrated. He didn't mind calling Miguelito. He had worked with him for years and with his father before that. The cartel leader hated to disappoint Miguelito. His father had been an amazing man—smart, loyal, bold, cunning, but Miguelito, he was all those things, too, but he was also crazy. The cartel leader looked around to see if anyone had noticed his musing. *Things best kept to yourself*, he reminded himself.

He put the call through and Miguelito's only answer was, "Get back here, quickly," and the line went dead.

DEE MOTORED SLOWLY UP THE HIGHWAY TOWARD THE E-5. "That guy said this thing would only do fifty miles an hour, right?" asked Dee.

Jamal nodded. "Yeah, that kid must have really souped this thing up," he replied.

"Let's hold it at fifty," Dee answered.

Back in the van the driver said to the team leader, "You realize this van only has a four-cylinder?"

The team leader twisted his head to look at the driver.

"It was all they had available that would hold five," the driver replied.

The team leader shook his head. "If they pull away, we'll shoot the driver. The other man, the one in the picture, probably knows more, anyway."

The driver sighed.

They were still on the A-5, which was winding around from the beach inland toward the E-5. They pulled into a stop sign, and Dee eased forward and waited. There were no other cars. He pulled through, and the van followed him immediately.

"They kept it pretty tight," he observed to Jamal.

"Yeah, I wonder what that's about, if there'd been another car?" Jamal replied.

"Mike," Dee called out, "You got your knife?"

Mike squeezed his shoulder. "Yeah."

"Can you very subtlety cut the cord on the canopy, the next time we stop, if I call out to you?" asked Dee. "You get the back and hold it down while Jamal gets the front?"

"I can try," replied Mike. "The way it's folded we could probably hold it down at a lower speed if we all put a hand on it. Everybody, reach up and see if you can grab it."

Everyone's hands went up slowly, and they acted as if the canopy was helping stabilize them.

"It might work," called out Angelic.

"I don't know how many chances we'll get," replied Dee. "Don't cut it until I tell you."

They wound around another curve, and Dee noticed that the traffic was picking up. *Now we just need a stop sign,* he thought to himself.

Around another turn, and he saw it in the distance. Traffic was picking up some, and the van was hugging his bumper tightly. That was actually a help as the van sat higher than the Thing. There were several cars perpendicular to the stop sign and one in front of Dee.

"Get ready," he called as they eased up behind the car in front of them. "Cut it and hold it."

The car in front of them rolled through. Dee eased up, the van tight on him. The car perpendicular to him pulled out and turned in the direction Dee was headed.

"Let it go and then hold on," called out Dee. He floored the accelerator, and the Thing jumped forward, the engine howling, the canopy snapped back and wrapped around the front windshield of the van, Dee swung the Thing quickly around the car that had just pulled in front of him, narrowly missing an oncoming truck, and then accelerated away as he happily noted there was a long line of traffic coming toward him. The Thing gathered speed around a long turn and then Dee had open highway in front of him. He pushed the throttle to the floor, and the VW shot away.

"Take a turnoff!" shouted Jamal. The others in the rear seats were frantically holding the roll bars and each other.

"Just a little further to the E-5 and I'll open it up. They'll never catch us. That was a four-cylinder Toyota van. I've seen them before. Let's get a little distance and then we'll make a choice. I don't think there's a shortcut to Faro. You have to go all the way to Seville," said Dee.

"Still," said Jamal, "You are one lucky individual."

"Yeah," replied Dee. "Almost like being in a movie."

40

SEVILLE (THE RETURN)

The van full of ex-military went to pull through the intersection at the same time as Dee and suddenly the tarp from the Thing was covering their windshield. The driver braked immediately, and the tarp began to slip from the window. The van was in the middle of the intersection and one of the perpendicular cars had nearly hit them. It blocked the van and the intersection up with traffic and car horns. By the time the tarp slipped enough to see, the driver and the team leader had lost sight of Dee and the others in the Thing.

"Get out there and get that bloody tarp out of the way!" the team leader screamed at the driver. "Back these people up so we can get by." The team leader was tempted to pull out this AK and clear the street, but then they would be stuck in place by all the abandoned vehicles. He waved at a couple of the men in the rear seats. "Get out there and help him."

Eleven minutes later they were racing down the A-5 toward the E-5. They could see no sign of the Thing.

"It's bright yellow. How can we miss it?" the team leader called out to the driver. "Can't we go any faster?"

"Got it floored now," replied the driver.

"Keep a sharp eye out," the leader called to all the men. "We'll go on to Seville. We know the bell is in the museum. Then we'll catch them, if not on the way. They're starting to get on my nerves."

Over on the N-4, the cartel leader texted Miguelito to get more instructions. They were headed back toward Seville, and he wasn't clear on their next step.

Miguelito came back quickly. "Go to the museum. I want to have a talk with the little man, the director, Diego something or other. Meet me there."

The cartel leader tapped his driver on the arm. "When we get to town, head for the museum."

The man nodded and pressed the accelerator a little harder.

"Can we stop for a minute? I really have to go to the bathroom, too much excitement, and too much bouncing around," said Keno.

"I second that," called out Angelic.

"Me too," added Gina.

Dee turned and looked at Jamal, who replied, "Wouldn't hurt, I about peed myself when you peeled out of the stop sign."

Dee nodded. "We can gas up and use the restrooms. Everybody be quick," he called out.

A few minutes later, Dee saw a sign for fuel and a café. Exiting the highway quickly, he let the others out and went to pull over to the gas pumps. As Jamal stepped from the vehicle, he pitched Dee his money clip.

Dee nodded and went about filling up the Thing.

As he stood there waiting on the others, he pulled out his phone. The ex-military team had tracking software, but it was probably GPS based and it didn't matter whether the phone was on or off. Dee wanted to check messages.

He scrolled to the texts and had one pop up from two days before. "This is EA—call me."

Dee stood looking at the text as Jamal walked up.

"What?" called Jamal.

"Message from EA," replied Dee.

"Elizabeth Adassa?" asked Jamal.

"She's the only one I can think of. You want to finish up and pay?" Dee said, pointing to the car and tossing the money clip back to Jamal, who nodded and one-handed the catch.

Dee stepped out from under the station canopy and dialed Elizabeth's number. He saw the others coming back from the restrooms and pointed toward the vehicle.

"Keys are in it," said Dee, and he climbed into the passenger seat as the call connected.

Jamal rolled back onto the highway, and they were under way again.

Elizabeth picked up on the third ring.

"Dee." she exclaimed.

"Hey, sorry, we've been busy, on the run," he replied.

"I want to hear about it, but let me share this, really quick," she answered. "I did some research on Cortes and his relationships here on the island."

"Please go on," replied Dee.

"I found a letter that says he made a list of gifts that were on the ship he sank in the Sea of Cortez. And that he hoped to return for them. That he marked the spot. But there were no details," she concluded.

"That's amazing, that's what we've been looking for all this time," he answered.

"I'll keep researching, but I wanted you to know. At least at one point in time there was an inventory of the ship," she said. "You were on the run?"

"We still are," Dee replied.

"Well then, let me let you go. I'll keep looking, take care," she said, and the line went dead.

Jamal raised his eyebrows at Dee while still watching the road.

Dee leaned toward him and motioned the others in the back to lean forward.

"That was Elizabeth, from the Canary Islands. She said that she found a letter that referenced a list that Cortes made about the ship he sank, and the items made from Aztec gold that were on the ship."

"Was that the list that guy was talking about back at the beach?" asked Gina.

Dee nodded and replied, "It sounded like Miguelito has the actual list. Elizabeth just found a reference to it."

Jamal nearly jerked the wheel, and Dee looked over at him sharply. "That's what we've been looking for. I've been chewing on that ever since he said it," answered Jamal. "All that happened so quick, I wasn't sure what I heard."

"What does that mean to us?" asked Mike.

Jamal looked at Dee.

"I think it means that we need to have a chat with Miguelito, or at least an opportunity to see if we can find his list," replied Dee.

"That's crazy," answered Keno. "He tried to kill us."

Angelic squeezed Jamal's shoulder from behind. "I know how much this means to you," she said.

Jamal looked at Dee again. "Maybe just you and me? Let Mike look after the women and let them all serve as our lookouts and getaway driver?"

Dee looked at him for a moment. "Okay," he replied.

"Are you sure that's a good idea?" said Gina from the back seat.

"No, I'm not, we'll have to approach it cautiously," replied Dee, and he leaned back and squeezed her hand.

The ex-military team leader addressed one of the men in the back of the van. "I thought you said that thing wouldn't go fifty miles an hour," he growled.

"My granny's would scarcely do fifty. We got to be closing in on them," he replied.

"There's a lot of traffic," added the driver. "We might have caught them on the open road, unless they tuned off somewhere. They could have continued on the A-5."

"That doesn't lead anywhere," snapped the team leader.

"Away from us," countered the driver.

"Go faster," retorted the team leader, and leaned back in his seat.

Miguelito anxiously awaited the return of his cartel men. He'd have to have them find the team and the tourists after they finished with the director, Diego.

There was a lot for the cartel men to do, and Miguelito congratulated himself on bringing them over to Seville. He had decided that the tourists must have solved the riddle of where the ship was located. They had given little heed to the painting. Miguelito had been looking for that ship for most of his adult life. His father had begun the quest when a historian from the National Institute of Anthropology and History had come to him with a story about a list, made by Cortes himself, that detailed all the treasures made from Aztec gold that had been on board the ship. The ship on which Cortes had tried to escape from the Spanish. When he couldn't escape, he sank the ship.

The humorous part, to Miguelito, had been when the man brought the list to his father, Miguel, rather than paying the man, Miguel had framed the historian with some fake sexual deviancy charges and watched him be dismissed from the Institute and made a laughingstock in his field of endeavor. The man had been greedy and had asked for too much money. Miguelito, nor Miguel, had any use for greedy fools.

Miguelito took the list from his pocket. He unrolled it and savored the details of the items. There, in the bottom third of the list, was a bell, stamped with the name 'Castillo,' the benefactor of the ship, and good friend and painter of Cortes.

The historian had a copy of the letter which he had brought to Miguel. Miguelito had taken the copy and had a hand printed version made in the calligraphy style of the time. The list included all the items on board and a note at the bottom which said, *Have Castillo detail the location.* Miguelito had always assumed that to mean the location of the ship and the Castillo painting had been seen as the key by Miguel. It was why Miguel had risked his own life to steal the painting thirty years before. All this time Miguelito thought the Europeans—Miguel's partners in crime—had the painting, but it had been lost. Now he wasn't sure he needed it. He had something better.

Miguelito thought of the tourists again. He couldn't be rid of them fast enough. He considered letting the cartel men handle it but decided that once he got the ship's location from them, he would go forward with the sacrifice. The men he'd hired on the ex-military team, his cartel crew, could take care of them, the sooner the better.

Thinking back to the tourists, it occurred to Miguelito

that the short, curvy, dark-haired woman would make a fabulous-looking sun goddess in full Aztec costume, even if she also had to be in chains. *He might keep her for a while*, he thought to himself.

THE EX-MILITARY TEAM HAD BEEN SCREAMING UP THE E-5 AS fast as the small engine Toyota van would take them. They'd seen no sign of the bright yellow Thing. The two things together had made the team leader extremely irritable. His men, sensing his mood, sat quietly and waited for the moment he would call them to action.

THEY HAD ARRIVED IN SEVILLE AND SWUNG AROUND THE city. The women weren't sure they shouldn't just keep going to Portugal and fly away from the whole situation.

The men had kept a close eye behind them coming up the E-5 as Dee worried that their stop for gas and a break might have allowed the van to catch up, but they saw nothing.

"Should we call Diego, let him know we're coming?" asked Mike.

"He usually works late," added Jamal.

"I think I'd rather take a chance and just catch him there," replied Dee. "No need to panic him." He looked around the group and they were silent, watching him. "We can drop in and out quick, see what he thinks about the list, and how we might get it from Miguelito. I say we just go to the museum. Jamal and I can go inside. Mike, you can stand guard, and the ladies can be lookouts."

"Make it quick," said Gina. "He can help us or he can't, then we're out of here, on to Portugal."

"I agree completely," added Angelic.

"Unanimous," said Keno.

THE VAN FULL OF EX-MILITARY WAS APPROACHING THE museum. "What's the plan?" asked the driver.

"Pull around back and we'll see if we can find the director, what's his name, he often works late. If anyone knows where the bell is, he will," answered the team leader.

THE CARTEL MEN HAD GONE STRAIGHT TO THE MUSEUM. They texted Miguelito and he met them at the back of the building. It was just before closing time.

"We'll go inside and filter out, find the director. I know where his office is, and we'll start there." He pointed to one of the men. "Be sure the museum stays open, no alarms, until we are through." The man nodded.

They marched around front and entered. The receptionist called out to them that the museum would close shortly.

"No problem," answered Miguelito. "We just want to take a quick look." He motioned to the man, who stepped over to monitor the receptionist.

Several of the men filtered out through the building to search for the director, if he was out and about. The balance of them followed Miguelito to the director's office.

DIEGO LOOKED AT HIS WATCH AND THOUGHT, *Perhaps I should go, stop and have a drink before heading home. It's my wife's bridge night. If I take a few minutes, I'll probably miss her.*

He shuffled some papers in a file and tried to decide if he should stay to consider a new exhibit for next month that had been proposed by one of the major patrons or worry about it later.

I think I'll go, he decided as he rose.

Miguelito and a raft of men stepped into Diego's office.

Diego's face turned pale. "What do you want?" he exclaimed. "You have the painting."

"How could you say such a thing," replied Miguelito. "It's mine, or my families, my father laid claim to it thirty years ago."

Diego sat back in his chair.

Miguelito leaned forward into Diego's face and said, "What I want to know is why you told those tourists I was here?"

Diego gulped.

"That was a terrible mistake, perhaps a fatal one, on your part," added Miguelito.

"They found me. I was tied up, bleeding. I had to answer their questions. What was I to say?" replied Diego.

"That is most unfortunate," replied Miguelito. "That awareness has made them difficult to apprehend."

Diego stuttered without saying anything.

"Tell me where they are," said Miguelito, leaning closer to Diego.

"I don't know," stammered Diego. "Honestly, I don't. I assume they are on the run if you are looking for them."

Miguelito sat on the edge of the desk, right in front of Diego. "Why don't I believe you?" he said.

Diego rubbed his forehead with his palm. "They came in a couple of days ago, said they were leaving, they didn't say where they were going, and I didn't ask. That's all I know," he whimpered.

Miguelito stood up and brushed his shirt where it had creased. "That's too bad," he said, then jerked his head toward his men. They stepped toward Diego, and there was suddenly another voice.

"Nobody move," said the team leader from the van. He and his men had arrived and seen the two large transport trucks. Suspecting some type of trap, they had cut the rear bell alarm on the back door and slipped inside. They had made their way toward Diego when they realized there was something going on.

As the five men, armed with automatic weapons, slowly circled Miguelito and his men, Diego rolled slightly forward under his desk.

The tension was high. Diego could see that Miguelito's men wanted to engage the five former soldiers and likely didn't care who got killed. But Diego had a plan, at least a short-term one.

He had a silent alarm under his desk. It was a robbery notification that rang directly at the Seville police headquarters. He punched the button twice, then paused, then punched it twice again. That was the signal for a robbery in progress. Send SWAT.

Now Diego could only hope for the best. If shooting broke out, which he was sure it would, he hoped to dive under the desk. Perhaps he'd survive, perhaps not.

The team leader from the van called out, "Step away from Miguelito."

When the men didn't do it, the team leader raised his weapon to his cheek.

Miguelito nodded, and the men moved away.

The team leader stepped closer. "Take off your jacket," he said to Miguelito.

Miguelito moved slowly but did so.

"Lay it on the desk and take a step back," said the team leader.

Miguelito stepped away.

"Cover him close." One of the other four ex-military men stepped up and aimed directly at Miguelito.

The team leader lowered his weapon and searched the jacket with one hand. He pulled the rolled-up list out of one of the side pockets. "This might be one thing I'm looking for," he said. The team leader unrolled the paper and smiled. "This will do. Now, where's the bell?"

Miguelito glanced at Diego, who looked at the team leader, and then back at Miguelito, and shrugged at both of them.

"I know it's here, where is it?" said the team leader, raising his weapon again.

Outside, Dee and Jamal had slipped from the Thing and were making their way to the rear of the museum. The door stood open, and they saw that the alarm had been disabled.

"What's going on?" asked Jamal.

Dee pointed a little further down the street. "There's the van. They got here pretty fast. They're probably shaking down Diego. We'd better see if we can help."

They waved to Mike, who was across the street, and to the women, who were up the street by the vehicle.

Dee and Jamal stepped inside the building.

"The tourists have the bell?" said Miguelito.

"They hid it here," replied the team leader.

Miguelito looked at Diego, who was near visibly shaking. "Is that true?" Miguelito thundered.

Not trusting his voice, Diego shook his head, and then squeaked out a, "No, it's not here."

At that moment, the man who'd been left with the receptionist and the two men who had been sent to wander the halls in search of Diego stepped up behind the five team members, automatic weapons to their cheeks. "Put down your weapons, or you will die," one of the three men called out.

The ex-military team leader quickly stepped closer to Miguelito and raised the barrel of his weapon to Miguelito's stomach. "Go ahead, your boss dies first," he replied.

Everyone stood still for a moment.

DEE AND JAMAL HAD WANDERED UP JUST BEHIND THE LAST three men with guns.

"What can we do?" whispered Jamal.

Dee held up his hands. "Watch?" he replied. Then his phone vibrated silently. He pulled it up to his face and read a text from Mike, "Sirens, police likely in route, get out of there."

MIGUELITO WAS THE FIRST TO SPEAK. "WHAT CAN WE DO TO resolve this?"

The team leader looked around. He laid the list he held on Diego's desk and placed his hand near the stock of his weapon. No matter what happened, this was a nasty crossfire. There would be many dead, and he was right at the center of it.

"We just want to be paid the balance of our fee and walk out of here. This job was a cluster from the start. We ought to get a bonus," he said.

"You'll stay alive," replied Miguelito.

"So will you," answered the team leader.

Then they heard it, in the not so distance, sirens, many of them.

"Times running out," said Miguelito. "We all need to leave."

The team leader nodded, as did Miguelito. "Everyone out of the building," called Miguelito.

Jamal and Dee saw the men breaking up and slid against the wall and back up the hall before they were seen. The men ran down the hall toward the door. They broke for their respective vehicles as police cars and SWAT trucks skidded into place.

It wasn't clear who fired first, whether the cartel men turned on the ex-military team leader and his men or the police or the SWAT unit, but the scene erupted in gunfire.

Mike dove under the nearest car. The women hid under the Thing. The air was full of sound and fire.

Back inside, Dee and Jamal creeped down the hall and called out softly, "Diego?"

They heard a whispered response, "In my office."

They hustled inside. Diego was still in his chair. He was still trembling. "Stay here with me until it's over."

"We got people outside," replied Dee.

"They are smart people. They will hide. Do not go out there. Wait until it's over," Diego answered. Then he handed them a rolled-up piece of paper. "I think you are looking for this."

Jamal took the paper and unrolled it. "It's the list," he

said excitedly. He laid it on Diego's desk and ran a finger down the items. "There it is, gold bell with *Castillo* engraved." He turned to look at Dee. "We found it."

Dee had a big grin on his face. "I'm glad that's over," he replied, slapping Jamal on the shoulder. Then he looked at the list and at Diego.

"That's not an original, is it?" he asked Diego.

Diego looked quickly. "I'm sorry, my friends. It's a copy, a few years old maybe. Made to look like an original, but not a good fake."

"What does it mean?" asked Jamal.

"I don't know," answered Diego.

IN A FEW MINUTES, SEVERAL OFFICERS CAME IN TO SEE DIEGO. He, Dee, and Jamal sat together in the office. Diego rose and shook hands and then introduced Dee and Jamal. "These men were in the building and came to my aid. What happened outside?"

"First," said the officer, "did they get away with anything?"

Diego shook his head.

The officer sighed. "Don't know how it started, but a gunfight erupted. There are several dead. Looks like a couple of groups of men, Americans and then Spanish or Mexican."

Dee and Jamal rose. "We have friends outside we'd better check on," said Dee.

At that moment, they heard voices and shouting as several other police officers attempted to keep Mike, Angelic, Gina, and Keno from gaining further entrance to the building.

Diego rose. "It's okay, they're with us."

EPILOGUE

The police remained outside and processed the scene for some time afterward. Diego eventually asked if it was all right for the group to leave. The police wished them well and said they would follow up in the morning.

"Let's go to a restaurant," said Diego.

"It's kind of late and I don't know that I have any appetite," replied Angelic.

Diego smiled at her and said, "I quite understand. I think the big thing is to get away from here, if not to eat, perhaps a drink."

"I could go for that," added Keno.

"Are there restaurants or bars still open?" asked Gina.

Diego nodded. "This is Spain, we are late night creatures, and we never close." He raised a hand toward the door, and they all trooped out toward the front of the building.

DIEGO TOOK THEM TO ONE OF HIS FAVORITE RESTAURANTS and they sat at a large table, looking out the front window and on to the street. Revelers strolled past, the city abuzz with activity.

"Hard to believe there was a major gunfight a few hours ago and people are back out in the streets," said Jamal.

"Things happen," replied Diego. "Life goes on. Speaking of which, what are your plans now?"

"I booked us back into the hotel we'd been staying at, on the way here," said Gina. "They had three rooms, but not together, we'll be all over the building."

"At least we have some place to go. Thank you," replied Angelic.

Keno squeezed Gina's shoulder. "You're a lifesaver."

"I'll walk back and get the Thing," said Mike.

"Why don't you just leave it on the street?" said Keno. "Abandon it, please."

"We might need some transportation. I kind of liked it, certainly goes fast," Mike replied.

"I think we should hold on to it for a couple of days, until we figure out what we're doing," added Dee.

"Agreed," said Jamal.

Diego surveyed them and laughed. "What a group you are! It's been so much fun, now that it's hopefully over. I don't think I can take much more."

They finished up and departed for the hotel, the vehicle, and for Diego, home.

MID-MORNING THE NEXT DAY, THEY GATHERED IN THE hotel's atrium for breakfast.

"Seems like we were just here," commented Keno.

"We were," replied Angelic, smiling. "There was just a lot in between time."

"What next?" asked Gina.

Jamal and Dee looked at each other.

"We talked about taking a cruise around the Mediterranean," said Dee.

"But there's something we really need to take care of first," added Jamal. "We need to turn the bell over, now that we can identify it."

"How do you want to do it?" asked Mike.

Dee and Jamal glanced at one another again.

"Quickly," replied Dee. "Jamal and I thought we could fly over and grab the bell from Ike and turn it over to the National Institute of Anthropology and History. Then fly back and join y'all for the cruise."

"How long will that take?" asked Gina.

"Three or four days, maybe five, tops," answered Jamal.

"And what are we to do?" inquired Angelic.

"Rest, shop, lay by the pool, be tourists," replied Dee. He looked around the atrium. "This is a nice place. A few days to recover and we'll be back and go again."

Keno looked at Mike. "What about you?" she asked.

He touched her hand with his and winked at her. "I'll stay here and take care of you," he replied, "and keep an eye on these two." He nodded toward Angelic and Gina.

"Three to five days?" said Gina.

"Tops," replied Dee.

"Not a day longer," she answered, and grinned.

JAMAL AND DEE MADE RESERVATIONS TO FLY TO KEY WEST. It was a direct flight to Miami and a connector. Talking it over, they decided to ask Elizabeth Adassa to accompany them. She had the documentation supporting the Cortes list and perhaps that would help convince the National Institute of the bell's authenticity.

Dee contacted her, and she excitedly agreed to meet them. She asked if she could fly to Seville and join them for the flight to Miami. They agreed, and she advised she would arrive that afternoon. That put them on a late flight to Miami, but thanks to the time zones they'd arrive in only a couple of hours, if you looked at a clock in Miami. It was a nine-hour flight, over seven thousand miles. It would be a sizeable chunk of day one.

Dee then texted Ike to tell him they would come back through Key West to pick up the bell. Ike came straight back and said he'd be there. There'd been a flu outbreak at one of the challenger tournaments and it had been cancelled. Ike had flown home for the week. Dee mentioned they were bringing Elizabeth with them.

It was a long flight. They booked three seats and put Elizabeth between them. She kept both men entertained with stories about her experiences and her past. She also filled them in on her Cortes research.

"I found a group of letters from late in Cortes' life. He was already back in Spain and reaching out to his man in the Canary Islands, within whose effects I located the letters, and Cortes was asking about various items he had left in the CI, and how he might obtain them. In one of the letters, he mentions the ship that he sank, the treasure, the listing of items, and how he likely could never return for them. It was actually touching, it reads as though Cortes was a completely broken man by that time, and quite humbled."

"It's amazing you found that," said Jamal.

"How did you know where to look?" asked Dee.

"Everyone has researched Cortes repeatedly. I thought about the people he dealt with and who might have something that Cortes had sent them or that originated with Cortes. I turned this man up by researching the time period. There were a couple of names and not much remaining documentation. I got lucky with this guy. He kept everything.

But the last time someone had looked at his papers was 1972."

They landed in Miami and made their way out of the main terminal, swamped with people, into one of the smaller regional terminals. There they would catch a small Air Florida plane that would ferry them into Key West. It was noticeably more relaxed in the smaller terminal.

"That was a relief," said Jamal. "I'd forgotten how crowded big terminals can be."

"Agreed, we've been on ships for a while now. I enjoy being on the water much better," replied Dee.

"Absolutely," agreed Elizabeth.

They boarded the smaller plane and landed in Key West a short time later. Ike was leaning against the wall as they deplaned and came into the terminal. He waved and started toward them.

Dee introduced them, "Elizabeth Adassa, Ike Mann, Ike, Elizabeth."

They were both smiling broadly.

Ike touched her arm, and she settled against him as Ike called out, "Come this way."

Jamal looked at Dee, and Dee looked back, and they grinned at each other and then followed along.

Ike loaded them up in his 'Conch wagon,' a 1953 baby blue Ford F-100 custom pick up, putting Elizabeth in the front with him and Dee and Jamal in the back in the bed. He made the quick trip to his house.

He parked, and everyone got out. Pointing at the house, he said to Elizabeth, "It's not very big, but it's home."

She smiled brightly at him. "It's beautiful, I love it."

· · ·

They got settled in the house and Ike called the treasure museum where he'd stashed their gear, including the bell. They told him to come by and they'd load it up anytime.

Dee and Jamal conferred, and Jamal elected to call the National Institute of Anthropology and History to schedule a meeting and delivery. Two days later was the best time they'd give him. In fact, they didn't seem interested at all until he said the magic words, 'Cortes' and 'Aztec gold.' Then they wanted all the details, but Jamal simply responded, "See you in two days."

They got on the phone and made arrangements for the flights from Key West to Mexico City. Again, it meant Key West to Miami and Miami to Mexico City. They made arrangements with the airlines for the one box and labeled it as dive equipment. When the airline asked what diving they were going to do in Mexico City, Jamal explained it was just a stopover.

Ike took them to dinner that night. They asked to go early as Dee and Jamal were feeling the jet lag. Elizabeth seemed fine. She and Ike paired right up, leaving Dee and Jamal as the other couple.

They boarded the plane the following day. Ike dropped them at the terminal and insisted they come back through on their way to Spain.

"I'd love to," replied Elizabeth, and the decision was made.

On the flight to Mexico City, Elizabeth advised them they didn't have to go back through Key West if they didn't want. If it was easier to fly on to Seville, they should.

"Ike is off for several more days, and he invited me back. I'd love to see the sites and you are welcome to come along.

It could be fun, but I thought you might need to get back to your group," said Elizabeth.

Dee nodded. "Yeah, we promised them five days or less. We're going to be out of time, but you should have fun. Ike is a great guy, you'll like him."

She grinned. "I already do."

After landing, they secured the cargo and their luggage and made for the National Institute of Anthropology and History. Mexico City was an enormous place, and they rode for over an hour in the cab, despite not covering that great a distance.

Approaching the Institute's headquarters, Jamal called and advised that they were arriving and that they would need a dolly or some assistance from maintenance. The speaker assured him there would be two or more guards available at the door.

As they pulled in front of the building, Jamal stepped out and waved at the entrance. Four large, burly men in uniforms and carrying guns approached. A woman in a business suit came running out the door after them.

She waved as she approached. "Hello, I'm Juanita Jimenez, we've been talking," she exclaimed.

Jamal stepped around the car to greet her as Dee and Elizabeth exited the cab.

She waved at the four men. "Please bring that to the conference room by my office," she said, and they stepped forward and hefted the box. "Come with me," she continued, while waving at Jamal, Dee, and Elizabeth.

The four men moved slowly with the box, their muscles bulging under the sleeves of their shirts.

Ms. Jimenez stayed close to them and to her visitors.

"Must be a hefty item," she commented, watching the men move.

"I think you'll like it," replied Jamal.

Ms. Jimenez led the way to the conference room beside her office, guiding the guards with the box and shepherding her guests. The men sat the box in the floor by the conference table. As they were retreating from the room, Jamal called out, "Would you have a crowbar or a claw hammer?"

Ms. Jimenez replied, "I've got one in my office next door, I'll grab it for you."

She returned with a crowbar and handed it to Jamal, and they all sat around the table.

"I'm all ears," said a beaming Ms. Jimenez.

Jamal and Dee glanced at each other, and Jamal stood up. He introduced Dee and Elizabeth.

"Let me start at the beginning," he said, and he quickly summarized the events of the past fifty days with Ms. Jimenez, starting from the Sea of Cortez to standing there in her conference room.

When he finished, Ms. Jimenez sat back in her chair and sighed. "That's quite a story. I don't think you could have made that up."

Jamal nodded and said, "Let me get more specific now." He pulled a small tube from his backpack and extracted a rolled piece of paper.

"I'm afraid this isn't original documentation. It appears to be a copy of some type." He unrolled the paper. "This is a list of items that Hernando Cortes had on board a ship that he sank in the Sea of Cortez. We discovered an item, as I mentioned, listed here as a bell with the name *Castillo* stamped into it."

Ms. Jimenez's eyes got big.

"Since it was a copy," continued Jamal, "that's why we

asked Ms. Adassa to accompany us, in that she found a letter from Cortes to his man in the Canary Islands, stating that there was a list, a sunken ship, and the items were made of Aztec gold."

Elizabeth flipped open her briefcase and pulled out a copy of the letter. She handed the letter to Ms. Jimenez.

"This is on file in the historical archives in the Canary Islands," she explained.

Ms. Jimenez glanced at it briefly and sat the letter down.

Jamal continued, "There was a painting by the artist Castillo, namesake of the ship, which provided the latitude, direction, and speed of where Cortes sank his ship. It was called the 'Numeric Madonna.'"

"I saw the article where you found the painting," exclaimed Ms. Jimenez.

Jamal nodded. "We'd already found what was left of the ship, so that wasn't helpful. We needed the list to verify the bell."

"Let me interject," said Ms. Jimenez. "Some years ago, it was before my time, there is a story about one of the Institute's historians who tried to sell a copy of the Cortes list to a crime figure here in Mexico. The historian was exposed as some kind of sexual predator, and they fired him. I don't think the Institute ever took any action against him. But it is possible that there were 'lists' floating around in the world."

"That criminal was Miguel Cortes, Miguelito Cortes' father," said Jamal. "That's why he was so frantic about the painting. He didn't have the location of the sunken ship. Apparently, he spent years looking for it. He was the one at the museum."

"Mr. Cortes is one of our biggest patrons, benefactors, and supporters. He is well thought of in government circles, we do not speak poorly of him," commented Ms. Jimenez rather primly.

"He's tried awfully hard to take the bell from us," interjected Dee. "He threatened the lives of some of our group and was involved in the deaths of several of our friends."

Ms. Jimenez looked aghast.

"How will you protect the bell, from him?" continued Dee.

"There will be no need to protect it from him. He has every right to see it as a Mexican citizen," replied Ms. Jimenez.

"What's going to keep him from taking it?" asked Dee.

"The bell will be well publicized, and placed on display, under heavy guard, at the capital here in Mexico City. No one, I repeat no one, would dare take it," she concluded.

"We're waiting to hear from our friends in Seville," said Jamal. "Perhaps Miguelito was one of the causalities of the shootout."

"We have a copy of the official police report. There is no mention of Mr. Cortes, or anyone known to be an associate of his, among the casualties or those arrested in that incident. It does appear there were a number of Americans involved," she replied in a short tone.

Jamal moved to the box with the crowbar and pried it apart. Dee stood to one side and assisted him.

Pulling off several of the runners, Jamal and Dee separated their dive gear until only the bell remained.

Ms. Jimenez came out of her chair, her hand to her face. She leaned forward slightly and touched the bell. "It is beautiful," she said, running her finger along the name *Castillo*. "It's real. I never thought the Cortes list was real."

"Why not?" asked Jamal.

Ms. Jimenez sat back down and looked out the window for a minute before turning back to them.

"If you'd brought this, this bell, to us, as you should have, we could have told you what it was. We, the Institute, have the original list. The historian sold a copy. We have closely guarded the list for hundreds of years. All of this could have been avoided, all these incidents." She paused and then continued. "I'll take this up with the governing committee and probably the culture minister himself, to see if you qualify for any reward. I think it's doubtful given your choices, removing the bell, taking it out of the country, holding it for so long. They will base the decision upon the totality of your actions and their costs."

There was silence for a moment. Then Dee said, "We didn't know that there would be costs or how great they would be. We're just tourists."

Ms. Jimenez sighed and ran her hands alongside her hair. "I'm sure this has been traumatic, but you must understand. The Sea of Cortez, or the Gulf of California, as we prefer, is a small ocean. It's only eighty miles at its widest. But it's technically a part of the St. Andreas Fault, a continuation of the Fault. It's over ten thousand feet deep. It does not have its own tidal pool but is driven by the Pacific Ocean. What that means is that the wave action depends on forces outside the sea itself. The sea bottom is very turbulent and in constant motion. It has one of the most abundant varieties of sea life in the world because of the extensive currents. Nothing in the sea would stay in the same place for long, even if you could reach it at those depths. A ship would never be found, except by chance."

"Why would Miguelito have spent his life looking for it?" asked Dee.

"He would have known the circumstances. He has such extensive business interests around the sea. I can only say, it must have been his dream," Ms. Jimenez replied.

"So that was Cortes' fate, both of them, to look for a

ship, for treasure, that could never be found. Cortes' Revenge really," added Jamal.

"There's no answer to that question," replied Ms. Jimenez.

Dee looked at his friend. "But you found your answer, Jamal."

THE END.

Get the next book in the series:

All for 1
Dee Sanders - Book 3

ENJOY THIS BOOK?

A NOTE FROM AUTHOR LP SNYDER

If you've enjoyed this book, I would be very grateful if you could spend just five minutes leaving a review (it can be as short as you like) on the book's Amazon page and on Goodreads or BookBub.

Thank you very much.

ACKNOWLEDGMENTS

I want to thank the readers who made my first book, *3 Hour Tour*, a success. That encouraged me to try again and here we are! I love exclamation points! Don't ever let anybody tell you they're excessive. I hope you enjoy the story.

I want to thank Vince Conti for the beautiful cover, Elizabeth Mackey for cover consultation, the editors at Frostbite Publishing for their invaluable assistance, my friends and fellow authors Kelly Utt and Shannon Brown for extensive insight, support, and patience, and finally my wife, Diana. She told me I could do it! She's also a great beta reader.

ABOUT THE AUTHOR

LP Snyder is a life-long reader who, at the last minute, decided to become a writer. It's been a great experience, and he wonders why it took so long to decide! Having read a little of most genres, LP decided to stick with his favorites—adventure, espionage, and crime thrillers! If you like fast-paced, humorous, action-filled, suspense thrillers, he's your Huckleberry!

Newsletter subscribers receive bonus content, including short stories and extended epilogues. Don't be afraid to ride that train!

Sign up at www.lpsnyder.com.

www.ingramcontent.com/pod-product-compliance
Lightning Source LLC
Chambersburg PA
CBHW031611100726

47898CB00006B/1751